THE
SWORN
VIRGIN

THE
SWORN
VIRGIN

A Novel

KRISTOPHER
DUKES

WILLIAM MORROW
An Imprint of HarperCollinsPublishers

HarperCollins
PUBLISHERS
Since 1817

P.S.™ is a trademark of HarperCollins Publishers.

HarperCollins books may be purchased for educational, business, or sales promotional use. For information, please email the Special Markets Department at SPsales@harpercollins.com.

FIRST EDITION

Designed by Diahann Sturge

Library of Congress Cataloging-in-Publication Data has been applied for.

ISBN 978-0-06-266074-9

17 18 19 20 21 LSC 10 9 8 7 6 5 4 3 2 1

For Matt

§ 38. A woman is a sack, made to endure.

§ 600. A man who has been dishonored is considered dead.

§ 601. A man is dishonored:

b) If someone spits at him, threatens him, pushes him, or strikes him.

c) If someone reneges on his pledged word.

d) If his wife is insulted or if she runs off with someone . . .

f) If his hospitality is violated.

> *—The Laws of Lekë Dukagjini, the code of the mountainous region east of Shkodra, Albania*

The past is always a rebuke to the present.

> *—Robert Penn Warren*

You could not step twice into the same river; for other waters are ever flowing on to you.

> *—Heraclitus*

THE
SWORN
VIRGIN

Chapter 1

Albania, 1910

The body lay motionless. His once bright brown eyes now as dull as the sucking mud beneath him, much like the sopping footpath they had traveled to reach this strange town. Thick blood flooded his white shirt from the deep black hole in his chest. Eleanora flinched as a tall, craggy-faced man touched her arm, telling her this was not something a young woman should see.

Where was her husband, her father, her brother?

"I am traveling with my father," Eleanora said.

She watched her hand rise, trembling as she pointed to Baba as he lay there in the dirt road, his eyes open and reflective, failing to see her or anyone else.

She gazed into his eyes, but for the first time she could remember, they did not crinkle as he smiled, they did not even meet hers. The scar down his cheek looked a deeper red than usual. She wondered when he would move. When she would move. She scratched the tears off her cheeks.

How could this be real?

Eleanora looked up and saw the townspeople staring at her and whispering, looking at her without meeting her gaze. Though they were all strangers, she felt as if she were looking at the people from her own mountain village, only some of these women covered their faces completely with lace, trembling elegant ghosts next to men who wore shoes turned up at the tips. Behind the townspeople, two-story buildings were pushed so tightly together they shared walls, their shuttered windows lined up like wood markers in a cemetery. If Shkodra was like the large foreign cities she dreamed of exploring in Italy, across the sea, perhaps she no longer wanted to go. How could she go anywhere, anyway, when Baba refused to get up?

Behind the town loomed the purple mountains where she had grown up. White streaks pierced the mountains—waterfalls, one of which was behind her home, the home she and Baba clearly should have never left. Home. Even with the windows and door closed, she could always hear the crashing water. She heard it now, roaring between her ears, and let it drown out the townspeople's whispers and someone's scream. Was it hers? Always the sound of rushing water.

Life was always the same until it was not.

Chapter 2

Two weeks earlier

"Why, Baba?" From atop her black horse, Eleanora watched a young bride weep, her silent family framed in the arched dark doorway of their stone hut as the bride was dragged away, held hand and foot, swinging between four grinning and grunting men, presumably her brothers.

Eleanora's father nudged his ivory horse, and they turned their backs to the scene. Baba smiled down at his daughter, the starburst of wrinkles around his eyes deepening. The sun broke through the ceiling of gray clouds and the bright beam washing over his familiar face smoothed the parentheses around his mouth, making his thick black mustache and his dark eyes shine. Eleanora was often surprised by his handsomeness. Were it not for his scar and thick mustache and white cap, he would look just like the etching of the ancient Greek bust pinned to the wall of his study.

"Why?" Baba repeated. "Are you asking me why I think they do it, or why they think they do it?"

"Why they think they do it," Eleanora said. Her horse, Tiziano, flicked his ears in tune with her growing distress. How could men laugh while that woman wept? Her small face was twisted tight with grief, her little ankles and hands gripped harder than necessary, and as Eleanora stared she became sure the woman was closer to a girl, younger than Eleanora's own eighteen years.

Baba rolled a cone-shaped cigarette between his long fingers, murmuring soothing words to his fair horse to keep her still as he put the sterling silver tobacco box back in a red leather saddlebag.

"They do it," he said, "because they think that everyone has always done it that way."

"And why do you think they do it?" Eleanora asked. Tiziano stomped his hooves.

She watched Baba raise his engraved silver lighter to his cigarette. Its curling etchings drew compliments wherever she and her father went, though Eleanora knew most men were as much intrigued with wondering how it worked. Eleanora herself had only ever seen one other lighter used instead of a match, and it belonged to a patient of her father's, one of the richest men in the mountains.

"Why, why do I think they do it," Baba repeated. His cheeks caved deeper as he sucked on his cigarette.

Baba exhaled, puckering his lips so his smoke shot up and away from Eleanora. "Because everyone else has always done it that way."

"Can't we stop them, Baba?" Eleanora asked, her hand hovering over the curved knife she kept tucked into her belt. "At least tell them to let her walk?"

The wailing bride wrenched out of her handlers' grasp, her moaning broken by the thud of her knees on the ground.

Baba did not turn his head at the sound; he continued to examine the front of his cigarette, tapping the fragrant tobacco back in.

"Yes, of course we could," Baba said. "When I was about as young as you, I interrupted such a scene, and the woman only cried harder and slapped me for the shame I had caused her."

The bride lunged toward her family, but her mother ducked into the dark house. The bride collapsed on her knees, sobbing. Two men grabbed her feet, while the other two snatched her hands from her face and held her wrists. The bride continued to writhe above the ground, without a chance of escaping, and Eleanora could not tell if this, too, was part of the ritual or if the bride was too tired to fight right. She sighed and looked down at the narrow rocky path, where her father's cigarette fell and bounced once, still smoldering.

Baba never finished his cigarettes.

His heels, polished and gleaming despite their days on the trails, dug into his white horse, and Eleanora looked back one more time before she and her horse followed.

HOURS LATER, ELEANORA paused at a sharp bend of the trail, behind which was her home, nestled into the rising cliffs the sun was about to sink behind. Baba had gone ahead, and she heard him open the creaking gate, clucking to his horse.

For the last hours, the trail had been too steep to ride their horses, so Baba and she had trudged up and into the crumbling pink shale that slid downward with every step. She took a jagged deep breath, let go of Tiziano's reins, and he trotted home.

He had known long ago where they were going and that it was dinnertime. Eleanora smiled. He was smarter than many of the villagers she met, including the men of the household she and Baba had just returned from. She would have thought their religion would have forbidden them from demanding Baba cut up their pregnant woman, but no religion was higher than that of Lekë, whose ancient laws ruled the mountains, demanding honor and blood, and not always in equal measure. How the family had wailed when they saw that their woman was pregnant with a dead baby boy! Much more than when the woman had passed away from the stray bullet, despite the fast and feverish work of Baba's and Eleanora's hands. A dead woman, killed by a stray bullet, might mean a hefty fine decided by the village elders, but a dead baby boy! A potential heir! Nothing could wipe that clean but blood from the shooter's family. Understanding that, Baba had argued against opening up the woman's belly, but the head of the house had insisted in loud violent language, shoving gold into his hands, while Baba looked at Eleanora as if to say, *They would do it anyway.* She had swallowed hard when she saw the woman's belly open, unable to look away, committing to memory anatomical details she might be able to use later in a painting or a drawing. His head was fuzzy with black hair, and his eyes were closed as if he were merely sleeping. Sleeping, though there had been so much blood.

Eleanora made herself swallow down her nausea, and continued to watch the sunset, taking out of her pocket a blue silk handkerchief, embroidered with her initials in brown to match her riding costume. She dabbed her damp forehead. She hated to sweat. Even when she had been looking at the baby, his father weeping and swearing revenge for his unborn son, she had dabbed at the sweat on her nose, her cheeks, without taking her eyes away.

She folded her handkerchief and put it back into her pocket. She would have to wash it when she got home, but she could not shove the damp silk back into her pocket when her costume was still relatively fresh, and she would hate to make the pockets bulged and misshapen. She had designed her riding costume herself, with an extra-full skirt in brown that split down the front, occasionally revealing matching tight brown pants. The women of the house they had just visited had stared, asking her if that was the special costume that healers from her tribe wore. When she had begun to say something sarcastic, her father cut her off, nodding and saying yes.

She laughed now to think about it. Her father had stymied her rudeness, while he looked back and winked at her. Baba encouraged her individuality. He gave her money for any clothes she designed, without asking, while he himself stuck to the traditional costume of a mountain man: snow-white woolen pants with the black braiding of their tribe; a matching cap and white shirt, topped by a cropped black vest; a scarlet sash around his narrow waist; and leather sandals laced together with rawhide. He kept his head shaved, like all other men in their tribe, with one lock of hair hidden beneath a white cap. His only difference was how often he insisted his wife wash his clothes; there was never a suggestion of a mark on them.

Eleanora absentmindedly dusted her full skirt, though hours ago in the early morning she had already checked for spots after taking off her sullied, bloodied nursing apron.

She stared across the darkening valley, shadowed by layers upon layers of mountains facing her. The foremost mountains were lit rose-gold by the setting sun, and she could see the steep terraces carved into the hills by farmers, their homes appearing as little more than dark dots with white smoke highlighting where they nestled into the mountain.

Eleanora crossed her arms tightly.

The baby boy had looked like he was hugging himself.

Eleanora kicked the trail, watching the pale rocks scatter, and walked on. When she turned the bend of the trail, she saw her home and admired all its glittering glass, imagining how startling it would be to see it for the first time. Surely one would think it was a mirage. She sometimes imagined it was something out of *One Thousand and One Nights*, though instead of being sculpted out of desert sands, its two stories were stacked rough stone—not unusual for her village. But such large windows, let alone with glass, were a rarity she had never encountered anywhere else, despite the many mountain chiefs' homes she had visited while traveling with her father for his medical work. In the pink sunshine, the windows winked at her over the tall fence woven of wood spears that surrounded her home and every other one in the village. Eleanora liked to keep flowers hanging in a brass vase nailed into the fence, next to the gate, though the feathery amethyst heather blossoms that were currently displayed were faded and sun-dried. What would she replace them with? Branches, maybe. The flowers' season had gone on unusually long; it was autumn already, and she doubted they would bloom for much longer.

She took the dried flowers out of the vase—they would be

useful for a medicinal tea. She latched the gate behind her, hearing the horses crunching hay beneath their hooves, while the goats bleated their greetings from the stable in the back, near the ivory cliffs that rose from their grassy yard into the clouds.

A gust of wind blew the lawn into a sea of swaying green, the hanging laundry into whipping white sails. Eleanora pushed her flapping hair from her face to behind her ears, and saw her stepmother, Meria. The woman's thin arms reached to tie escaping clothing back to the line. Her stepmother then tried to smooth her flaxen braids back under her white lace headscarf, which she changed often, but one would never know for they all looked the same. Meria wore the traditional costume of a woman of their tribe, a billowing white blouse tucked into a bell-shaped white wool skirt, smothered by a gold-embroidered, black-fringed apron and beaded cropped vest. A wide, heavily studded belt sat upon yards of scarlet silk wrapped around Meria's tiny waist, denoting her status as a married woman.

Something of her stepmother's pale-blue eyes reminded Eleanora of the young bride, though she thought Meria much more beautiful, mostly because she remembered the Meria of her childhood, when her papery thin cheeks had been pink pillows for Eleanora's baby ones, and her lips had been less pinched and pressed often against the child's forehead. When Eleanora's eyes met hers, Meria looked away back toward the laundry, though she leaned close to the younger woman so she could kiss her cheek.

Baba came out of the stable, brushing off his palms.

"What a sweet picture you two make," he said, squeezing Eleanora's shoulder. "You look like you walked out of your own painting."

He nodded to Meria, and she followed him into their house, while Eleanora went to the stable to brush down her horse.

Chapter 3

$\mathcal{M}$eria's husband's house had more windows than even the home of the village chief, letting in more light, letting out more heat, and letting in more rain when the skies wept waterfalls, which would be any day now as fall slipped in. She did not imagine she knew anything of building, but was it not common sense that to have holes instead of walls would weaken a house? She worried when the snow piled onto the roof, crossing herself when her husband, Fran, and Eleanora were not looking, praying that the wood-shingled roof—another unnecessary strangeness, when everyone else's homes were thatched—would not cave in. Sometimes Meria mumbled about having to gather extra firewood or asked Fran how she should stop endless leaks. At night she was careful not to walk in front of the high, wide windows, feeling defenseless against vengeful gunfire, though who would shoot at her when she was the wife of a man who had saved many lives? She never criticized her husband for building a rather foolish house. Because as foolish as it was, it was admired throughout the mountains, and the rare times she went out visiting, her neighbors always asked her, collective breath held, what she would do if a window were to break and how long it would take to bring the glass in from Shkodra, the nearest town. And though that would worry her—could she not just board up a broken window in the meantime? What would the villagers think? She would not let it show, but would merely smile into her cup of hot coffee. So what?

And so what if she had no other women to help her with the housework and if her stepdaughter sat with guests instead of serving them as she should? So what? If her stepdaughter did not lessen her load around their home, she was loving in other ways, ways her own mother would not have counted for much, God rest her soul, but ways Meria still found charming. While Eleanora's smooth hands never lifted a wooden spoon and shrank from touching a goat except to pet it, her cool palm often patted Meria's cheek, tugged her hair teasingly as if they were little girls, and her stepdaughter wore the same trusting smile as when she was a baby. Though Fran bragged about Eleanora's being braver than most men while they practiced their healing arts, as far as Meria could see, despite the exaggerated curves of Eleanora's figure, she was still the same young girl who shrieked at a spider. Meria often found herself admiring the beauty her stepdaughter had bloomed into, made slightly uncomfortable by the suggestive, womanly body Eleanora had grown while she was still a girl and so far from marriage. Meria never commented on her beauty; she would not risk spoiling the girl into vanity. Fran spoiled her enough. But so what?

Meria could be careless about sugar and salt, she wore as

many rings as she liked, and her home was so much larger than the cave-like hut she had lived in before she met Fran. He and Eleanora may have left her alone and lonely for weeks at a time, while they traveled the mountains practicing their healing arts, but her husband never hit her, never even threatened to. Fran was a good man, and she still enjoyed making him little dishes he liked, either ill-smelling things he swore kept him healthy, or dainty delicacies Eleanora described to her and she usually managed to figure out how to re-create, earning their cooing praise.

Meria stepped back from the curling steam rising from the hammered copper pot she stirred over the hearth. Eleanora had requested a simple stew for dinner, and as Meria looked up, her stepdaughter smiled at her, the sunlight hitting her straight black hair, shiny as if it were dyed and drenched in oil, though she knew Eleanora would never bother like other women did. She had always had a fascination with clothes, even as a toddler gurgling and pointing to pictures of women's foreign costumes from her father's books, but Meria had to admit the girl was not proud of her looks, even while she managed to keep her complexion like milk, the whitest white even when she was a wriggling baby.

Meria remembered holding Eleanora when the girl was a tiny toddler, proud of and worrying over her pale skin, imagining she was her very own. A son, of course, would have been infinitely preferable—some men refused to marry their brides until they bore them one—but Meria would have settled for giving birth to a daughter, especially one as lovely as Eleanora. She cringed when she recalled how shameless she had been, even dancing in their home, her hands hugging her narrow waist, suggestively letting her lace headscarf fall off her flowing fair hair. Anything to get Fran's attention—the end result of which left her flat on the floor and flustered and hopeful for days, until the moon changed and she had to stuff her skirts again. But there was to be no other baby but Eleanora, Eleanora who was not her own, which became clearer every year.

Eleanora's looks were so different from hers no one assumed they were related, and eventually the only connection Meria felt to the girl's dramatic allure was this: as her own faded, it seemed to feed Eleanora's. Each bit of beauty that trickled into Eleanora carried power, and with each passing year, Meria felt her hold over her husband lessen. Fran was kind to her, but he was kind to everyone, and kindest to Eleanora. Fran loved his daughter so obviously, Meria was sure the villagers laughed about him. Once Meria said to her husband she could understand carrying on about a son. A son would be his heir; a daughter was merely sold into some other tribe. And why had he not yet secured a betrothal for his daughter? Fran responded by walking out of the house, carrying Eleanora with him, though she could walk by then. Meria still thought of that scene, years later, replaying it in her head and holding back her words, for then perhaps she might have borne him a son. After that he ignored Meria's cautionary words, answering instead Eleanora's silly questions: Why did the sky not get closer the higher they climbed into the mountains? Where did the sun disappear to at night? The river ended in a lake, but where did it begin? He answered questions Eleanora did not even ask, teaching her his healing arts, so that they would become partners. It became as if she were the son he did not have, but also maybe the wife he wished for . . .

Before Eleanora was old enough to travel with him for work,

he would bring fabric from his travels to complement Eleanora's white skin, her black hair, her gray eyes; sometimes there was extra for Meria to also make herself a dress. Fran did not seem to notice Meria only made herself hidden petticoats out of this colorful fabric; she preferred to keep to the traditional black and white wools of the village, though she would have indulged in embroidering her skirts with gold thread if he would remember to bring it more often.

If only Meria could have given him a son. Then Fran would not embarrass himself by spoiling his daughter and flaunting his peculiar treatment of her across the mountains. He bragged her beauty and special skills were recognized by chiefs days' hikes away, but Meria was sure people also gossiped about other aspects of the girl. It was fine for a small child to sit with the men among the floor cushions as they talked business and politics with Fran. But for a marriageable woman, nearing nineteen years old, to sit with men? It did not matter that Eleanora was an exceptional healer. The villagers whispered. Some said it was worse her father sat with her, openly condoning her eccentric behavior.

Was it possible Eleanora had inherited such airs and attitudes from her mother? Fran might laugh at her, but Meria believed the stories she had heard of spirits possessing people unknowingly, especially women and girls, and especially women and girls who traveled at night. And had not Fran come to her and her mother at night, with Eleanora swaddled onto his back? Perhaps Eleanora was just like her mother, though she could not possibly have remembered her mother and never mentioned her to Meria. Nor did Fran.

Early in their marriage, Meria had walked in on Fran sitting in a dim room, weeping over a photograph, and as moved as she was by the tears of a man, she was more curious about the picture. She had never seen one, and she lifted it out of his trembling hands, her fingers moving to touch the dress in the photo. He snatched it back.

Meria still remembered parts of the photo: how intricate and careful the curling embroidery on the skirt was, how piles of coins were woven into the woman's dark hair, and how her pale eyes, shadowed by slanting brows, stared directly into the camera, at Meria. That was all she recalled, though sometimes a look from Eleanora reminded her of it. Meria supposed the photo had come from the same place as the woman had come from, as Fran had come from, as Eleanora had come from. Or had the photo come from someplace else? Had this woman traveled outside the mountains? Who knew what this woman might have done if she could give a photograph of herself to a man.

Meria had once known a girl in the village who was shot by her betrothed's family, with her own family's permission, for running outside her home, bareheaded and alone, to talk to a strange man walking by. A woman could not give a photograph to her betrothed, let alone another man, without dishonoring her family. And what husband would bother paying for a photo of his wife when he already had her in the flesh? Where had Fran put that picture, anyway? Locked away somewhere, forgotten, though forgetting would be unlike Fran . . . Meria's thoughts were fleeting, like sticks floating, carried fast by the river. Fran himself had come as a surprise from beyond the river, with that tiny baby bound to his back.

Meria remembered him knocking on her mother's gate, where only the two of them had lived. He stood there in the rain, tall and not much thinner than he was now, with the mewling baby, a lost traveler in the night. It was dangerous to welcome anyone, who could be anything, into one's home at night, but it was more dangerous to refuse a guest—it was unquestionably dishonorable. Meria's mother exchanged greetings with Fran. She and her mother had of course asked him to stay for dinner, though they barely had anything to share beyond stale cornmeal. They were even out of coffee. But the stranger produced some from his bags, along with a sad smile, and his eyes kept finding Meria's even under her lowered eyelashes. He was amused by her, and she was fascinated by him—he knew things she did not. His look reminded her of her father teasing her when she was a girl, before he was killed. And there was something comforting in that look, while it also unnerved her.

Fran's smile had widened as he watched Meria fuss over how small and pale the baby was, and she even had the boldness to criticize the way he had wrapped her and correct him about the cause of the baby's cough. He stayed the night, then a few more, while the baby's cheeks grew rosier under her care. Her mother cooked them meals she had not had the reason—or ingredients—to make in years. Fran would leave early in the day to heal people, she learned, and would return in the evening with sour goat's yogurt, cornmeal, and sometimes even sugar. Sugar! She had had honey occasionally, as a few villagers kept bees, but sugar? Oh, it gave her the sweetest buzz that was only heightened when Fran met her eyes and laughed with her at her surprised joy. Weeks passed and he had begun to leave his belongings around—carved wooden bowls that were shockingly smooth to touch or a strange, heavy silver pipe—and hang his gleaming rifle near the door.

"Did you see how much silver there is on his gun?" her mother asked her as the door closed.

She smoothed Meria's hair with a dot of oil, finally stirred from the lazy depression that had oppressed their home since her husband and sons had died. She would lean near her, both of them sweating over the open fire in the middle of the small room, and whisper to Meria, "How good it is to have a man in the house again!"

Fran and Meria were married by a gnarled priest in the house that winter, in a quiet ceremony, far from the usual three-day festival that distracted entire mountain villages. Their only guests, besides a few neighbors, were members of the extensive family of a rich man whose life Fran had saved. Meria's older sister had married into a faraway tribe, and her brothers and uncles and grandparents had died.

Her mother passed soon after, sick with a knifing in her chest from drinking rainwater, and though Fran had changed the little house so much, he built another house in a quiet corner, right next to the only footpath leading in and out of the village. He built most of the airy two-story home himself during the spring, using irregular gray stones he found in the mountains for floors instead of the usual packed earth, and the village gathered to watch as he brought in glass for the windows, provided by a merchant whose leg—torn by gunfire—Fran had mended so well the man barely limped. Fran chose everything, from plush rugs he hung on the walls instead of layering on the floors, to little copper cooking tools a man ought not to concern himself with, and when he was done, he turned to Meria, holding Eleanora while she kicked her little lean legs, and asked, "Do you not like it?"

"Do you not like it?" Eleanora repeated.

Meria blinked herself out of her reverie. The sun had caught her eye through the window; it had been shining behind Fran's head, and when he moved to show her the fabric he and Eleanora had brought from another village, the sun had blinded her. She squeezed her eyes open and shut, and in front of her was Eleanora, standing straight with her legs wide like a man's. Her arrogant pose was obvious even under her extra-wide skirt, sober black wool but embroidered with swirling purple in yet another strange pattern. Eleanora had paid a local girl to make the skirt for her, sending it back twice before she was satisfied. Women still debated what was more audacious: the bizarre designs, or paying someone to do one's own sewing. Eleanora sent the work out so as not to bother her stepmother, but next time Meria might insist on doing the sewing herself. She sighed. Who gave the girl such odd ideas, and why did Fran allow it?

Eleanora's long fingers cradled and stroked a bolt of pale-blue wool. Meria pretended not to notice as the girl scrunched the fabric close to her face. There was something sensual in the way she rubbed the thick fabric between her fingers, but then Eleanora laughed like a child, and Meria could not help but smile in reply.

"I thought it would make pretty aprons for you and Eleanora," Fran said.

"Did you, Baba?" asked Eleanora, her voice teasing. "Because I chose it. It reminded me of Meria's eyes."

She batted her lashes at Meria, giggling.

"Either way, it is lovely," said her stepmother.

She thought of the last time Eleanora had worn such a flashy fabric, and she already dreaded the looks from the other women.

A deep voice bellowed from the gate. "Oh master of the house! Are you receiving guests?"

Meria folded the blue wool and laid it in a carved wooden chest as Fran went to answer the gate. Then she walked to the hooded hearth in the back corner of the room and began making the coffee, stirring a muddy mix of ground beans and sugar and water, her eyes on the copper pot hanging over the open fire, while she listened carefully to more ritual greetings at the front door, gleaning from the voices it was Lulash, the man she expected.

She did not look up from the pot. Fran ought to make coffee as the head of the house, but he left all the cooking to her. She glanced over. Lulash did not seem to notice the break in tradition. The tall man wore a white cap perched on his shining shaved head, a ballooning white blouse constrained by a cropped black vest, and white woolen pants with black braiding down the sides. His costume was the same as Fran's, the same as every other mountain man, except for the silver chains piled over his chest and turquoise rings jammed onto each of his thick fingers. Meria suspected he dyed his full black mustache with henna and indigo, and if he did, so what? He was still considered as handsome as when he was the age of his youngest son, and he was tall enough to carry his extra weight gracefully.

Lulash collapsed into a sloppy sit on a large silk floor cushion, facing the window and Eleanora, and Fran followed silently, his back as straight as a pine trunk. Meria set up a low table between the men, careful to keep its etched brass top from jangling against its polished wood base. She brought fresh red-and-white towels for the men to wipe their hands with, and a large bowl of cubed goat's cheese, her eyes never meeting the visitor's, never inviting a greeting, let alone intimating her meeting with Lulash's wife earlier that week.

Eleanora sat by the window nearest to the men, sketching what looked like a sleeping baby, his fingers curled around a skin-colored cord. It was magic the way she made images appear on paper, but hopefully Lulash would not notice the drawing. There was something disturbing about that baby, and it was not quite proper how she was making it clear the baby was a boy. Eleanora's hair escaped her purple headscarf as she leaned forward, smudging a black line with her thumb, casting a shadow where there had been none. Now her hands were dirty, and it was such a loud scarf, but the fabric was noticeably rich; surely Lulash had never seen such a color. No matter. He was staring enough he would not soon forget it, though he seemed equally put off by Eleanora's hands hovering over the paper. Meria walked over to her stepdaughter.

"Would you please come help me in the back?" Meria whispered.

Eleanora did not look up as she continued scratching at the paper with her tan pastel, though she grinned.

"To make my specialty, burned bread?"

Lulash looked past Fran, his furrowed brow pointed at Eleanora.

The girl plucked a brown pastel from her leather box.

Meria squeezed Eleanora's arm. She looked at Fran. He had not seen. He was watching Lulash with an amused smile. She patted Eleanora's elbow, and the girl grinned as she let out an exaggerated groan and followed her back into the cooking area.

Meria handed Eleanora a copper bowl and a wide wooden spoon. The ingredients were set out and measured. Eleanora cracked the brown egg on the side of the bowl, dumping in the amber yolk, picking out eggshell shards. At this rate they would have corn bread in spring. But Meria could hardly care; she was listening carefully to the men's low tones. Lulash named a sum. She watched a large puff of smoke rise from her husband's mouth as Fran asked, incredulous, "Do you not think that a bit high? After all, I have found my daughter to be rather useless for housework."

Fran called for Eleanora. Even as Meria mixed in the cornmeal, her eyes followed the girl as she crossed the room to the men.

Eleanora plopped down on a cushion between the men, her posture as straight as her father's. Meria would have remained standing until they dismissed her. Oh well.

Eleanora turned to Lulash, smiling.

"My name is Eleanora."

Lulash continued to face Fran, though he tightened his crossed legs so Eleanora's spreading skirts would not touch him.

"Your daughter's beauty is praised throughout the mountains, and now I see with my very own eyes why," Lulash said. His eyes took in Eleanora from her neck down. "A waist as wide as a man's palm," he murmured.

"Indeed." Fran nodded. "Her waist is even smaller than the neck of my horse, and my horse is a very fine animal." Fran winked at Eleanora, and Meria was relieved Lulash did not notice.

The man leaned forward, his protruding stomach rattling the tabletop, and rapped his ringed knuckles on the brass surface.

"I am prepared," he said, adjusting his vest, "to most gladly pay twice what I offered to have her for my son Edi."

"And we have not even negotiated! Let's triple the sum, and not a Napoleon less!" Eleanora laughed.

She was so loud sometimes, but her giggle was infectious. Meria moved so she could see Lulash's smiling face; he had the look of a man watching a dog walk on two legs, though perhaps a little less delighted. He took the pipe passed by Fran, hesitating before he inhaled deeply.

"Tell me, Fran, dare I hope you will accept?" But Lulash's question was really the statement of a man who took for granted getting what he wanted. "What do you think?"

"Me? What do I think?" asked Eleanora. "Yes, I am afraid I do have thoughts. Here is one of them—I have seen your son Edi." She popped a piece of cheese into her wide red mouth. "He is almost as handsome as you are."

Lulash raised his tangled eyebrows at this, his heavy black mustache lifting as his smile widened and his blue eyes met Fran's.

"I have also seen your daughters and your fine horses," Eleanora continued, "and the way you allow your son to treat the ladies and the beasts. Tell your son, 'No.' I would never marry him."

Lulash coughed, smoke sputtering from his mouth and nose. He sprang up, his knees nearly knocking off the brass top of the table.

"How dare you," he said, still addressing Fran.

"Me?" asked Fran. "But I have not said anything, so I am

not sure what you may be rebuking me for, except for raising a rather spirited daughter. I did insinuate she was unlikely to be a suitable wife."

Eleanora looked at her father, then back at Lulash.

"My father speaks rightly," continued Eleanora. She popped another chunk of cheese into her mouth, taking her time before swallowing. "As we have already established I am ill-mannered, please go ahead and tell your son if I were a man, I would show him what I thought of his proposal and how he treats his sisters."

Lulash tugged on his necklaces.

"Long may you live," Lulash stammered to Fran, as his father had said, and his father's father had said, and his father's father's father had said at the end of every conversation not punctuated by a gunshot.

"Long may you live," Fran returned, grinning as he walked Lulash to the door.

"And long life to you," Eleanora chanted. She stood with her legs wide, watching Lulash with a smile as he slammed the door. The gate creaked open and banged close, and she and Fran laughed over the sound of his horse galloping down the trail.

Meria watched from behind the fire. The coffee's steam covered her face, making her hot. It was one thing to throw away an opportunity like that, but must they have insulted Lulash, too? For some dream of that foreign school she and her father babbled about? Who even knew a man who had gone to that school, much less a woman? The coffee began to boil over. Meria grabbed the pot and dropped it onto the floor before it could burn her palms. She dipped her hands in a wooden bucket full of cool spring water, twirling them, worried they might blister. There was a clank as one of her rings slipped off and bounced on the bottom of the pail. Meria fished it out, admiring how it was extra shiny in its wetness.

It was the large turquoise ring Bubci, Lulash's wife, had admired when Meria had visited her house days ago.

It had been Meria's pleasure to speak with her old friend. She had known her as a girl, when Bubci came to the village as Lulash's bride. When she had come of age, within less than a year, she had borne him a son and Lulash's extensive family had accepted her and married the young pair. Bubci had borne him many more children after that, each son leaving her a little heavier and much prouder. She had given her friend cornmeal and bricks of butter after Meria's brothers and father had been killed, and her plump hands patted Meria's still-thin hands, smiling, nodding to show she was listening while she kept glancing at her daughter-in-law, sighing at her clumsiness as more dishes of dried apricots and cubes of cheese and honeyed almonds thudded onto the crowded table.

"I am so very happy for you, to see you doing so well," Bubci said. "And still so skinny after all these years! I guess this is how you keep a husband as good as yours without having children!"

Meria laughed, looking down, her ears impossibly hot.

"Children." Bubci sighed. "Yes, yes, thanks to God for having so many and still having my health, but the way they torment one. You know my youngest son, Edi. His first wife, she seemed to be a fine girl, from my own family's tribe, except she ran off, in the middle of the night! No one has found her yet, and her family and ours have looked to the ends of earth. Now he tortures me, Meria, absolutely tortures me, telling me he needs a wife with spirit. He has in his head that he wants someone to spar with. He uses such language with me. I tell him to take it up with his father, but if he must ask me he should marry a young girl, someone delicate but not too weak, hardworking but quiet, very quiet. I could use quiet in this household. Please, must you rush me like so!" Bubci snapped. She slapped away the hand of her daughter-in-law so she could take the last piece of dried apricot before her daughter-in-law took the dish away.

"Sons! How they torment one. It is even worse if you have more than one son, trust me, my friend, because then they gang up on you! Edi is absolutely obstinate. Refuses to let us pick his wife this time since the first one ran off. Have you ever heard of a man choosing his own wife? No, no," she answered Meria before she could finish, "we have not found her yet. Edi says"— Bubci laughed—"he says he would like to marry your Eleanora! But I told him there are enough men in my household."

Meria laughed, crossing her arms over her chest, shaking her head to let the young woman understand she did not want any more cheese. "Oh, Eleanora, it is only in her work with her father she is so exceptional. In her manner she is very feminine, and my husband tells me she was asked again as a bride for some rich merchant in Ipek."

Bubci snorted. "He is a Serb, no doubt. And?"

"And my husband's decision to say no is his own. He has grander plans for her, I assume."

"Too good for our family, hmm?" Bubci pushed away the hand of her daughter-in-law again so she could lick her finger and dip it into the sugar of the empty dish before it was lifted away.

"It is not that at all, Bubci! You know—"

"I know that Eleanora is getting older, and I would be proud— grateful!—to receive an offer such as my family's."

"Well, yes, of course. It is not that."

"It is because Edi has a temper? The bullet only scratched that stupid man's leg and we paid, we paid even without the council of elders asking. That is nothing. I hear Eleanora swears like a man while she works like a man. Somehow Edi likes this. You know he always liked near-wild Arabians instead of some stupid soft mule. Me, I prefer a mule. Maybe Eleanora is beautiful, maybe she is not. All I know is Edi is a sure offer and she would remain close to you and your husband, who is so fond of his daughter. Suppose they even keep on with their healing together? I would not mind, I have plenty of help here."

"You make many good points," Meria said. "Edi, he is a good match. You know we all still talk of how handsome he is, and just the other day I heard someone saying he was the most beautiful singer."

"Glory to your lips," Bubci said. "You speak the truest truths."

"And I will speak to my husband, I promise," Meria said, mostly to soothe her friend, but as she walked home she warmed to the idea, thinking her husband would be grateful to have Eleanora's future settled and safe, while she remained near and continued her work with him.

So Edi had a temper. Even Fran might yell when he was drunk on raki, which he had her distill from plums and only plums, until the liquor was so strong she did not know how it did not burn his belly. Well, Eleanora could keep Edi in line. And if she could not, well . . . plenty of people would think Eleanora was finally getting what she deserved, after being too good to fall in line with everyone else. If she were the man she acted like, surely someone would have shot her by now.

Meria's friend had not questioned if Eleanora would accept

the marriage offer—it hinged on Fran. Why would Eleanora not accept what her parents had arranged for her, just as her parents had accepted what their parents had arranged, and as their parents had accepted . . . Life was a stream of people accepting arrangements by other people, washing away the resisting few.

But Fran had made his decision. Meria only wished he had not had to insult her friend's husband while doing so.

Meria cursed when Eleanora's bloodstained apron fell from the pile of soiled laundry jumbled in her arms. She kicked the apron before picking it up, giving it a grass stain she would have to deal with now. Fran insisted on spotlessness.

Meria waddled out to the laundry lines in the yard behind the house. Fran insisted she wash the linens before he and Eleanora returned from a trip, though he could be days or weeks earlier or later than planned, and with the soiled clothes and bandages they brought back, Meria almost always had something to wash, a stain to scrub, rugs to beat. Winter was the worst, when she had to bring the boiling tub inside and make the air sticky and her hair frazzled. But at least the hanging laundry was invisible from the footpath—and neighbors always eager to note another eccentricity of her household. The lush yard encircled their home and was surrounded on three sides by a fence. A cliff overhead formed a steep wall on the far end of the yard, rising out of the mountain shelf that was the foundation of the village. Beside the house, a narrow footpath led down into the village in one direction, climbing farther into the mountains in the other direction. A small waterfall fell from the cliffs into the yard; Fran and Eleanora often took turns showering in it after traveling, and Meria often washed the laundry there. Despite the pattering splash of the waterfall, which collected and over-flowed from a large wood and metal tub Fran had fashioned, Meria could hear Fran and Eleanora still laughing.

The wind probably carried their laughter down the trail to Lulash, too. Meria sighed. If they were not careful, those two might get what they deserved.

Chapter 4

The unrestrained rush of the river bothered Eleanora, mesmerized her. It slid forward without stopping, constantly changing but always the same. It was like time itself, and its babbling filled her head as she watched it from atop her horse, Tiziano, as if speaking to her: *How could you think you had captured me in your pictures? I have always been white, I have always been blue, I have always been green, I have always been clear. I have never been any of these, and all of these, and I am always all of these things, and how could you ever hope to capture such a truth? Your paintings, all carefully rolled and packed into your satchel, might be improved by my truths sliding all over them, do you not think so? Even if I ruined them, what would it matter what would it matter what would it—*

"Watch how I do it, Eleanora, so you might repeat it," Baba said, Tiziano's reins loose in his strong tan hands.

She tried not to stiffen in her saddle as Tiziano snorted and shook his sleek black mane. Her father murmured to him, trying to persuade the horse to step off the bank. She bragged

Tiziano was braver and more intelligent than most people she had met, but he hated the water. Once, early when she had gotten him, he had even thrown her off near a stream. She liked that about him. He was like her—he could work hard, galloping until he foamed, but he did not do what he did not want to.

But Baba would coax him across. She clutched her leather satchel of watercolors and pastel paintings close to her chest, away from the churning green. It made her laugh to think the very thing that inspired so much of her art might ruin it. The river had no vanity; it was indifferent to everything, even its own nature. Eleanora focused on a lone sage bush leaning toward the sandy shore ahead, not breaking her gaze until her horse's hind legs were out of the water. It had been deeper the last time she crossed it with her father, but the frothy current still made her uneasy.

Oh, if the men who praised her nerve, her coolness under pressure, were able to see her now! She laughed at herself. Thanks to the God she did not believe in, they could not see her. She had enough trouble ordering them around even with her father there to back up her requests for fresh air, for boiled water, for space.

Eleanora hopped off her horse and let him shake off the river's water from his deep black coat. He grazed on the sparse grass dotting the gritty sand, as Baba splashed through the water with his own horse. She scanned her legs, reassuring herself there was not a drop on her navy wool pants, which, along with a matching navy blouse and a turban-like hat, she had designed especially for this trip. Her costume was beautiful, and spotless.

Eleanora's smile vanished when she saw Baba had already hiked high ahead on the narrow trail, his calm ivory horse climbing behind him. She hurried up as he continued quickly ahead, and when she looked back, the river was a green-blue streak far below the trail. The track was steep but monotonous, and her thoughts wandered to Shkodra, the city they would soon visit. Her father said he had not been there since before she was born, and she knew only one other villager who had visited. In Shkodra they would meet with a priest who could help her get into art school in Venice. L'Accademia Reale di Belle Arti di Venezia. She rolled the name around in her mind. Giovanni Battista Tiepolo had worked there. Antonio Canova's right hand rested there in a vase. Alessandro Milesi! To even walk down the same hallways as him. It was madness to imagine she was worthy.

Eleanora painted so many people from her memory, patients with faces twisted and red, or slack and pale, blissful mothers clutching babies unaware they were no longer in the womb, but the detail she used to try to capture such expressions was really merely practice for her more serious work, *en plein air* landscapes inspired by masters she admired, which was the bulk of the work she had quickly and carefully rolled up for the priest. She had painted only two true portraits: one of her father twisting his black mustache as his eyes followed whoever looked at his picture, and one of the foreign woman who had changed her life.

Eleanora had seen her years ago when the woman passed through their village, and even five-year-old Eleanora caught the queer whispers about her: this woman had been floating through many tribes, entertained by chiefs, paying homage to ruins, staying one night or two, and then moving on. She was a curiosity, but to Eleanora she seemed an elegant queen from a faraway country. She wore thick purple socks and stiff brown leather sandals like the mountain women, but her skirt was a plain tan cloth, her wide waist free of the traditional apron and heavy studded belt of a married woman, her simple white blouse buttoned up to her sunburned neck. Her face was shaded by a strange straw hat that sat like a plate tied to her head, and when she took it off for an eager child to touch, she revealed frizzy hair cropped like a little boy's.

Eleanora stared as the woman drew pictures in a book she carried. Eleanora had approached with the few other children whose mothers had not pulled them away, eyes growing larger as the woman's deft hand scratched a pencil across the page. She was a magician—soon the blank page held a miniature version of the hut in front of her. Eleanora reached out to touch the page, to see how it might feel, and the woman turned and smiled.

"Do you like this?" she had asked.

She spoke slowly, stiffly, but clearly. Her twangy voice was unlike any Eleanora had ever heard.

Before Eleanora could respond, the woman turned the pages of the book, and Eleanora saw faces of familiar-looking men and women, tiny towers men might hide in during a blood feud, and then something completely alien. The woman pointed to it.

"You have seen this?"

Eleanora shook her head, chewing on her thumb.

"You know what a"—the woman put her finger to her lips—"train, you know what a train is?"

Eleanora nodded. She had heard Baba's friend talk of trains, which ran faster than any horse, created cities wherever they paused, and charged through mountains. The other friends of her father had called that man a fool, but Eleanora had believed him.

"Like a train," the woman explained, "small . . . but flying like a bird. Earth . . ." She paused and floated one hand over the other.

"It flies over the earth?" Eleanora asked. She was good at guessing games like this.

The woman nodded, grinning.

"A train that flies!" Eleanora exclaimed, her eyes widening. She traced the woman's drawing with her finger. This thing floated men above the clouds?

That night, nestled near Meria, Eleanora dreamed she had the wings of an eagle, and she and the foreign woman soared over a beautiful country, though she could not remember how it looked when she woke. But seeing it had given her the same pleasurable pang she sometimes felt when the night sky was so clear the stars seemed to shimmer within reach.

The next morning Eleanora climbed the stairs to her father's study, sometimes stumbling in her excitement, always pulling herself forward. She found his fountain pen, tugged a leather-bound book off the lowest shelf, and began scribbling in the margins of random cream pages. When she showed Meria, her stepmother tried to take the book from her, but her father smiled at her ink-stained hands. He gave her paper that had numbers scrawled on one side but was blank on the back, and took another book from his shelf, opening it to a picture of a primitive statue.

"Try to copy that," her father said.

Eleanora spent the rest of that afternoon and countless others exploring how to turn pen scratches into shapes, shapes into landscapes, and landscapes into glimpses of other worlds. After-noons bled into evenings, and soon Eleanora was excused from the little housework she did so she might draw and paint, teaching herself techniques from studying other drawings, and, later on, after her father taught her how to read Italian and Turkish, he would surprise her with fresh books with detailed instructions on tricks to re-create light and shadow and perspective.

Now, as Eleanora followed her father up the path, she wondered what her life would be like if she had never seen the woman, if the woman had not shown her it was possible to choose another path in life. What if Baba had not been of the unique disposition and position to support her passions? Eleanora shuddered. The standard life of the mountain woman was, at best, a never-ending chore: wake before dawn, gather firewood, cook food, sweep the floor, care for beasts, discipline children, serve men, weave fabric between other tasks, and then escape consciousness through a few hours of sleep. Sheep had more freedom and were less likely to be hit by their owner. Eleanora meant for each day to be an adventure, whether she traveled on foot or merely in her mind. She was lucky, so lucky. The cool breeze whispered as it blew across her damp forehead, and the sharp sunshine beaming on her face made the rocks crunching beneath her feet sparkle like crystal. The shrubs clinging to the mountains glowed green and vibrated in the breeze, as if mirroring the ecstasy at the core of her young being pulsating with the full potential of her life before her, with the joy of youth that knew no reason why it could not meet every opportunity it faced.

She beamed at the straight back of her father before her: she was so lucky, and lucky enough to know it and be grateful.

She would miss Baba if she went to Italy, but surely he would visit her. Or perhaps after her schooling she would move back, living in the city they would visit tonight, bringing new techniques to her old subjects, creating a fresh vision of art for her country.

It was night when they arrived at the priest's house, which sat on a hill perched above the city. The lights glowing in the buildings below were like another constellation of stars. How could such twinkling brightness exist outside the sky? Eleanora had known a rich merchant who had kept so many candles burning in his home it was as if it were the brightest daylight at all hours, but this, this was extravagant! She looked at Baba, who met her eyes, smiling.

The priest's humble home felt familiar though; it was two stories high and built of rough, round stones, like her home, but with few narrow glassless windows and a crude wooden staircase leading up to the front door on the second story.

They tied their horses to knobbly wooden posts in the grassy yard and climbed the creaking stairs. Her father knocked, and a bareheaded servant cracked open the door, his bony hands gripping its scarred wood as if it were a blanket pulled to his jutting chin.

"Yes?" the servant asked, his eyes narrowed. "Who are you?"

"I am Fran Aganis," Baba announced, "from Arbër, come to see Father Aberto."

"Please, one moment."

The door slammed shut.

Baba raised his eyebrows and grinned at Eleanora.

The door creaked open to a dark room lit by skinny candles hanging against white walls, highlighting their rough plaster and framing a faded print of Saint Peter nailed to the wall. The brown back of the servant receded into the darkness.

Baba hung his gleaming rifle on wooden pegs near the front door, and a dark, willowy priest in a black-belted robe came forward from the back of the room.

Eleanora raised her brows as her father knelt for the priest's blessing. Baba, who often teased Meria when he caught her crossing herself at the wind whistling through the canyon. But a stern glance from Baba and she followed suit, the priest's thin hand surprisingly heavy on her head. With her head still bowed, she looked to her father to watch for when he rose.

Father Aberto laughed, a deep chuckle surprising for his frail frame. "Forgive me for the welcome my servant gives you." He lowered his voice. "He is not right in his head, but loyal he is, and good he means."

Baba rose, smiling. "I am sure he is kind."

"I am sure you are, too," said the priest. "So you are Fran Aganis."

His words were slow and fluid, with a singsong accent Eleanora found charming. His prominent hooked nose hung from his face, shiny and pink at the tip, and his heavy lips dipped in the corners, though there was a smile in his black eyes as he looked at Eleanora.

"I am Father Aberto. I am happy we meet, finally." He grinned, and this revealed radiance, along with his red cheeks, saved his face.

"Father Gianni," the priest said, "he writes to me, he says he would not survive his first winter without your help. How do you say, *la tosse* . . . his cough is with him always, but better now many thanks to you."

Fran bowed his head.

"*Prego,*" Baba said.

Father Aberto beamed. "*Come parlare bene l'Italiano?*"

"I am afraid that you have heard all of the Italian I speak. I can read and write a little, as can Eleanora, but that is all." Baba laughed. "As for Father Gianni, anything I can do to help him and his parish is my pleasure, Father Aberto. As much as I try not to, I still remember how difficult my first winter in the mountains was."

The priest chuckled, handing Eleanora and her father copper tins of red liquid.

Was this wine? Eleanora sniffed, the fruity fragrance tickling her nose. She had only once drunk raki, the crystal-clear liquor of the mountains, when her father handed her a cup after they had finished an especially grueling surgery. It had burned her throat and her stomach, and she had hated it until it left her mind floating above the sad fact that the bloody bandaged woman would probably not wake up and maybe that was best considering the evidence of her other ill-healed injuries. Baba drank raki as often as other mountain men, during the elaborate and long toasts when he visited patients, but she knew her father preferred this rare beverage. She stared into her dark cup and took a tentative sip, wrinkling her nose.

As the priest led them into the large room, Eleanora could see the servant stirring a large copper pot over the open fire in the back. She sipped her cup, watching the flames' shadows dance on the walls, then took in the rest of the space. The windows were small narrow holes, with a large stone placed in front of each, covering them for the night; most houses she visited did the same to guard against gunfire from feuding families. An unusually high wooden table flanked by two benches took up half the room, and dented square cushions were scattered across the rough wooden floor. The priest lowered himself onto a cushion with a groan. When her father sat down, she followed.

Baba raised his cup to the priest. "This wine is delicious, thank you. It has been so long since I have had any."

The priest waved his compliment away with his sinewy hand. "It is nothing, nothing. If I could give you a casket of it for Father Gianni's health, it would not be enough."

"That, again, is my pleasure. Father Gianni is well loved in our village now," Fran said.

Eleanora said nothing. Her strongest memory of Father Gianni was him chastising her for reading a novel, and asking her why she did not learn Latin and read the Bible. As if it were not convenient for him that no one read, so he could dictate to others what the Bible decreed. She took a deeper gulp of her drink. Its pleasant buzzing erased her tiredness from their long hike. She would become a Catholic if that was what it took to get into the academy! She covered her smiling mouth, looking at her father and the priest with politely grave eyes as she listened.

"Ah, I am very glad to hear this," the priest said, his large head bobbing. "He has a most difficult time, no? He wrote me about the blood feud in his parish. Between tribes Thethi and this . . ." His hooked nose wrinkled. "The other was who?"

"Gjojika," Fran said.

Baba raised his tin but seemed to find it empty, and the priest beckoned the servant with a crooked finger. "Those two. They are always at war," her father said.

"Yes, yes." The priest nodded, holding out his cup to have it refilled by the servant. "Why for?"

"They continue to fight because no one can remember why they began." Baba smiled. He swirled his refreshed cup. "It goes on because no one can remember it not existing."

The two tribes had fought for many generations, for so long that everyone told a different story about the origin of the blood feud. Eleanora had heard the latest from her father. After swearing peace for a few months, the fighting began again: a Gjojika man was shot, and as revenge a Gjojika sworn virgin shot a young Thethi man, really no more than a boy.

Baba shook his head.

"A child never should be killed," he said. "This is something I can agree with tribe elders about. But will they punish a sworn virgin?"

Punish a sworn virgin? As if they did not already live a life of penance, trapping themselves even further in tradition than other women. Eleanora did not care how loudly they might curse and laugh while drinking with men—there was something sad and fruitless about sworn virgins, forbidden from ever acting on love. Eleanora had not been in love, other than with a young man who had been to Budapest and Bucharest, whose image she carried with her for weeks until she met him again—and found him coarser in tongue and looks when compared with fair-haired heroes from her books with whom she had confused his memory. But she thought it to be the highest hope of living—the starved sensualist in her said so, and the doctor's rational daughter asked why were so many stories and art inspired by true love if it were not so fundamentally important? It did not matter that supposedly wise men said marriage had nothing to do with love and happiness—to forgo love seemed the biggest sacrilege against the self, though she supposed the loveless lives of sworn virgins were no emptier than those of most of the passionless villagers she knew. Eleanora had spent time with a sworn virgin many years ago. The sworn virgin was a friend of Baba's, and exactly like any other mountain man—except missing a mustache. And what man would go without a mustache?

Baba had answered on the way home. A sworn virgin was a woman who had vowed to remain chaste in order to gain the right to live like a man: she could inherit property, earn a living, drink and smoke with other men, carry a gun, and kill for vengeance. Though she could kill, she herself could not be killed during a blood feud. Except for that, she was essentially regarded as a man; even "she" was always referred to as "he." Women who had known sworn virgins as little girls giggled with lowered eyes around them, as shy as if they were strange men. Sometimes a sworn virgin shaved her head and dressed in pants, sometimes her name was changed to something more masculine, sometimes not. Eleanora understood some women chose this path as the only honorable way to escape an arranged marriage, but no matter the reason for their vow, if they decided to be with a man later, the sworn virgin and her lover—even if he was her lawful husband—could be shot by her family or her former betrothed's family for dishonoring them. Her family would carry shame, and her former betrothed's family had the right to shoot the men in her family, too, and both families would go to war with the sworn virgin's lover.

"So very complicated, these customs," said Father Aberto, shaking his head. "For me, so many years and Albanian ways can still feel foreign. Myself, I worry for my friends, for my colleagues. It is almost anyone, they can get shot. I know the rules are strict, I know these mountain men are honorable, but you just see their past catch up to them. I worry, I worry . . ." He dabbed his napkin at his frown, then turned to Eleanora, his eyes crinkling in the corners. "But you, Eleanora, you need only worry yourself with your beautiful art."

The priest led them to the high table, where the servant had laid out dishes. Eleanora took a seat next to her father on the hard bench, stroking the edge of the plate with her finger. It was not made of carved wood or hammered copper, but a glossy version of something like plaster. And instead of sharing large bowls of stew and yogurt and corn bread they would dip into with their hands, the priest used silverware to serve her a pile of red sauce–covered strings on a plate set in front of her. Fran and the priest twirled the strings around their pronged spoons and put them into their mouths. Eleanora tried to copy them, succeeding with only a few strings falling back onto her plate, grateful she had not splattered sauce on her blouse. The little white strings were doughy and delicious. She leaned closer, inspecting her plate. She had never tasted something so delicate. Tomatoes like crushed blossoms, the little strings like hair of an angel. A revelation, that food could be more than fuel for her body. It could be turned into art, too, and feed her spirit.

The priest poured Eleanora another cup of red wine, and under the close candlelight the tan leather of the spherical decanter gleamed. The bottle was covered with illustrations, one of a dragon pinned down by the thumb of the priest. The priest met Eleanora's eyes as she leaned forward for a better look.

"Do you know this?" Father Aberto asked.

Eleanora wanted to say it was a bottle for wine, but even

her humming head knew that was too obvious an answer. She shook her head and wondered if her cup would be filled again.

The priest set the decanter on the table and slowly spun it. Brown-green areas were labeled in Italian, separated by blue areas that sailboats floated on.

"This, it is the whole world, you see?" the priest said.

"But it is round!" Eleanora said. She had had a glimpse of a map once before, but it was flat, like the world.

"Yes, it is round. The Earth is round."

Eleanora looked at her father.

"I have read such things," he said.

"Yes, yes," the priest said with a chuckle. "Now, see, we are here." He pointed to a part of a green area bordering the blue. "And you wish to go here." His finger crossed the blue to the green space labeled Venezia. "And this blue space between, that is . . ."

"The sea," Eleanora finished for him. Her eyes widened. "So what is green are countries? So this is Albania, and that is Italy? What about the rest?"

He showed her where Costantinopoli was, Grecia—with so many sculptures and stories, Francia—with the best painters now, yes—and Inghilterra, and she gasped as suddenly the world became both big and very small. The space between Italy and Albania was nothing compared to the mass of Africa, and yet resting within Albania were cities she had not known of. The town below where she now sat, a mere walk away, was still an unknown reality. How much more might the world contain?

Eleanora pinched spaces between her thumb and index finger, trying to see how the distance between Albania and Venice measured against the length of all of Italy. "Baba, have you traveled to any of these places?"

Her father shook his head and squeezed her shoulder.

"I am too old now, and I fear so many of them, even were I to go, would not live up to my lifetime of imaginings. But you, my soul, should see it all." He turned to the priest, smiling. "And you, Father, should see Eleanora's work."

Baba rose from the table and fetched the heavy satchel she had left at the door. He unpacked the pictures and unrolled them on the empty end of the table, holding down their curling corners with two pewter candleholders, careful not to let the wax drip from the sparkling candles. The priest walked to the other end of the table. Eleanora put down her utensil, then picked it up again. She was too afraid to stand near him and explain what she had been trying to achieve. She held her breath as she watched his face. Only his black eyes moved as he examined her pictures. Finally Father Aberto spoke. "Her work has this feeling, no? There are these lines. They are all correct and make this picture I want to walk into, but it is as much something about the lines she chooses not to draw . . ."

Eleanora closed her eyes. Did he think her work good?

Father Aberto continued to examine the drawings on the table as he spoke. "Were she a man in Italia, I do not doubt she would have a patron already. A young man I know, he has a smaller talent—and he was accepted to Accademia di Belle Arti di Venezia. We will get her in, yes, yes, we will get her into the academy."

Baba went to her, hugging her shoulders from behind. He kissed her head, and Eleanora felt a rush of warmth shoot through her.

"Thank you, Father Aberto," she whispered. "Thank you."

Had she said the words aloud? What did it matter? She was going to the academy. She was going to Italy. She would really become an artist. She squeezed her father's hand so hard he winced and laughingly shook out his hand.

The priest grinned at her father.

"Yes, yes, this academy will accept her. It must be. And you remember the fees I wrote of?"

Baba nodded, his eyes glistening.

"Of course. I will have the money by the end of the month, before her studies begin."

So everything was certain and settled! Eleanora let out the breath she had not known she was holding. The men returned to their seats, utensils twinkling against plates, their gay voices discussing details that drifted away from her. She stood and walked toward her paintings, hovering in front of them with her legs wide and her hands on her hips. She was really going to become an artist and study with masters she had admired. If she was celebrated for her work half, no, a quarter as much as Rosalba Carriera! And despite what her father said, she was sure, sure she could convince him and Meria to join her. In Venice there would be beautiful shop windows and giant cathedrals for Meria to admire, books and thinking men for her father. They would be so happy there, and Meria would forget her disappointment in Eleanora for rejecting the proposal of her friend's son. A lightning bolt of joy shot through her. There was so much happiness ahead of them. Tonight she knew it, and her whole body hummed with anticipation. She stretched her arms above her head before she let her hands drop like stones against her sides. She felt a sleepy satisfaction. She raised her heavy hand to her painting of the river, tracing its current with her wavering fingertip. In the flickering candlelight it was as if the river ran beneath her touch. She supposed it was always running, even if it looked still from a distance. It moved eternally forward, dissipated into the air, rained back on itself, and it mattered not to the river if she understood or drowned or enjoyed the ride. She pictured herself floating forward on the river and wished she had her pastels with her so she could capture the rapt expression on her own face. It was so rare she dreamed up a completely new picture she wanted to paint, but tonight, tonight she knew she could do anything.

She looked around, and finding no paper or pastels, she plopped onto a floor cushion, forgetting the men were still at the table. They joined her soon with cups of coffee. Eleanora held hers with two hands, breathing into it so the steam warmed her cheeks, tired from smiling so much.

Eleanora watched the smoke from the open fire rise into the ceiling as the men continued to talk. She joined in with them occasionally and they laughed with her, though she could not remember what she was saying, only that she felt sure of herself and so happy, happier than she had ever been. She tipped her head back and watched the smoke curl up into the thatched rafters, making little shadows, swirling into peaks of the mountains she lived in, melting into a white bird's wings, with a woman's head nestled between. Or was it a man's?

She did not have long hair. She waved her feathers as if to say hello, hello, and Eleanora saw she was looking at her own face. She tried to say hello back, but found she was without a voice. She watched herself tumble through the air, and when she hit the ground, Eleanora jerked against the cold floor and realized she had fallen asleep. Her father was not strict about many customs, but she was never to be so rude as to fall asleep while sitting as a guest. She straightened her tired back, grateful when the wiry priest stood and led her through a dark narrow hallway. Even in her drowsy daze she was surprised by his strength when he caught her arm and kept her from stumbling. He paused at the doorway of a small room, gesturing her to go in. It was empty except for a bed of two thick, plaited reed mats piled upon each other and a red cotton pillow, topped by a heavy wool felt blanket.

"Thank you, thank you, *grazie*," she mumbled, smiling, continuing to thank the priest even as she fell upon her bed.

WAS THE POUNDING in her head or at the door? Eleanora squeezed her eyes shut at the sharp sunlight, rolling over to escape it, but the pounding continued.

"It is a new day, Eleanora."

Ah, Baba. Did she have work to attend to? Where was she?

She shot up from the bed—Father Aberto's home! He had said she would go to the academy! And today, today she would see the city. She stretched her arms above her throbbing head while looking out the small window. The sun's silvery tint slid over the dewy grass, and she heard Tiziano neighing below. She was going abroad, and she would be an artist! She grinned as she folded her blanket. She straightened the waist of her navy pants, tucked in her blue blouse so it was tight and straight, and picked up her navy turban from the floor and adjusted it onto the back of her head. She wished she had her looking glass from home so she might make sure every detail was right. Even she was not oblivious to the stares she received when she wore pants and a masculine turban instead of the traditional headscarf so long it nearly dusted the ground, but she felt in the city her costume would be accepted, maybe even admired. Perhaps she might even see another woman wearing something similar. A future friend? She smiled. Today, anything was possible. This was even better than the day, years ago, she had received a letter back from a friend of a friend of her father's, telling her that yes, the esteemed Accademia di Belle Arti di Venezia still existed and they sometimes accepted women students. And now they would accept her!

She smoothed the front of her pants as she walked into the main room where the fire smoldered. She thanked the servant as he offered her coffee, humming between her sips. The rocks had been removed from the windows, letting the rising daylight shine through the room. Baba and Father Aberto already sat on the floor, and she joined them, wishing them *buongiorno*.

"We have this settled," said Father Aberto, patting Eleanora's hand, grinning at her father.

The priest rose and went to the table, nodding as he looked at her drawings once more before rolling them up and handing them to his servant, with low words about how important these items were and how careful he must be.

Father Aberto turned back to her father.

"I send these to my colleague, and let him know the payment follows soon. I am very proud to be a help in the, what is the word, the career of this great artist. Oh, and how I envy you, if I do say, a life in Venezia." The tips of his fingers touched his smiling mouth.

Words about a great artist living in Venice, and he was talking of her! She finally found her tongue.

"Father Aberto, how can I thank you enough? I cannot, and so I will merely say *grazie mille*."

"Ah!" Father Aberto exclaimed, bowing. "You will soon be at the elegant city you already belong to."

After she and Baba finished their coffee, they thanked Father Aberto at least three times, the priest laughing and clasping their hands as they bade him goodbye for the day.

Baba and Eleanora rushed down the stairs like playful children. Eleanora held her father's arm as they began the walk into town. She felt as if she might float down the lightly sloped path if her father was not holding her hand.

Baba beamed as he greeted strangers they passed.

"We must celebrate," Baba said, squeezing her hand on his arm. "There was a café I visited a lifetime ago. Perhaps it is still here."

The packed-dirt road was wide and framed on each side by paths of slippery embedded rocks—the Platonic ideal of a dry riverbed, though she had to try not to trip while walking on them. She remarked to her father how similar the two-story houses scattered between olive groves were to the ones at home, and after passing a swaying grass field she admired a large, smooth cream building shaped like an oversize house, protected by a delicate white tower that seemed as tall as the mountains behind them. Across the street was another cream building of two stories, both levels an arcade of endless arches facing the street and continuing into the horizon. Its red-tiled roof slanted over its extended balcony. The roof was supported by carved wooden arches, and the balcony, by wide white marble columns below, planted into the street. She ran her hand over one of the smooth white columns. It was out of an illustration of Italy, or ancient Greece. The stones that paved the sidewalk of the pavilion were flat, and the white stones that framed the arches were near-perfect rectangles. Eleanora stroked them to see if they felt as smooth as they looked.

The wide road was empty in the calm early morning, except for a skinny brown dog trotting. Eleanora held her hand out and he came to her, his moist nose tickling her fingers. She patted her pockets, wishing she had something to give him. He licked her hand and pranced off onto a side street.

Eleanora smiled as she watched him, almost walking into a high dark wooden table and chairs that had been set in the pavilion.

"Here we are again," Baba said. "The café is the same. It is out of my memories. I celebrated many things here. Becoming a doctor. My sister, God rest her soul, marrying a man far from here. And then finding out that she loved—" He sighed. "Well, today is the most important celebration. The biggest. You have worked so hard, my Eleanora, and deserve everything that is coming to you."

A brass bell jangled as Fran pushed the café's door open, holding it for Eleanora to walk in first. The short dark man behind the polished wood counter put down his newspaper to greet them.

He scratched beneath his red skullcap, then his dark eyes lit up.

"Fran? Fran of Gucis? You look nearly the same. But I have not seen you . . ."

"In almost twenty years, Mark. You look well," finished Baba, smiling. "I was telling my daughter how often I used to come here. This is my daughter, Eleanora."

She nodded at the grinning man, her eyes narrowing. Gucis was not the name of where her father hailed from. Why had Baba not corrected him?

Mark and Baba kissed each other's cheeks. The café owner scanned Eleanora's face, grinning, patting Fran's arm.

"So you married her after all, Fran? Where is she? Dueling with some disrespectful man?"

Fran's face dimmed. "No. I married a woman from the mountains. I live there now."

"Ah, I understand," said Mark. He cleared his throat, his smile reappearing, though it no longer reached his eyes.

"Would you like coffee and cakes?" The man laughed. "I am still here, serving the same things. You must tell me if they taste as good as you remember, but memory is a harsh judge!" He laughed again, while motioning for them to take a seat.

Baba told her to go ahead. He continued to talk to Mark in low tones.

The café's four tables were empty. Eleanora sat nearest to the window so she could watch the townspeople outside, the crowds growing with the warmth of the day. Most men had the same thick mustaches, shaved heads under caps, white woolen pants and shirts, and cropped black vests as the men in her village, but some wore turbans or red caps like Mark, and robes that fell to their feet or shoes that curled into a point. Some women were merely echoes of the women in the mountains, babies swaddled on their backs and spindles weaving thread in their hands, while others' faces were obscured with lace veils, creating a mystery Eleanora admired until she was distracted by two women who were covered in rich white fabric from head to toe, except for a curving cutout around their brows and eyes, revealing a sliver of sidelong glances.

Her father sat down, placing a cup of coffee and a piece of cake before her. It was corn bread from heaven: a glistening golden diamond, sprinkled with chopped green nuts on top. Eleanora leaned into its buttery citrus fragrance.

Baba watched her with a wistful smile.

"I wish she could see you. Your mother would be so proud of you," he said, his voice cracking. He sipped his coffee.

"My mother?" Eleanora repeated. Her hand hung in the air, a piece of cake pinched in front of her open mouth. Baba never spoke of her mother. Never. And she had never asked him. It was a lifelong, silent agreement they had had. Eleanora sometimes wondered who her mother had been and if she was anything like her, but she felt a pain hidden behind Baba's silence, and furthermore, to breach that silence was to breach her loyalty to Meria, who had kissed her finger when she was stung by a bee, who had sponged her through fevers, who was as much her mother as any woman who may have birthed her but whom she had never met. Her mother? Was this the woman Mark had referred to? Eleanora realized that as much as she loved Meria, she had imagined herself as simply her father's child, perhaps having sprung out of his forehead as Athena came to life from Zeus. Eleanora bit into the cake, suppressing a cough as it crumbled and stuck in her dry mouth.

Baba still had that wistful smile on his face, as he looked past her. "She would be so happy you are escaping all this"—he waved his hand in the air—"this smallness."

Eleanora asked without thinking, "And did she?"

"Escape all this?" His smile sank and he leaned his chin

against his fist. "In a way, I suppose. All that matters is you will have the freedom she wanted, that her family would not give her—and would not give me, for that matter."

He took a bite of cake, chewing slowly, looking at his plate.

"Fran! Fran! Where is Fran?"

Out the window Eleanora saw the priest's shouting servant across the street, holding her father's shining rifle in the air, standing on his bare toes as he searched the crowds. He continued to yell her father's name, and others stopped to stare, some laughing.

Baba smiled, shrugging.

"Apparently I have forgotten something undoubtedly important."

He waved at his friend behind the counter.

"Mark, bring her another piece of cake—one more for me as well, please." He winked at Eleanora, his old joking self again. "I will be back before I am gone, and when I return I have something to give you."

The door jangled as Fran let it slam shut. Eleanora ate her last bite of cake, wondering what little gift Baba had in store for her, and if the man would really bring her more cake. It was sweeter than anything she had ever tasted. And Baba? Had he thought the same thing, years ago, before she was born and he had his first taste? Had her father shared a piece of cake with her mother?

Now that her surprise had worn off at his mentioning her mother, a million questions bubbled up at once to ask him when he returned. What was she like? Where was she from? How old had she been when she met Baba? Was it love at first sight? She thought of what she knew of her mother. Nothing really. She supposed her mother must have died long ago. She wondered if her mother had known Meria. She hoped they had been friends. No one had ever said if they even had met each other in passing.

"Here is your cake."

Eleanora turned to smile politely at Mark.

She heard a crack, a booming bang. She shot up out of her seat. No doubt that was a gunshot, and training with Baba had taught her to rush to scenes most women fled.

The plate brushed her fingertips before it shattered on the floor.

She ran out the door, her reflex to save whoever might be hurt. Likely Baba was already there, tending to this poor person.

Chapter 5

*E*leanora stared into Baba's unblinking eyes, and he stared back. But his deep-brown eyes were unseeing and she saw all: the black braiding down the sides of his white trousers was splattered with mud from the road; his white shirt clung to his chest as it turned a deep maroon darker than the red sash slung around his waist and almost as dark as his black vest; the scar on his cheek was an angry pink under the burning sun; his mustache held more gray in it than she remembered; and his cap had fallen off to reveal he was overdue to have his head shaved.

Eleanora knelt, reaching to put her father's cap back on. That was stupid of her. She needed a compress to stop the bleeding. She tugged off his sash and began stuffing it into his bleeding chest, and the greedy cavity sucked almost all of it in as she pressed it and more blood gushed out, thick and staining her hands. What should she do now? If only Baba would tell her.

She patted his cheeks to see if he would wake and respond, repeating his name over and over again.

She flinched as some strange man grabbed her arm, and she tried to wrench her arm away. Always, always stupid men interrupting the important work she and Baba had to do. They never understood, even when they had begged for Baba and Eleanora to come.

"What do you think you are doing?" a man's rough voice asked. "I believe this is too much for you. A woman should not see something like this. Where is your husband? Your father? Your brother?"

"I am traveling with—with"—Eleanora swallowed her sob—"I am traveling with my father. Baba?" she cooed. "Baba?"

Baba did not even blink. She must remain calm. She took a deep breath, choking and gulping and on the verge of panicked sobs. Perhaps someone had smelling salts for him?

The maddening man continued to tug at her arm. "Please, if you will rise and leave this man's body in peace for his family's sake. Where is your father?"

She pointed to Baba as he lay there, continuing to lock eyes with her father until that stupid man's hand clenched her shoulder, this time pulling her up and twisting her away. She clawed the tears off her cheeks, but it was like trying to stop a waterfall with her hands. What was the point? She wiped her bloody palms on her pants and faced the tall strange man, she without curiosity, while his small eyes, buried in his craggy face, widened.

"This is your father?" he asked. "And he was shot while you were with him?"

"No, no, no . . ." Eleanora said, shaking her head. "I was in the café."

It was too late. She was too late. She might have gone into the streets with Baba. Eleanora stared at the dirt road, imagining how her father would have said he was going outside, and she would have said that she would of course go with him, and then they would have returned, arms hooked as they walked, to their cake. She kept her eyes on the ground. Mud caked on her knees; a red smudge on her new leather sandals; a tear fell from her face and shattered into another stain on her shoes. She must try to get that out before Meria chastised her later.

"You were not with him? I thought not, but one must be sure," the man said, twirling his white mustache, frowning. "No man would ever shoot another while he was with a woman or child."

As if she did not know that. What would he tell her next in his sad, apologetic voice? That water was wet? That the sky was blue? That she should not have left her father's side?

"Well, you must return to your family," he said. "There is nothing else to do."

"Nothing?" Eleanora repeated. Baba had drilled into her there was always, always something to do, even if one did not immediately think of it. She took her handkerchief out of her pocket and wiped her forehead and scrubbed her sticky cheeks. She would not move until she thought of what she might do to save him.

"There is nothing to do," he repeated.

If only he would shut up so she could think. She imagined her feet had roots buried deep into the ground, otherwise her foot might just swing into this stupid man's knees and kick and keep kicking.

"Your father owed this man blood. He said so. It was an honor killing. He—"

"Owed him blood?" Eleanora met his eyes now, almost screaming, "Who? Who? Who was he and how could you have heard such a thing and not tried to stop it?"

"How would one stop something like this? This is the Law of Lekë since the time of Lekë, which is to say, always." He began to warm up to his subject, as a few men nearby nodded approvingly. "The Law, as you know—"

"Who was he?" Eleanora asked.

"Who? Oh, as for the shooter, I do not remember his name. Though he called it out, as was right. He did seem a little drunk, but he did what was honorable, and then he fled," said the man.

He scratched his scalp beneath his cap, dented but white like her father's. Eleanora crossed her arms tightly so she would not be tempted to knock his cap into the mud, too. The sympathy in the man's eyes was cooling.

"I want to speak with the elders—no, the chief of the town," she said. She would find this shooter and make him pay for what he had done. When the elders found out who had been shot . . . Her tone was hard, but not brittle. She would not be a stupid hysterical woman. She would be calm as Baba had taught her to be. She wiped her eyes and took a deep breath, squaring her shoulders. "Now, please. Take me now."

The man swallowed and crossed his arms. Did she face fear or disdain? Both, a combination she recognized but had stopped trying to understand, had never needed to understand, so long as Baba was with her to laugh at it. She knelt next to her father, holding his hand, hoping to pull him up, but he was too heavy for her and his arm flopped down and splashed back into the mud. Another spot on her sandals. Since her father refused to get up, she must do what he would have done. She wiped the tears off her cheeks. Stupid tears. Why was she crying when nothing was wrong that she could not fix? This was her fault but she would make things right, and then . . . She stiffened her back and hugged her arms across her chest.

"Please," she said, pronouncing each word as if it were its own statement. "Take me to the chief of the town."

The man raised his snowy caterpillar eyebrows, spun, and started walking down the road. Eleanora focused so completely on the back of his short black vest as it wove through the crowd that when the man paused she almost bumped into him. They were in front of a building, part of the seeming infinity of buildings leaning against one another, though this one was slightly whiter and wider, with delicately carved window frames. Under a broad, high arch was a tall wooden door that opened with a grunt.

In a high-ceilinged white room, a scribe slumped at a heavy wooden desk facing the front door, guarding another glossy dark door behind him. Eleanora found an empty seat among the waiting men, leaving her escort standing. He greeted a man, the same age, the same costume, the same dumb look on his face, and began to inquire about his sons and his sons' sons, and as his conversation rolled on with his back to Eleanora, she realized he had helped her as much as he meant to.

That was fine. She did not need him. She did not need anyone. What had she been waiting for anyway? She must speak with the chief so they might catch Baba's kill—the man who had done this.

Tears were suddenly sliding down her cheeks, and she scratched them away. Standing before she thought of it. Feeling almost wonder as she saw she was walking up to the young man slouching behind the desk, who continued to flourish scrawls with his engraved silver reed pen as her shadow moved over his papers.

"Excuse me," she whispered through her clenched jaw.

He squinted at a letter in front of him and dipped his pen into its jewel-encrusted inkwell.

"Excuse me," she said more loudly.

He raised his chubby chin and stared at her expectantly. She felt the other eyes bearing down on her back.

"I need to see the chief of Shkodra," she said.

"We do not have a . . . chief," he said, his thick mustache drooping with his frown. He looked her up and down. "I am not sure where you are from. But this is not like those little mountain villages. I believe you are referring to—"

"I wish to see whoever is in charge." Her eyes began to well up, but if she did not blink, if she ignored that wetness, it must disappear.

The scribe's pale lips tightened, and his mustache half drooped with his disdainful smirk.

"Regarding?"

"Baba was, my father was . . ." Eleanora felt the tears about to spill over, and she focused on the blank wall behind him. "He was shot."

He looked back down at his desk, picking up his pen.

She kept her eyes wide and unblinking, digging her finger-nails into her palms.

"My father was, he was murdered."

"Well, if what you say is true . . ." He put his pen down, stood, and knocked on the door behind his desk.

"Come in, come in." A loud sigh sounded as the scribe opened the door.

A heavy man with a coiled red turban drooping over his fore-head looked up from his gleaming desk at Eleanora, the thick gold rings on his fingers glittering as he continued to scribble onto papers that another scribe shuffled in front of him. The desk scribe walked over behind the desk and whispered into his master's ear. The ringed hands never stopped dancing over the papers.

"Her father, you say? Yes, I believe I have heard already. If his family is here, we must speak about moving the body immedi-ately, it is in the middle of the road . . ." the head of the town said, his sentence another loud sigh, his right hand continuing to jiggle and jot, his left hand holding a stamp that pounced on random pages his assistant slid onto his desk while he glanced at Eleanora.

"If you think I have not heard already about Fran of Gucis, and have not heard of such a thing happening many times be-fore . . ." He waved at his assistant. "Show me that paper again." He cleared his throat. "It is a shame, but I am afraid this is another example of why women should not wander from men's sides. He was your husband, right? Oh, your father, I see. Well, either way, he would not have been shot then, of course, were a woman with him. It was an honor killing, I was told. This sort of thing happens so often with these mountain people, they make such enemies of each other and for what? I have always said—"

"But my father had no enemies," Eleanora interrupted. She was vaguely aware her hands hurt, and she looked down to see one was wringing the other. She forced her hands to her sides.

His eyes stayed downward, but his mustache lifted beneath a tight smile.

"The man who shot him might beg to differ." He stamped another paper his scribe pushed in front of him. "Why else would he have shot your father like that, in the daylight and so publicly? This was no mere murder, though I have heard the shooter was, er, intoxicated. No money was taken. He left your father's rifle placed against his head, an expensive gun at that. And he announced his deed, according to your traditions, your law . . . of Lekë, is it?" He murmured something to his assistant.

"And did he announce why?" Eleanora asked. That he would not meet her eyes made it easier for her to speak.

"Oh, something about some woman, of course." He shrugged. "Women are almost always at the bottom of this sort of trouble."

"Who was she?" Eleanora demanded. "Who?"

"Must you shout? I have such a headache." He rubbed his temples, sighing again. "Who was she? Who knows? This man's wife or sister or cousin? His mother's mother?" He chuckled. "From what I understand, such things may go back to the time of the Prophet himself." He kept squiggling his pen as he lifted his eyebrows at his scribe. The scribe stepped toward her.

Eleanora stood still, pressing her lips together.

"At least tell me who the shooter is," she pleaded. "Please."

"So you might gossip with your brothers and uncles and cousins and start some endless feud? I have enough to deal with without another one of those on my hands." He shrugged without his pen pausing. "His name is Kol, of . . . I do not recall from where. I am sure he probably already fled to the mountains. What does one expect me to do? Am I to handle everything? Now my scribe must show you to the door. He can help you to find someone to transport the body, or if you wish, my cousin has funeral services here, Muslim or Catholic, and if you use my name his price will be quite fair."

Eleanora went to see his cousin, Alek, and she knew not if his price was fair. All she cared, as she stood in the shabby room a few doors down from the chief's office, staring at the dirt floor, was that she would not have to see her father's body again. She stood there, watching her right hand twisting her left fingers, while Alek's two sons fetched her father's body, and handed over Baba's prized rifle and a leather pouch jangling with gold and silver coins, and a sterling silver bracelet of a ruby-eyed serpent biting its own tail. Was this the present Baba meant to give her? Alek said it was a beautiful bauble he would be willing to take for payment, but she snapped at him, refraining from slapping his fat hands away. She slipped on the bracelet, exhausted and bewildered and numb as Alek's plump brown fingers plucked half the silver and gold coins out of her palms. She walked away from the service in the overgrown cemetery when the cheap pine coffin was about to be lowered into the ground by Alek's grunting sons. That had not been Baba's body in the coffin. Baba was on an extended trip for work, he was busy healing and helping people . . .

IN THE DYING sunlight of late afternoon, she stood in the middle of the bustling city street, her thumb rubbing the sterling-silver-and-enamel pattern on her father's rifle. The crowd strolled around her, a river current momentarily diverted by a stubborn boulder, while Eleanora wondered what she should do next, besides try not to cry and desperately wish her body were in that cheap pine coffin instead.

Chapter 6

Even in the murky twilight, the townspeople turned to look at Eleanora as she trudged up the hill to the priest's house. Who had not heard about the foolish, selfish daughter who had left her father's side? Who had left him to—

She still could not use that word.

She had played in her head so many different scenes in which she had stopped Baba with a light touch of her hand on his arm, asking him to wait so she could go outside with him.

"I have had enough cake and want to see the city with you. Why not leave together now?"

Or perhaps she merely said, "Let me get that for you instead." Even if she had only asked him to wait a moment, stalled him with some foolish talk, "Baba, remember the time when—"

Oh, she loved to point out the foolishness of women, but most every one of them but her would have had the feminine instinct never to have allowed this to happen.

Eleanora kept her eyes down on the beaten trail as it crunched beneath her heavy feet.

"Are you an honorable man or a woman?"

Was someone talking to her?

"Are you a man, or are you a woman?"

She looked up to see a pair of mountain men, twins in their snowy wool pants and caps and blouses tied down by black cropped vests, except for their mustaches—one was a boring brown and the other a shocking red, which its owner continually twisted.

"I am a woman, of Arbër," she answered automatically. It was odd to be addressed by unknown men, even if their greeting was a mere twist on the standard greeting between strangers, "Are you a man?" or for women, "Are you a woman?"

The red mustache was tugged down. "You are a woman?" His hand lazily gestured to her father's rifle. She realized then people might be intrigued by the unique image of a woman carrying a firearm.

"A woman?" said the brown mustache. "You are not a sworn virgin? Then why are you walking alone with this gun?" he asked. "Have you stolen it?"

Did she look so guilty? Her sin was her business. The only person who had ever had a right and the right mind to judge her was Baba, and he was gone. She rubbed her thumb into the etched silver of her father's rifle.

"No, I have not stolen this gun," Eleanora said. "And even if I had, what business would it be of you two old maids in britches?"

Eyes at their widest. The red mustache turned to his shocked friend; he twisted his mustache as he eyed Eleanora's gun.

"If she is not a sworn virgin now, she will be a sworn virgin soon," the red mustache said, nudging his friend, "though maybe not by her own swearing. Who cares about her beauty? Extra beauty in a woman is only extra trouble, as you can see. What man would stand for such an attitude in a wife?"

And they chuckled, not at her but with each other; she had already ceased to exist for them, though they walked a little faster away when she tilted the front of the rifle toward them.

It was dark when she found herself at the bottom of the staircase of the priest's house. She heard her and Baba's horses neighing as she trudged up the groaning stairs. She stood before the door, wiping her nose with her handkerchief, straightening her shoulders.

Before she could knock, the door creaked open; the servant's lowered eyes floated in the dark before he slipped away. His retreating back wore the same sleeveless brown tunic he had worn that morning and the night before, and Eleanora felt perhaps nothing had changed and when she walked through the door she might find her father suddenly guiding her again.

Father Aberto appeared in front of her, hands out, his wiry brows slanted toward heaven.

Eleanora stood planted in the middle of the room. She shuffled her feet and realized she had forgotten to take her shoes off. Baba would think that rude, but she did not care. How could he accuse her now, when—she turned her head and roughly wiped her eyes with her handkerchief.

The priest gently lifted her father's gun from her hands and tilted it against the wall near the door. He pressed a cup of raki into her trembling hand. No wine tonight? What did that matter? What did anything matter? Eleanora downed it in one burning gulp, like she had seen men do after Baba had given them bad news about their sons, their wives, their brothers, their fathers. Her father. She held her empty cup a little farther out, hoping he would refill it, and he did. Eleanora sipped it slowly, looking at the high table. She wondered if the priest had eaten those doughy strings again for dinner.

"I am very sorry, so sorry, for this loss, dear child," said Father Aberto.

Eleanora said nothing, looking at her shoes. She drank the rest of the raki, welcoming the stream of hot pain into her belly. She deserved to suffer more. She fingered the knife tucked into her belt. She had forgotten it was there; it was always there. Another missed opportunity. She might have run out into the street and caught him after at least, punished him for—

"Please, you are most welcome to stay here." Even under her lowered eyes she saw Father Aberto's wringing hands.

She remained standing, letting her fingernails dig into her palms. She was so stupid, so very stupid, she could think of nothing to say.

Finally his hand touched the middle of her back, guiding her to the dark room she had slept in last night. Just last night she had been smiling and making plans with Baba. She shook her sloshing head. It was not until the door closed that she let herself remember how often her father's hand had brushed her back like that. She sat down on the mat, hugging her knees, screaming into her thighs.

She did not realize she had been sleeping until she woke up, whimpering. "Baba!"

She had been trying to warn him. She stared in the darkness, rubbing her cramped neck, still seeing her dream. She had been sitting in the café again. Right outside the window was her father's back, suddenly a rifle pointed at him, at her, as he faced Eleanora, blood gurgling from his unmoving mouth, though the words rose up: *Where were you?*

She sat up in the smothering darkness with her hair wet and matted to her forehead. She threw the clinging blanket off her thumping heart. She would not fall asleep again. Whoever had come for Baba might come for her. He was coming for her. Was that a creak? He was already at the stairs into the house. She must sit up; sit up until the sun would make this nightmare impossible . . .

She squeezed her eyes shut at light breaking through the narrow window, burning onto her sweating face. She threw her arm over her eyes, feeling a point pulsing between them, and lay still, willing her headache away. Where was she? Alone on stiff bedding smelling of incense, without the heat emanating from the fireplace or her father's low humming as he read an old newspaper.

She was on a trip with her father, yes, but not for work. She rolled on her side and drew her knees up to her chest. She felt she had arrived here a long time ago. She sat up. But how could that be when her father and she had only come here the night before to meet the priest?

She remembered.

Her face scrunched into a cry, then froze—to what end? No one would or could comfort her. If only she had Meria to hold her. But to have to tell Meria her guilt, to explain to her what she had let happen. How she had been so slow and simpleminded.

She slammed her fist into the pillow. Maybe she should hit the stone floor instead so she would really feel it? She shook her head, grinding her fists into the floor as she pushed herself to her feet. She rolled up her mat carefully, folded and refolded her blanket twice until the corners lined up, and when the pillow fell from on top of this pile, she balanced it on the dead center of it again, forestalling facing the priest and his pity that would make her weep at the realness all over again. He had known her father for an evening. So he had complimented her paintings. What was her unimaginable tragedy to him but another sad story brought to him to be murmured and prayed over? But perhaps he would have news about her father's—no, she could not use that word yet. Baba was merely gone, and naturally she was a little lost without him, but she would tell him how she felt soon enough, while he held her hands and laughed, apologizing for leaving without an explanation. That was the trick she would play on her mind, the story she would tell herself, like when she often told fathers in a low, soothing tone that their sons were merely gone, that they had floated away to a peaceful place. Not that they had choked on their own blood, that pneumonia had suffocated them in their own fluids, that the gunshot had—

Enough. Eleanora plucked her turban from the floor and dusted it off, straightened her clothing, and crossed the hallway into the main room. She stood in the doorway, rewrapping her turban on her head, feeling foolish about it, but she had nothing else to cover her hair. She sighed. There was the eternal fire with its pot of coffee over it. She took a cup from the servant, willing her hands to keep calm though she was tempted to toss the coffee in his stupid face. He was to blame, too. She walked away from him, cradling the cup. At least it warmed her hands against the slight chill in the morning air. Summer had slipped away.

Father Aberto greeted Eleanora with open arms and palms spread, as he had last night. The windows remained covered, and Eleanora wondered if she had dreamed going to sleep. Perhaps she was dreaming now. If only she were! And when she woke, she would never, ever leave Baba's side.

"About your father I am sorry, very sorry," the priest said. "Such a good, good man. Tell me, I want to help if I can."

Had he said this last night? How had she replied? Thank you, but there was nothing he could do? She continued staring into the brown-black depths of her coffee.

She gasped and looked up into the priest's frowning eyes. Her heart hammered with the fear she might have forgotten to say this: "You can help me secure my place in the academy. I still wish to go. In fact, more than ever."

School! What had been a holiday dangled in front of a child was now the answer to everything. She had not known what an opportunity it was—to fly from all this, to begin a new life, to let this one float away.

The priest looked down at his bare feet.

"Of course, I still send your pictures to my colleague in Venezia. Of course, of course I do that. But the payment . . . you see, your father was to send it in a month, two months."

She felt the weight with which he said that, but surely the money must be somewhere. She chewed her lip. Whatever she had asked for, her father had always given her twice that and a smile; she and Meria had never wanted for anything. There must be money hidden at home or things she might sell. The two horses downstairs! What did she want with her father's horse, anyway? To watch his drooping head and sad, intelligent eyes wait for Baba each day, another reminder of him never returning?

"Perhaps my father's horse would pay for my schooling?" Eleanora asked.

Baba's horse had loved him deeply, and Baba had loved his horse; he never said so, but he was prouder of nothing, except for Eleanora. He would have been saddened to see him go, and who else would brush him and feed him with Baba's care? Well, it was his fault for abandoning her, and leaving her to figure out all these things she had depended on him for. Her lip trembled, but she made herself stare at the high table in the distance, where the wine decanter sat.

"Pardon me, I do not know the price of a fine horse like this one." The priest cleared his throat. "But I believe it is only a small beginning."

"Perhaps my horse would cover the rest?" She closed her eyes, nodding, relieved at the thought. She could leave both horses here and flee today across the sea, if she could only leave this all behind. She would write to Meria later, explaining everything, and Meria would meet her in a new city, a new life for both of them.

"Maybe this is half." His hand covered his mouth as he coughed. "You see, it is not only the academy, the school supplies you must have, but there is, too, the large price of living in a very big city like Venezia." Then his dark face brightened. "Your father had brothers?"

"My father has no family I know of, and all of my stepmother's has passed away."

She stared at the trembling blackness in her cup, the priest's blushing silence heavy on her throbbing head.

She had come to this house as the daughter of a man in the unique position to send his daughter abroad to study art, and she would leave as an unprotected orphan. She had seen families decimated by a bullet before, and she had patted hands and told them, convincingly, everything would be all right. What a fool she had been, then, and more than ever, yesterday, as she had sat in that café like a child greedy for a sweet. What else was there? She must not stand here and think of all she might have done. She must not let the priest's pity crack her strength. Any moment and it would be too many taps on a frozen lake, and she would find herself suddenly thrashing and drowning in ice-cold water. She remembered a mother, hugging her young daughter, who had kept her back straight and cheeks dry while listening to Baba explain that all three of her sons would not live.

"A brave woman," Baba had said admiringly.

Eleanora set her cup down on the high table, forcing herself to look at Father Aberto in his mournful eyes when she thanked him for his help with the academy and his gracious hospitality. As she turned to the door, she thought he started to step toward her, but she grabbed her father's gun and dashed downstairs to fetch the horses.

It was hard to walk the wide dusty road, winding through the grassy plains back to the purple mountains looming ahead, with one horse's lead in each hand and her father's rifle slung across her shoulder, but it distracted Eleanora from her mind spinning through what she might have done, and who the evil man who did the deed was, and why people were staring. Perhaps it was because they knew, they knew who she was and what she had not done. She trudged on until the path narrowed as it began to rise steeply into the mountains. She stopped, her breath heavy already. She could not lead both horses across the river alone.

She was not sure what her father's prize stallion was worth, but she would have to find out what someone would pay for it. And if someone paid much less than her father had, the blame laid with him, leaving her so suddenly alone in a strange town.

Eleanora tugged the horses' leads around, shouting at them to turn faster, yelling at them when they bumped into her, suddenly sobbing, "Baba! Baba!"

She would do anything to have him back. Anything. She crumpled in the middle of the road and pressed her forehead to the ground, choking on the dirt she inhaled. Nothing would bring him back. Not even carving up the evil man who had done this, if she even found out who he was and why he had ripped her father from her life. No, not even that would help. Eleanora had seen men consumed by revenge and knew how lives were twice ruined that way. She must go on as her father would have encouraged her to. She must get back to Meria, and they would plan together what to do. She ground her teeth and started walking, blinking back her tears.

When she caught herself speaking to her father in her mind about how the swaying fields reminded her of the lush valley below their village, she shook her head so hard she was dizzy and clucked at her horses. She came down the same road she had traveled with Baba, intent on avoiding even a glance at the priest's home, and she wandered onto a small path bordering the fringe of the town, hoping to find a way into the city's heart while not passing yesterday's café.

She came across a young woman sitting behind a few pieces of rough pottery for sale. Her sun-browned face and bright scarlet headscarf reminded her of the women from a village on the edge of hers.

"Long life to you," Eleanora greeted her.

"And to you, long life," the woman replied, surprise written on her face even as she did not look up from the vest she embroidered. "How could you get here?" she asked politely.

"Slowly, slowly, little by little," Eleanora replied, continuing the courteous formula. "Are you a woman?"

"I am a woman born of Shala married into Shoshi."

"Might you tell me where the market is?"

"Market? You mean bazaar? Which bazaar? The covered bazaar, the flea market? It is not market day, but you will find people there nonetheless, though if—"

"Which is the closest one?" Eleanora interrupted her. She was afraid if she did not hurry she would lose her nerve. "I mean to sell a horse."

"Ah, well, then why not the covered bazaar?" She shrugged and offered seemingly simple directions, and Eleanora soon found herself lost in a labyrinth of slippery cobblestone paths walled in on both sides by one- and two-story stone buildings that all looked the same, with entire walls cut out as storefronts. Within these man-made caves hung glistening guns, hammered copper cups and pots, and flowing fabrics. Her horses nearly bucked as a small man walked by, pulling the chain leash of a bristling black animal larger than any dog she had ever seen.

As she turned to calm her horses, she saw the disintegrating large arch the woman had described.

She was too shy to enter the actual building, the largest in

Shkodra and certainly the largest she had ever seen, and so she lost herself in the crowds.

People crawled stall to stall, everyone staring and jostling but staying out of her way, so that she had gone down half the arcade before she realized she would have to approach potential buyers. She saw a stall with rolls of white bread and brown loaves, and she was drawn to it for its empty calm and the perfect shapes so different from the crumbling corn bread she knew. The baker came out from the back shadows, yawning, tapping a wide knife onto his palm. Eleanora took her eyes away from the cloud-like rolls and asked him if he knew anyone who bought horses.

"We all buy horses at some point." He smiled, pointed teeth showing, but the smile did not reach his dark eyes. "Are you selling the white one? It is a very beautiful horse."

He offered what even Eleanora knew was a large amount. She considered this while watching him finger the shining blade. He stared unblinking into Eleanora's eyes.

A tiny shirtless boy, ribs showing, darted from behind the cart to snatch a loaf. The baker tried to grab him, the knife swinging in the air, and hooted when his fist pounded the small shoulder before the boy scampered away. The baker cursed, swearing he would kill the boy and all his family.

Eleanora backed away. It did not matter if the baker would give her enough to build her own academy in Rome. If he treated a starving boy that way, she could not bear to imagine what he might do to Baba's strong-minded horse.

She walked a few paces, until a man and his young son approached her. The boy came up to his father's chest; that and his lack of a mustache and slightly askew snow-white cap were the only differences between the two. They both wore traditional white costumes of mountain men. Eleanora did not recognize the pattern of the black braiding up the sides of their white woolen pants, so she was unsure what tribe they came from, but the father's eyes were relaxed with kindness.

After they dispensed with the usual long greetings, he was direct.

"I overheard you are selling your horse," the father said. "For how much?"

Eleanora repeated the price the baker had offered.

He shook his head.

"It is a beautiful horse, but more than I can afford."

"What can you afford?" Eleanora asked.

"A little more than half."

When she accepted his offer, he grinned, patting his son's shoulder, asking his son how he would like to ride this horse to school. It reminded Eleanora of a long-ago scene she refused to let surface on the stage of her mind for fear she would weep. She emptied the satchels on her father's horse, packed them into her own, and did not look back.

ELEANORA SWUNG HERSELF onto her red leather saddle, urging Tiziano to a fast trot back toward the priest's home—but for what? His pity meant nothing; it was his job to offer consolation to anyone, for anything. He had stumbled over her name when he had said goodbye. He had barely known her father. How would he know directions to her village? She could get home alone. It was simple enough—a single path crossed the river, and only one footpath led into her village. She pressed her lips together. Might as well start now.

Traveling to Shkodra had taken almost a week with her

father, but they had visited old friends along the way, who had then told her father of an entire family overcome with a rash, which Baba quickly diagnosed and left them with a detailed recipe for a tincture for it. He had left them so happy, so quickly! She wondered how they were doing . . . She shook her head. They were fine and she was fine, and if she hurried, she would be home to Meria before dark.

And if she did not, who cared? No one. As far as Meria knew, she was still with her father, safe.

Eleanora sighed, staring at the purple-blue mountains soaring over the city, and urged Tiziano on faster. When she reached the grassy plains on the outskirts of town, she encouraged Tiziano into a loud and hard gallop, never hitting or whipping him but merely speaking to him. He understood her, and she felt comforted by his warm bristling coat. Clusters of men and women with bundled babies jumped out of the way and turned to look at her, and Eleanora urged Tiziano to go even faster, only slowing him when she remembered she had much farther to go.

Where the plains ended, the craggy mountain sharply rose, and the path was narrow and steep all at once.

She hopped off Tiziano and led him one sliding, steep step after the other on the stair-like path of crumbling white rock and pale-green shale.

She allowed Tiziano and herself to rest only when she was sure, if she looked back, she would no longer see Shkodra. She squatted in the dirt path, taking deep breaths and petting Tiziano's foaming muzzle. She had already climbed high into the sky, the deep-green valley thousands of feet beneath her; even the sun seemed beneath her. Cream cliffs shot out of mountains carpeted in green shrubs or blue with distance, all of them peaking on top of one another like craggy waves midcrash, the highest, farthest ones ending in crests of white snow. Each mountain was a jagged, ever-climbing, never-ending layer upon the other, their depths a hazy blue, and their purple-blue slanted tops streaked with silver-white waterfalls, which made a soft, steady murmur all around, the waters' roars softened by distance. Until now, Eleanora had not realized how she took the constant white noise for granted and that she had missed it while in the city.

Across the valley was the mirror image of the mountains Eleanora crouched in, their shadowy purple cut only by the curling white smoke from the dim dots of houses buried into cliffs and those silver streaks of waterfalls. She wondered if there was a girl nestled in those cliffs, too, weighed down by the same sharp heartache.

No. Surely she was alone.

Eleanora heard quick crunching footsteps behind her. Her horse's ears stiffened. The path of crumbling green shale had become so narrow and nearly vertical it was almost impossible to overtake anyone, so she urged her horse to start scrambling up again, looking for a place she might let the other hiker pass. Oh, and how she hoped he would pass, without a look her way.

What if it was *him*, what if *he* had followed her? She gripped her knife, ready to whip it out, trying to shake the thought away. For all she knew the man who had killed—who had done what he had done to Baba had made a tremendous mistake, no matter what anyone said. No one was coming for her.

Ahead, the path appeared to pause into the air; it must bend upward to the right. Eleanora crawled closer: before the sharp curve a small patch of grass jutted into the sky. A weathered wooden cross had been planted in the center, held there by piles of rocks around its base, and underneath the cross a dark man sat rolling a cigarette. He stared at her as she stopped.

The gravelly steps behind her paused, too.

The dark man tossed his cigarette, sprang up, his hand on his pistol.

"Are you traveling with this man?" he spit at Eleanora.

Eleanora glanced behind her. The man was much younger than she, but his head was shaved, and he wore the beginnings of a blond mustache, almost the same shade as his fair face. She squinted; the braiding down the side of his pants differed from the dark man's. The blond man's eyes widened, and his hand trembled over his gun, until she said on an impulse, "Long may you live. Yes, I am traveling with him. He is my cousin."

The dark man looked doubtful but let his hand drop to his side.

"Well, then, we meet in peace," he said to the younger man. "Would you care for a cigarette?"

So the two men were from feuding tribes. She despised meaningless violence, but she clenched her jaw to fight angry tears as she watched them gossip like friends. Death skirted so simply, thanks to unthinking tradition. Why had she let her father go into the street alone? Because she thought she and her father were above tradition? Because she thought she was so superior to everyone else's laws? She had made such a stupid, fatal mistake. It could have been so simple. Eleanora walked to the edge of the cliff, kicking a spray of rocks, watching them silently disappear into the blackening valley below. She tiptoed closer to the edge, kicking a larger rock, her ears straining for any noise. She was so high up she supposed she would not be able to hear even if something the size of her body fell. She shook her head. More foolishness. She had her horse to look after, Meria to return to, and she must at least wait for this young man to be safe again.

"Safety? Do any of us ever know safety?" asked the dark man, taking the fragrant cigarette back from the young man. "As for peace, we may know that, and I hope soon. Likely twenty-five men from your tribe and mine ought to wipe out the blood debt."

She looked across the valley's deepening shadows—surely somewhere, tucked into one of the hundreds of cliffs, was another pair of undeservedly lucky men like these smoking cigarettes, though she could not even make out the smoke of the chimneys anymore. She could barely see anything. The sun would set soon, and she had not even reached where she crossed the river with her father yet, which he had said was the halfway mark between the city and home.

She looked at her supposed escort, smiling as he chatted in low tones with his new friend.

"Dearest cousin, could we be going?" she asked.

The men stopped talking, the older one twisting his inky mustache and raising his eyebrows.

What might her alleged traveling companion say to that? Eleanora tapped her foot. He shrugged and smiled at his would-be murderer, thanking him for the cigarette.

"Long may you live," he said. "Go on a smooth trail."

"Long may you live," the dark man answered. "God take you safely home."

When Eleanora and the fair young man were out of earshot of the other, he turned to her.

"Thank you for helping me," he whispered. "I am not afraid to die, and it would have been an honor to die if I might have killed that fellow. But you see, I am my father's only son now. If it were not for that, I would have told him the truth and let fate decide who lived."

"It was nothing," Eleanora said. "Why are your tribes feuding?"

Eleanora generally disliked men from either tribe, as they were the strictest adherents to the ancient code. But when the young man looked back to talk to her, his rosy cheeks and bright blue eyes evoked a cherub in an Italian fresco. His sparse mustache wiggled every time he smiled, which was often.

"Some silly woman, naturally!"

He turned back and grinned at her again, proud to share such exciting news with a stranger.

"She was from that fellow's tribe and betrothed to a good man in my tribe. Before she was born, their fathers agreed their children would marry. They were great friends, you see. But instead she ran away with another man."

Eleanora frowned. "How long ago was this?"

"Oh, I guess a few years now. Her family has been hunting for her and her husband since the night she fled, but they still have not found her! Those poor men, they cannot be friends now. And the shame is enough to kill them."

So let it, Eleanora thought. Her weak interest in such a standard story was dissolving into distaste for its players, but talking with the boy distracted her. "But the woman," she asked, "she at least ran away for love?"

"What does a girl know of love?" He laughed, his head slightly tilted back and exposing his skinny throat, which Eleanora had the sudden urge to grab and shake.

To think this was the life she had saved. This instead of another, one who might have smiled from an opposite feeling at the romance of a woman deciding to flee from being traded as a token of affection between two men who cared nothing about her life, so long as she did not disgrace them.

"It is such a shame," he continued, "how many men have died over this. If only they would catch the girl and her husband. My two brothers were killed by that fellow's tribe."

"So why not swear peace?" Peace was often reached by the tribes' elders coming together and negotiating a monetary settlement.

"Peace?" His step quickened, and he did not look back. "Too many men have died to swear peace now."

Of course, that too many men had died meant more should. Eleanora sighed and changed the topic.

"So, cousin, where are you going?" she asked.

He chuckled again. "Home, home finally! I have been visiting so many villages. I have seen so many villages! And I know it is rude of me to say so, forgive me, I have not tasted anything so nearly as good as the food at home. There is a way the corn bread is made, it is light as air . . ."

He only stopped praising the meals of stewed goat and roasted skewered pork that he would soon enjoy again to ask Eleanora where she was going.

She named her small village. "Did you go there during your travels?" she asked, hardly caring for his answer as she looked ahead to make sure Tiziano was fine.

"That is so far! I have heard of a strange and powerful healer and his daughter—a daughter!—from there. Is it true they live there?"

Her throat tightened. If her father's work was done, then hers was, too. "I have never heard of them," Eleanora answered.

"Ah, perhaps it is only a story. Who ever heard of a woman healer?" he asked. "Nonetheless, your village is rather far." He put his hand to his heart. "In our house there is always a welcome for a stranger. The door of the house of my father is open to you."

"Glory to your lips and to your feet," Eleanora replied politely.

She knew he invited her out of courteous habit and deeply ingrained custom that made gods of guests, and it was a dishonor to turn a stranger away for the night. It all came back to stupid honor. Still, she was grateful, because she had hiked farther than she remembered walking with her father. The trail's decline had steepened to an ongoing slide, her heels digging and slipping in the crumbling green shale that slid into her socks and rose as choking dust into the air, for what felt like hours, though she still had not reached the river. The sky above was a deepening blue, but night had already flooded the valley below and she could no longer see how much farther away its bed was. It was bottomless in its blackness. Though the idea of trying to charge home tempted her, resting her horse and aching body—and delaying explaining her guilt to Meria—was tempting.

"Thank you," she said. "My name is Eleanora, by the way."

"I am Veli, a man of Pulti, of the village of Plani, of the house of Marke Gjonni," he replied.

When Eleanora said nothing, Veli began singing of courage in the Land of the Eagle, continuing to bellow even as Eleanora choked on the dust their steps kicked up. His tune about being a mountain eagle remained steady as he grabbed the tail of her horse to keep him from tumbling headfirst. She could hear the river rushing beneath Veli's songs, and thought she would see it when they paused at a fork in the widening path now level with the floor of the valley. But the gurgling water remained invisible. She felt relieved to follow someone whose feet were so unquestioning of the path before him.

If only he would stop singing of how glorious an honorable death was.

The ground melted away into the inky horizon and shadows of the canyon. She stumbled over hidden rocks while Veli's pace began to race. She flinched at a deep bark in the distance. She was sure villagers would release near-wild guard dogs soon. Ever since she had been nipped by a seemingly friendly beast as a child, she had to smother shrieks when she saw even a chained dog, and despite Meria's insinuations that she would prefer even a four-legged male guardian to being left alone while she and Baba traveled, her father had always refused to keep a dog.

Her eyes scanned the low shadowy shrubs for glowing eyes, and she almost bumped into Veli when he stopped suddenly. Her horse snorted. Her ears strained above her thumping heart for a rustle in the shrubs, a low growl—then she exhaled. Ahead of them a tall fence of woven wooden spears wrapped around a low mud house with a thatched roof, its small windows blocked by rocks outlined by the light escaping around the edges.

Veli looked back at Eleanora, his eyes gleaming, and put his finger to his lips.

"Oh master of the house!" he called in a boy's imitation of a deep voice. "Are you receiving guests?"

The gate slowly cracked open, a gun appearing before a face, that of an aged version of Veli. Narrowed eyes shot wide open with joyful recognition. The older man kissed both cheeks of his son and hugged him, slapping his back. He kept grinning as he was introduced to Eleanora, took her horse's lead, and begged her to honor them by sharing their dinner.

The house was a single room like a large cave, its packed-dirt floor layered with worn rugs, their faded patterns shifting in the crackling firelight from the central open hearth. Eleanora hung her father's rifle on a splintered wooden peg near the door, by which several goats and two thin sheep grazed on dry-leaved branches, their bells tinkling.

After the men realized Eleanora was merely an unmarried woman and not a sworn virgin, out of respect for their potential boredom and her honor they seated her with the four other women, who waited for the men to finish eating so they could clear their table and sup on their leftovers.

When Eleanora had traveled with her father, she sat with him and the other men, listening to their talk of border wars and shifting business alliances, often interjecting her questions and opinions, but she did not resent these women's artless chatter and curiosity about her costume, because it veiled her silence as she declined their repeated offers of corn bread and warm goat cheese. Though the women raised their eyebrows to each other at her rudeness, they offered her hot raki after she had asked, and kept refilling her cup, which she guzzled without thinking, grateful for the burning warmth pooling in her stomach and the dull buzzing in her head. Raki was not nearly as fine as wine, another thing her father was right about, but she would drink anything that would blot out the constant replaying of that afternoon in the café.

The wind wailed outside, an otherworldly sound she had grown up hearing almost as often as the waterfalls. Across the low light of the open fire, the women crossed themselves for protection from wandering spirits, and Eleanora startled as she felt a slight tug at her pants.

"Was that a fairy?" a little girl asked.

That gale whistling through the canyon must have made the child think of mountain fairies, those strong spirits of the ancient trees that took on the form of women, able to protect warriors or petrify a man with a glance. They were not real, her father had whispered to her when she was the girl's same age, after someone had spooked her with stories of them. But had he not called her his fairy often?

Eleanora nodded with a half smile on her face as the girl, blue eyes wide, told her she wished she were a fairy. So did Eleanora. She wished she could soar through the cold air above the mountains, untethered from the pain barely numbed by raki. At least she was free from the guilt of her father chastising her for falling asleep before her hosts. But she could not fly. She fell back, down into the welcoming floor cushions, unable to fight the warm darkness . . .

He was hitting her with the butt of his rifle, with a steady, unrelenting rhythm that she did not mind so much because she had saved Baba from being shot by the same gun. It hurt, it hurt, and she was unsure where her father was but grateful, even in her pain, that he was safe he was safe he was safe—

The pounding of her head woke her up. As she squinted at the dawning sunlight sifting through the lightly smoking air, she desperately wished she could go back to sleep. She rubbed her throbbing temples. The house was nearly empty; almost everyone was gone for the day's work.

She rose and folded a thick red felt blanket someone had laid across her. Veli's father offered her a tin of steaming coffee.

"Beauty and good to you," Eleanora said as she took it. She drank the sickeningly sweet coffee in one burning gulp. "Good trails to your feet."

The little girl was a few cushions away from her, her skirt in her mouth, still staring until Eleanora smiled at her.

"Are you a fairy?" Eleanora asked the little girl.

The girl giggled and hid behind her mother's skirts. The woman pushed her daughter away so she could grab the pan of corn bread batter, crossing herself before she put it over the hearth.

Eleanora stared into her empty cup. She must get home. She would have to relive it all as she told Meria and burn with the shame of having been the fault of it all, but at least she would be with Meria.

The fire in front of Eleanora began to blur and melt. She blinked, her lashes heavy with tears. She handed back her empty cup and stood. Her host, Veli's father, stood as well, and they walked to the crude wooden door, where they pulled on their shoes and Eleanora took her father's gun.

She followed her host through the field to the tall wooden gate.

"How may I thank you for what you did for my son?" Veli's father asked. "I sent him to stay as a guest of cousins so that he might escape the worst of the feud here. I know fate must decide these things, but sometimes fate needs a little nudge. I bore the loss of my first and second sons, but I could not bear to lose my last one." He looked off in the distance. "I am very fond of Veli, and it is too late in my life to raise another heir. When I think of that girl and what havoc she has wreaked for being weak . . ."

"Is it not always a shame when a woman makes her own decisions?" Eleanora said, squinting in the unbearable sunlight, one corner of her lips lifting.

"Glory to your lips," Veli's father said uncertainly, while his eyes shifted back toward his home. He broke into a grin, still facing Eleanora but looking past her, and she turned to see his son bringing her horse to her.

She stroked her horse's mane, its shining darkness warmed by the sun. Her host unbolted the gate, telling his son to bring him his rifle, so he could escort Eleanora to the village walls. A guest was the sacred responsibility of a host until the guest reached a boundary or stayed at a new home, and until then any insult or harm to a guest must be avenged by the host.

Eleanora told him she would rather go alone.

His eyes widened, but his stubborn traditionalism was no match for her independence and her impatience to hurry home.

He shrugged and advised her which path to take and how to most safely cross the river, where the path would continue on the other side.

Eleanora thanked him. "Long may you live!"

"And long life to you," he replied, his lips pressed into a white line. "Go on a smooth trail."

The gate shut behind her. She knew he was annoyed that she risked his honor by traveling alone instead of with him. She was sorry to add further worry to the gentleman's life, but she was desperate to be alone before she reached home, so she could think of how best to tell Meria everything that had happened.

She yanked her horse's lead toward the sound of the rushing river and did not look back.

When she reached the sandy riverbank, she stood hypnotized by the steely blue-green water, its depth masked by the froth streaming against boulders beneath the surface. The river was at least three times wider than the length of her horse, and moving faster than when she met it last.

Her horse's lead was tight in her white knuckles; she leaned forward as she tugged Tiziano onto the wet sand. The horse neighed and backed up.

Letting her horse graze the sparse grass dotting the sand, she paced the riverbank, trying to decide where her host had recommended she cross. She felt a twinge of jealousy, thinking of the happy family she had just left. Veli's father would live to an old age, old enough to teach his son everything he knew, so Veli could take care of his father in his old age. Veli himself would have a son, and Veli's son would have a son . . . All while Eleanora stood here alone. She dug her fingernails into her palms.

She could not think of this now. She walked faster, coming to a square boulder three times as tall as she, inches away from the river, dry and immovable. As she walked around it, she saw it held a cave. She stepped to its blackness, yelling into it because its damp darkness made her afraid. No echo answered. She returned to her horse, then sat on a rock half-buried in the sand, slouching as she made meaningless twirls into the dirt with a stick.

Why not wait for the river to rise and wash over her, let time decide? She shook her head, sat up, and faced her horse.

Tiziano had backed farther away onto drier ground, his black eyes narrowing as she approached. She snatched the lead and pulled him toward the river, but soon he refused to budge.

So she would ride Tiziano. She mounted and, while perched, tightened the straps of the rifle so it was secure across her shoulders. She dug her heels into her horse and he relented, one stubborn step at a time until the water was rushing over his hooves.

His front hoof pawed the water a few times before he simply stood, his ears back. Of all the times for Tiziano's stubbornness to kick in. Well, had not her father said hers matched her horse's? She ground her heels. He took another trembling step, and as his hoof hovered over the river, she slapped his haunch with her palm.

His hoof splashed in, then the riverbank in front of her flipped sideways before dissolving into a crashing blur of blue-green water, the weight of her horse slamming her underwater as she screamed.

Chapter 7

*E*leanora desperately kicked to escape her horse's thrashing hooves. Blurry blue darkness overcame her, and a sweeping terror and the water's indifferent power sucked her downstream. Her chest throbbed. She twisted until she saw a light gurgling through the water. She clawed toward it. With her chin barely above the river, she gasped for breath. Was that Tiziano ahead, twisting sideways, dragged forward by the torrent?

"Tiziano! Tiz—"

She was washed under by another current, and she choked on water flooding into her gasping mouth. Her father's gun struck her in the back of her head, the leather strap tangled around her arms. Her heart hammered a soothing pulse marking the rhythm of her mind's chant: *You are going to drown. You are going to drown. You are going—*

Her ribs slammed against something hard and cold, and she squirmed so her belly pressed against this hardness, and she tried to crawl to the rippling sunlight. She panted as she clung to the boulder, each breath a piercing pang. Her eyes stung, but she forced herself to peer over the rock she clung to. Hundreds of feet below, the river dashed into thousands of frothing pieces before calming into a fathomless blue-black pool.

Was that Tiziano's mane sloshing below, or only foam from the waterfall? Her heart twitched looking so far down. She rested her cheek on the slimy rock, forcing a deep breath before a spasm of pain. Her boulder was the largest in a natural dam before the waterfall. She inched her way left to the shore. She grabbed on to the next rock, but it teetered and tumbled below. She took a shaking breath and continued to slither sideways, her leather sandals slipping on the slimy rocks of the bottom of the river. It was not until every inch of her body was on dry land and melting into the rocky shore that she felt any sense of safety, though a pain shot through her at each breath. She gingerly pressed her side, holding back a howl. She had cracked a rib.

She squeezed her eyes shut, shooting them open again when her mind replayed Tiziano thrashing in the river. She retched, her wet hair slapping her face. She had had Tiziano since she was a child, and he had tried to protect her. Another stupid, fatal mistake she had made. Dare she peek over the waterfall's edge? She had not seen anything in that dark pool moments ago.

"Tiziano," she called in a singsong. "Tizzie?"

She made little cooing noises, yelled angrily, threw stones into the shrub, and fell to the rough ground, wanting to sob but only choking on her heaving, stabbing breath.

"Tiziano!" she screamed.

Only the river's rushing and the waterfall's crashing answered.

She told herself her horse had made it back to the other side somewhere, panting, resting. He was safe. He must be safe. She clawed the tears from her cheeks. Like Baba. She nearly broke into sobs again, but instead she ground her fist into the sand and staggered up. She could not afford to break down now.

The thin, stretching oak trees were nearly rooted in the river, and the forest was carpeted with deep-green bushes that sprouted between the boulders that tumbled around and in the water. Eleanora was forced to hike inland, though each step was an effort and she knew the path she had left was upriver. Her soaked pants sucked against her thighs, and every step she pushed forward was a little battle against choking wetness. It was as if the river were still with her, its current still fighting her and trying to mold her movements to its own as she wandered through the forest. Perhaps she would come upon Tiziano. She choked down her tears and continued forward, fighting her body's desire to crawl.

Eleanora was sure the trail would appear, floating at the horizon, but she was continually disappointed by another layer of oak trees topping her line of sight. Her wet clothes were a smothering cold in the forest's shade, and her legs began to tremble despite her short steps. She was tempted to sit and rest, except she feared she might not get up again. She told herself if she would only walk a little more she might find Tiziano.

Her heavy steps became automatic; she forced herself to keep pushing forward through her pain, chuckling bitterly at herself. Was this what she asked miscarrying women to breathe through? Was this how people who were no longer parents felt while she cooed at them that everything would be all right? She laughed bitterly and pain racked her chest. Time, time would heal all, she thought sarcastically. What time was it anyway? The amber leaves of the oak trees wove a lacy ceiling above her head, closing out most of the sky; she only knew it was not night.

She stopped.

On the horizon stood a squat stone house with smoke puffing from its sun-grayed thatched roof. Eleanora pushed her matted hair away, scratching her forehead. Had she been here before? She trudged toward the clearing circling the house. She would ask for directions and hurry home.

From the gate Eleanora called, "Oh master of the house! Are you receiving guests?"

She stood on her tiptoes, searching for movement behind the tiny glassless windows of the still house. Nothing. She looked around. Some of the fence had fallen, nearby was an uncovered well where a dry bucket hung over the side, and the door her fist hovered over was splintered and grayed. She slipped through the creaking gate, looking up at the house every few steps as she followed the ribbon of dirt leading to the crude wooden door, standing staring at its cracks, suddenly embarrassed by her soaked clinging clothes.

The door groaned open.

Eleanora stepped back, her hand shielding the ache in her side. She noticed bright blue eyes first, irises so light they were almost lost in the whites of the eyes. The door opened farther, revealing a darkness that sucked in the sunlight. A sunbeam set off specks of dust floating through the black air like little stars, and in the blackness hung a pale face, a dusty moon. Its thin lips were surprisingly red, as if all the blood in this face coursed to those lips. Eleanora only thought of this face as female because it had no mustache above those lips; no man would be without a mustache unless he was a sworn virgin.

The eyes scanned Eleanora bottom to top, lips downturned as the gruff voice tumbled out. "What is it you want?"

Yes, she faced a sworn virgin, and sworn virgins often disdained women even more than men did. Eleanora crossed her arms, shivering. Those eyes continued to scour her. What did she want?

"I want—" *to know how to get back home*, she meant to say, but her mouth filled with hiccuping sobs. "I want—" *to get to my life of three days before, I want Tiziano, I need Baba, I—*

"Oh, what—come in."

A rough hand grabbed Eleanora's arm, pulling her inside, shutting the door. Eleanora's eyes adjusted to the dim light. It was a small room with an open hearth in its center, and curled near the smoldering fire lay a dark body blanketed in rough wool.

Eleanora tugged off her sopping shoes and sat on a lumpy floor pillow as she was told, wincing as she lowered herself. The sworn virgin wore all white like most mountain men, only her pants looked thin with wear at the knees.

"Beauty and good to you," Eleanora murmured as she took the cup from the sworn virgin's gnarled hands.

"Beauty and good to a donkey's ass, and glory, too," the sworn virgin muttered.

Eleanora chuckled to herself. Glory, indeed. The coffee was thin and bitter, but she was grateful for its warmth. She held the cup close to her mouth. The steam warmed her face and her mind, and a memory rose with the mist from her cup: she had been here before, with her father, so many years ago. Eleanora remembered it as the first trip on which she had assisted her father in his work, and then only by boiling water to sterilize his instruments. She had burned herself with the water.

She had stood behind Baba at the sworn virgin's door, then sanded smooth, and after tossing back many cups of raki while Eleanora joked with them, her father and the sworn virgin had shot at a tree trunk, her father laughingly acknowledging the sworn virgin struck closer to the broken branch in the center.

Eleanora and her father left, Baba firing his rifle three times as a respectful goodbye.

"That is the sort of woman I would like to be when I am older," Eleanora declared. She had never known her father or any other man to show respect to a woman by firing farewell shots. "Strong and independent, and not having to bother with all these skirts and waiting to be spoken to before speaking."

"That is a good sort of woman to be, but she is sort of not a woman," Baba replied, laughing, his cheeks still red with raki.

"But she had no mustache!"

"If there were any way to grow a mustache through sheer willpower, she would have. Or maybe you would," Baba said, pinching her cheek. "She is a he, nonetheless."

Baba had explained the sworn virgin had vowed to remain a virgin to avoid a marriage arranged by her brother and had thus earned the right to live as a man. Hardly unusual. The sworn virgin had not bothered with her vow in front of witnesses, but simply had changed her name to Pjetër, shaved her head, and begun wearing pants and carrying a gun. Pjetër kept mostly to herself, but when a drunk man joked about Pjetër not having a mustache or testicles, Pjetër had beat him nearly to death with the butt of her rifle and won the respect of mountain men, including the one she had beaten, who, when he awoke from his coma, immediately told everyone he wished he could marry one of his daughters to Pjetër.

But the admiration for Pjetër soured to exile when she chose to live alone with a woman who was not her relative.

Eleanora's father tossed an unfinished cigarette to the ground as he finished his story, his lips curling into a wry smile.

"Sure," Baba acknowledged, "mountain winters are hard, but was your neighbors' letting you alone really such punishment?"

Eleanora's wistful smile at the memory of her father froze when Pjetër's hooded eyes caught hers. The sworn virgin moved stiffly around the low fire, muttering to herself, but her back was straight and shoulders wide. Pjetër said nothing to Eleanora, and she thought at first it was to let the blanketed person in the dim corner—Pjetër's woman?—rest in peace, except the sworn virgin carelessly dropped logs into the hearth.

Eleanora cleared her throat.

"I admit I am lost. How might I return to where I came from?"

Pjetër said nothing but snatched the empty cup from Eleanora's hands and tossed it into a pail full of water.

Eleanora continued, "I came from—"

"Yes, yes," Pjetër interrupted. "I know, I know. I remember your father, girl. You came from Arbër? It will be dark soon. And you do not know the trail. You will stay here and share dinner with us."

At her last word, Eleanora looked back at the covered body, watching the blanket rise and fall subtly but steadily with silent, shallow breathing. What if the blanket stopped moving while she slept? Eleanora looked away. She had the touch of death now, while so few days ago she had prided herself on spreading immortality and feeling above the illnesses she cured.

"There is not much here, and on top of that what little we have I must cook! And what do I know of cooking? It is a woman's work." Pjetër rubbed her brow as she looked back at the blanketed body. "But even she must rest. She has been so unwell these days." Pjetër sat on a floor cushion across from Eleanora.

"What ails her?" Eleanora asked, half afraid but hopeful she could help.

"Her? Ha! She is merely pretending to get out of her work." Pjetër laughed, but her brows knit. "Your father is a healer, right? Perhaps he could come? I do not have much to pay him, but . . ." Pjetër looked down and twisted her sash.

"He always liked you. He would come if he could," Eleanora said, trailing off. "He would, but, well—"

"Spit it out, girl."

"My father, yesterday, he was—" She clenched her jaw as Pjetër's bright blue eyes bore down on her. "He was killed."

Pjetër paused for a moment, then sprinkled tobacco into her cigarette paper. "Shot? Truly your father was a good man, the best man I knew. No false honor with him. A man of few and strange traditions but real honor, the kind that counts. Why was he killed?"

"Why?" Eleanora echoed. "Why? I do not know."

Pjetër's silence spurred her on.

"I only know that it was my fault, that if I had been smarter I might have saved him."

"Your fault? Did you elope with a man or something?"

"Elope!" Eleanora exclaimed. "No, my father would not have stopped me from marrying for love."

Pjetër rolled her eyes, licking her cigarette paper. "Then?"

"It was an honor killing," Eleanora said. "For revenge."

"Who? Someone shot him even though he was with you?"

"I was not—" She picked at the rough edge of her fingernail until she tore it off. Blood welled in her cuticle, and her finger throbbed. "You see, I was waiting in a café . . ."

Pjetër tilted her head as she sucked on her cigarette.

"That makes the killing questionable," Pjetër said. "Did the man know your father was traveling with you? What will your family do? You have brothers?"

Eleanora shook her head without looking up. She was trying to pull down her sleeve to wipe away the blood on her finger.

"Your father has brothers?"

Eleanora shook her head again.

"Surely another man is in your family?"

Eleanora stopped to think. "Not that I know of."

"Well, at least your mother has brothers that are alive?"

"I never met my mother," Eleanora said. Pjetër drummed her fingers on her lap.

"And my stepmother's father died long ago."

"And you are not betrothed to anyone? So you are without family. Your tribe may help you, but believe me, I can tell you what a tribe counts for when you act in a way they do not like."

"Oh, and how many times have I done that!" Eleanora laughed a little. Pjetër's blasé attitude reminded her she was not the only person to ever endure such a tragedy. She sat up a little straighter. "No, I am not betrothed, at least I have that. And I at least have my stepmother, Meria. Though she does not know yet what I let happen to my father." She covered her mouth so Pjetër could not see the sob she smothered. She swallowed hard.

Her host merely shrugged, smoke puffing from her weathered dragon's face. "Perhaps you will become a sworn virgin? Why not? Then you may tell your stepmother whatever you like."

Eleanora wiped the mutinous tears from her cheeks, and even with blurred eyes she saw Pjetër look away with disgust. That hardened Eleanora more than pity could—Pjetër was dead to her family and village and tribe, her only companion extremely ill, and still her life went on. But Eleanora's life would not go on as hers had. She sat up as straight as Pjetër.

"I will not become a sworn virgin. I will still go abroad for schooling."

"Schooling?" Pjetër asked, the gray smoke wafting out of her open mouth. "What sort of an education do you need, besides one in a little more modesty in front of men like me?" She cackled.

Pjetër squinted at Eleanora, her cigarette jabbing toward her. "Now seriously. What does anyone need school for? Especially a woman."

Eleanora saw the blanket shift in the darkness behind Pjetër. How did one explain being schooled on drawing pretty lines to someone living like this? Would it heal that body beneath the blanket? No. Eleanora knew all this. But art would help her escape such concerns. She pinched her torn, throbbing finger to try to stop the bleeding. "I am going to become an artist. My father wanted me to go."

Pjetër nodded. "I do not know what it means to be an artist, but if your father wanted this . . . He was a good man. One of the few I respected."

Pjetër rose, dumping handfuls of twigs into the hearth before stepping to the back wall of the room.

Behind the growing fire's twisting flames lay the shrouded body, and Eleanora could not tell if the body stirred or if it was the shifting shadows of the blaze. The fire's crackling was punctuated by the clanging of pots and bowls, the breaking of eggs, and though those noises went on, Eleanora flinched when the body whispered and beckoned with a pale, bony hand.

Pjetër bent over the body, then dug around until she found a rectangular pan to pour the mixture into. While the corn bread baked over the fire, Pjetër took a low tarnished tabletop that had been leaning against the wall and set it up on wobbly wooden legs in front of Eleanora's lap, and on top of this she placed a towel and a shallow bowl of sloshing water Eleanora cleaned her hands in. A crude carved bowl of sour goat's cheese clattered onto the table.

The corn bread was more like a burned, bitter pancake. Eleanora broke off a small shard, and even swallowing that sent a piercing pain through her chest again. She tried to remember what Baba had done about broken ribs. She believed he said they just had to heal, but she remembered him telling that to a small boy who had fallen out of a tree whose branches he was feeding to his goat.

"Sometimes time is the healer," Baba had said, in such a way his soothing words were a balm.

Her eyes welled up, and she looked away so Pjetër would not see her.

"Oh, God, yes, you are not meant to be a sworn virgin, you are most definitely a woman." Pjetër got up from the table and poured something in a cup she shoved into Eleanora's hands. "Take this."

Eleanora gulped the raki. Stiffening her lip, she looked Pjetër in the eye, and held out her empty cup.

"More, please."

Pjetër smiled.

Chapter 8

Since you are without a man, you should become a man," said Pjetër. "Sure, you would have much to work on in terms of your demeanor, but you would not be the first to have a gun in your hand as a complement to your cowardice."

She held out a cup of coffee to Eleanora, tapping her bare foot as her guest rubbed her bleary eyes. The coffee sloshed onto the dirt floor as Pjetër put the tin down with a sigh, walking to the front door where Eleanora's father's rifle leaned, inspecting its silver etchings.

"Oh, yes, I remember this so well," Pjetër said. "I dreamed of this after the first time I saw it. The finest gun I have ever seen. It is a Mauser, you know? And silver filigree, the best of Gjakova. As beautiful inside as it is out. And for you, right now it is merely a most expensive walking stick, no?" Pjetër let out a throaty chuckle.

Eleanora drank the coffee in one gulp and rose, grabbing her father's gun from Pjetër and holding it to her chest.

"Oh, God, are you trying to kill yourself? You do not hold a gun like that!"

"Show me how then," Eleanora said. "If anyone could make a man of a woman it is you. Teach me how to shoot it."

Her father had taught her to knee a man in the groin, and had her carry a curved knife in her belt when they traveled, in case she was stolen to become someone's potential wife. He had taught her how to thrust the blade to the best effect, but he had never shown her how to shoot. No woman knew.

Pjetër raised her tangled eyebrows and grinned like an imp.

Eleanora and Pjetër stood outside in the damp gray dawn, facing the inside of the fence on which Pjetër balanced thick pieces of firewood. Was this where Pjetër and her father had competed for the best shot years ago? Eleanora blinked away her tears. She could not remember, and it did not matter. What mattered was whether or not she could defend herself and Meria now. She forced herself to focus on Pjetër's thick hands, as she showed Eleanora how to pull back the bolt of the rifle, put three rounds into its magazine, and push the bolt back to load the chamber. Pjetër shook the bullets out and made Eleanora try it. Her cold fingers fumbled a bit, but Pjetër nodded her approval.

Pjetër shook out the rounds.

"Do it again," she commanded. "And again. And again and again and again and again. Do it so many times you cannot imagine it being done any other way."

Eleanora repeated the movement, faster and faster until her hands loaded the gun as if by their own volition.

Pjetër whistled. "You are almost as good as a man!" She chuckled again. "I like to tell you things like that because I see how mad it makes you! Oh, as soon as I show you how to shoot, you will shoot me if I say that again."

Eleanora laughed despite herself, feeling light and fast and young until she thought how if she had not been so foolish she would have learned this years ago and been able, at the least, to avenge her father's death. She pushed the rifle back into Pjetër's hands. "I promise not to shoot you. Now show me how to use it."

Pjetër took the rifle from Eleanora and raised it to her shoulder, squinting at the far-off target. She passed it back to Eleanora and told her to raise it as she had.

"Do you see those two pieces of iron?" Pjetër asked.

Squinting, Eleanora jerked her chin yes.

"They are like a canyon and a river," Pjetër explained. "Their tops must be even. And you put the center top, the river, at the center of your target. The center of the center at the center. It is like a little infinity, you see? Forever and ever and ever. Just like life is." She cackled again.

Eleanora centered on the target and pulled the trigger, hard. She had heard gunfire all her life. Her father was often welcomed by all the men of a village firing three shots each, but she was not prepared for the violent noise so near her head. Eleanora's wrists flipped back from the recoil.

The firewood thumped onto the grass.

"Ha! We will make a man of you yet!" Pjetër exclaimed. "Now . . ."

She showed Eleanora how to release the hot shell from the chamber and slide the bolt back into place, loading another round.

"Again."

Eleanora aimed, pulled the trigger again. Without thinking she pointed the rifle lower as she fired, correcting her aim in anticipation of the recoil. The second piece of firewood remained atop the fence.

Pjetër clucked, "You are reacting to something that has not occurred yet."

"But I could not help it," Eleanora said. "It is funny how your mind anticipates the same thing happening again, which has not happened yet. There is a lesson here."

"Yes, you are right, there is a lesson here. The lesson is to stop doing that! Is that what you will say," Pjetër asked, "when you have killed your goats weeks before, and you are starving? You will find a rabbit in the forest and tell it"—Pjetër raised her voice to a nasal squeak—"'I could not help it. Yes, it is so funny'? That will not put meat back on your table, girl."

Eleanora emptied the chamber in a flash, loaded the third round, and took aim.

"Now, aim as I told you," Pjetër directed. "And keep your arms loose."

Eleanora breathed deeply, then fired.

The firewood toppled onto the grass.

Pjetër grinned.

Before the sworn virgin could speak, Eleanora emptied the chamber, loaded another round, aimed, and fired again. Thump.

"How is that for a girl?" Eleanora asked. "Maybe a competition this time?" Perhaps she could beat Pjetër, as her father had not.

"No, I would rather not waste the bullets, and I do not

want to shake whatever confidence we have built today." Pjetër grinned. "You will be all right, girl. Though I think you ought to start home if you wish to arrive before dark."

Eleanora nodded.

"I will go get my things and my horse . . ." She blinked hard to shut the tears out. She had nothing, absolutely nothing but her father's gun. But at least she could use it now. She slung it across her shoulders, clenching her jaw.

"You are your father's daughter after all. Long may you live," Pjetër said. "God take you safely home." She reached into her pocket and held her gnarled fist out to Eleanora. "Well, I am trying to give you something, girl!"

Eleanora opened her palm, and Pjetër dropped three rounds into it.

"Thank you. For everything," Eleanora said. "Long may you live. Go on smooth trails." She turned back. "Oh, you can give your woman a tea of valerian root for her pain!"

"Ha, enough with you and your flowers, girl!"

The gate slammed shut.

After climbing high enough on the ribbon of a rocky path Pjetër had told her to follow, the gold-green clearing that surrounded the sworn virgin's home was a pale dot. Eleanora raised her rifle, considering firing three rounds as a respectful goodbye. She lowered it and slung it across her back. Who knew what might happen to her on the way home?

ELEANORA CRACKED OPEN the gate of her home, fingering the wilted flowers drooping in the vase. Meria's fair head was bowed behind the window, probably over delicate embroidery, and then her figure disappeared deeper into the house. Eleanora watched as her head reappeared, dipped, and when she looked up out the window, Eleanora looked away, as if what she could not see could not see her, like when she was a child and she had hidden her face from her father.

Would she never stop crying? She clenched her fists until she could not feel the pain, then admired the red crescents her fingernails had dug into her palms. She might stand there, staring at them until it was too dark to see, only—

"Eleanora!" Meria's voice was a soft singsong. "Eleanora, what are you doing out here? Did you run ahead of your father?" she asked, her voice teasing.

Eleanora looked up, but she could no longer see Meria, she was crying, blind. She reached for Meria to bury her head into her shoulder, like when she was younger and she had been stung by a bee or cut by a branch.

Meria made soothing hushing noises at Eleanora, as when she was a baby, and did not even chastise Eleanora for her bare head but petted her hair instead. She was grateful even as she felt her stepmother's body tense.

Meria pulled back, her eyes searching Eleanora's.

"What has happened, my child?"

Eleanora looked at the tips of her soiled shoes.

"Baba, Baba—" Eleanora's words were swallowed in a choking sob. Though Eleanora was taller than Meria, her stepmother pressed her head down into her shoulder again. "Baba was killed for honor."

Meria let out a low wail, a deep and mournful animal sound utterly unlike anything Eleanora had ever heard. Hearing her own sadness vocalized braced her. She took a deep breath.

"We went to Shkodra as planned," she said, keeping her voice from shaking. "Everything was going so perfect, and the priest told me I would go to the academy. We went to celebrate at a café in town, and I was waiting for him there. He told me to wait for him. He told me to. So I waited as he said, and then he was shot, and I tried to find out who did it, I tried so hard, but they would tell me nothing. And then I had to sell his horse but lost the money when my horse, Tiziano . . . Tizzie . . ."

The vision of her horse flailing downstream assaulted her anew. She swallowed.

"My horse may have drowned in the river. I have lost everything, I lost everything, and all of it is my fault."

She kept chanting "my fault" under her breath and before Meria could respond, Eleanora dashed down the path and through the open door, curling into a ball, her head on the bare floor next to a pillow, hearing her stepmother sobbing and hovering behind her.

ELEANORA WAS SURE her stepmother blamed her, as she was right to.

The next morning, she stared out the front window, her chin tucked into her knees. She imagined walking casually out of the café with Baba, fetching his gun and holding it properly as Pjetër had taught her, touring the town, clasping Baba's arm when she saw the crazy dog-like beast chained to its master's wrist, visiting with the sworn virgin. Baba would admire how well Eleanora had shot, and then he would go on to work, urging Eleanora home alone. *You must practice and prepare for the academy*, he would say, chucking her chin. At any moment, the gate would open and frame Baba's joyful figure, loaded with trinkets from his travels. Eleanora would run to him, like when she was a young—

"Eleanora—" Meria's voice broke. "Do you have any idea why your father was killed? You are right. It may have all been an incredible accident, but . . . Did anyone tell you anything? I would like to know." Meria's head was bowed over yarn wrapped around her carved wooden spindle. Her long three-pronged distaff was tucked under her arm, spearing clouds of gray fleece hanging near her head, though for once the tools were motionless in her thin hands.

The vision of Baba swam before Eleanora. Suddenly her nose and cheeks were warm and wet, and she muttered in a dead voice between gulping breaths as if she were forced to repeat a lesson, "What can it matter? The official answer is it was an honor killing somehow related to a woman. So as such, no one gives a damn." Eleanora looked up to see what effect her words had. "No one gives a damn."

Meria widened her eyes. "Eleanora!"

"Was it that I cursed," Eleanora asked, rubbing her fists into her wet eyelids, "or that Baba had something shameful to do with another woman?"

"Your father had a life before I met him, but the man I knew was a very good man." Her thin lips twisted into a quivering smile. "A man of strange ideas, to be sure, but a good one nonetheless."

Meria's nimble hands started twirling her spindle again, and she leaned her head forward so her thick tears fell onto the floor instead of her yarn.

"He had no reason to go to the city. He always turned down

people even begging him to come work there. I thought perhaps he had been avoiding someone. He—" Meria stopped when Eleanora looked up sharply. "He did what he believed he had to do. He may not have cared about rites, but I am terribly sad we cannot bury him and mourn him properly."

The spindle trembled as she attempted to swallow her hiccuping sobs.

"And to think we have no one"—Eleanora gulped—"no one to avenge his death, to punish that wicked man who took him from us."

Meria tossed her spindle to the floor, retrieving it immediately and fondling the polished wooden thing, seeming satisfied it was not broken.

"Eleanora, we have each other," Meria said. "It is very sad, yes, but people die and unfortunately for the ones left behind, life often goes on."

"Well, in that case we are lucky your damn spindle is not broken," Eleanora said. She turned back to the window.

"In that case, we are," Meria said. "God forbid I must make and sell cloth to a spoiled girl like you."

She was spoiled, she was, and her father had sheltered her from ever knowing it until now. Meria was suddenly hugging her from behind, weeping, and Eleanora cried into her knees, begging her stepmother to forgive her, not knowing she had stopped until she woke up in the middle of the afternoon, with a pillow beneath her head. Meria was better to her than she deserved. She squeezed her eyes shut, trying to quiet her mind, pretending not to hear Meria asking her if she wanted something to eat, though she reached out and clutched her stepmother's hand.

It was dark when she woke again. She had heard a cracking footstep outside. Had the wicked man come for her, too? Her heart thumped so hard her broken rib throbbed. Perhaps it would be easier if he killed her, too, then at least she might be with Baba again . . .

When Eleanora woke in the morning, she was relieved to see the sun high in the sky, not minding she was hot under the thick, stiff blanket. She turned onto her side, gasping at the pain, but not caring as she faced the wall.

So Baba had been drawn outside the safety of the mountains to help Eleanora into the art academy. And to what end? Meria had never said anything about the trip to her, but Eleanora felt she had been against the plan. Her stepmother had been right.

Eleanora did not draw or paint for several days afterward. Normally the first turning of the leaves was her private ceremony; she would sit outside with her box and easel, sorting through her orange and yellow pastels and attempting to capture the trees' transition. She sat outside this year and found herself staring at the blank paper, and left her treasured easel outside to be drowned in the first rains of the season.

She picked up her pastels again only after another nightmare of eyes staring at her, judging and accusing, screaming. She only realized later that she was hearing her own screams, and that was why her stepmother shook her awake nearly every night. Oh, that nightmare was even worse than when she dreamed of Baba's killer finding her. She never slept through the night anymore, and when she awoke the unblinking eyes bore down on her until the sun rose. One dawn, without thinking, she went to her paper and pastels and found some relief as she drew what haunted her.

Eleanora traced over the thick straight eyelash again; she had made the eyelash as long as her finger. The pupil was a deep gray, not yet black, and she watched as her hand made a little figure of a man inside it, much like the silhouette of a man going into a cave, holding a walking stick at his side, or maybe a gleaming rifle—

She crumpled the drawing and threw it into the fire, remembering as she watched it burn that she was running low on paper. Of course she had not thought to get more while she had been in town, when she had had money. And now she had practically none. She was so stupid. But what did it matter? She snapped the black pastel in two and threw it across the room, feeling foolish as she knew she would pick it up later and fix it.

She got up and walked over to the hearth. She started to reach for the corn bread, but Meria reminded her it was for dinner tonight. Her stepmother had slaughtered one of their two goats weeks ago when men searching for Fran had stopped by. The guests' sadness at not finding Fran was great—almost as great as their appetite for the roasted meat. Meria had hid the other goat in the shed so they would at least have cheese when winter came. They had never kept their own chickens or pigs, as Baba had always been given pork and chicken and eggs as partial payments for his work. Were they never to eat flesh again? But who cared. Baba had been the one in the family who loved pork skewers.

Eleanora sighed, her feet like weights as she climbed the stairs to her father's study. She let the door slam behind her.

The room was less than half the size of the first floor, but what worlds it contained within the bookshelf lining the entire wall facing the windows. Thanks be to God—though she doubted his existence more than ever—for the books, which she spent hours immersed in now. She had abandoned Dante's *Inferno*, which she had long admired for its symmetry, after realizing Baba would be stuck in limbo for being a nonbeliever. She reread, instead, Euripides' *Electra*, *Phoenician Women*, *Medea*, envying Medea's revenge and daydreaming about the chariot of Helios flying her away after she had punished whoever had taken Baba from her.

The worlds of the books saved her from this one, and she was grateful.

As Eleanora sat down on a cushion, embroidered with one of her own designs, she was overwhelmed most by the world of her father. She pressed her forehead onto the maroon Qom rug, breathing in the faint smell of his clove-laced cigarettes. She looked at the white cap waiting for him on top of a massive walnut chest with claw feet. Her father had told her it had been made by her great-grandfather in Italy, and she felt a familial pride studying its baroque carvings now, though in the past she had often sat on it and carelessly stacked books and art supplies on top. She wondered what it looked like inside; maybe it was velvety blackness with the word *Hope* embroidered on the bottom. She laughed bitterly. She had already opened Pandora's box and had found no hope at the bottom, just a bitter surprise that she could go on and only feel a dull ache where there had once been a piercing pang, the same as her rib, which had seemed to have healed itself. She rattled the chest's curvy iron padlock. To her surprise, it easily popped open.

She smiled. How like Baba to assume no one would challenge the lock's dense appearance. Then again, perhaps he had put nothing in this chest in a long time. She lifted its heavy top, the hinges creaking, and peered into its wooden darkness. She reached in and felt a chestnut shaggy fur coat. She tossed it aside. Underneath were etched sterling silver boxes—she shook them, must be bullets and tobacco—piled upon a cracked leather notebook. She stacked the boxes against the wall and opened the notebook.

My soul was written so clearly in Italian by her father's careful hand that her heart jumped as she heard his voice in her head as she read it. She thought perhaps he was addressing her, until she noticed the date above the greeting was a month before she was born.

Chapter 9

I doubt I will ever read you these letters, but I write them to myself to read one day when you are as old as I am now, and I have grown used to your smile and perhaps even our occasional bickering. I will read these words and remember how I was wracked with anxiety while I almost lost you. How you made me promise, no matter what happened, that I was not to take us to any village where we might be found out. So I recall each moment I watched your heavy fluttering eyelashes as you twisted in your sleep, and I held my own breath as I waited to see if you had stopped breathing, releasing my sigh as you finally took a deep, rattling inhale. How even in my relief I cursed myself for not having planned better so we might have escaped across the sea immediately . . . As soon as you are well, we will go deeper north into foreign country where we know no one and where we might live amongst other people but not bound to them. I know how you hate the idea of us living in another claustrophobic village—"It is not living but slow suffocating!" you shout—but how can we escape that when you are far along with child, and that is what holds us here now? Would you blush at my mentioning it? Oh, no matter how unconventional you are and how often you try to shock me, I know that is something you tried to keep to yourself, raising your belt and skirts higher and higher to cover your growing stomach, waiting for it to become an undeniable physical fact that would announce itself. Well, it has, my soul.

I will probably have to break my promise to you.

The yellowed page trembled in Eleanora's hands. She chuckled bitterly. She was a greater fool than she imagined, having assumed she had known her father completely, at least before he was gone. What questions she wished she could ask him now! What a lazy simpleton she had been to wait, imagining she had an eternity with him. She merely knew what he had chosen to reveal to her—yes, he had always wanted to be a doctor— and what she remembered about him—oh, how she had felt so happy and hateful when he would tickle her awake. If only he were alive, she would never be irritated with him—or anyone else—ever again. She smirked even as tears welled up. What a ridiculous bargain to try to strike with a god she never believed in. She was still so naive.

Had she ever truly understood that Baba was not merely years older than her, but that he lived a life before hers? He had once been her age, with dreams she would never know. Had he wanted to escape to Italy? Perhaps. He had loved her mother rather desperately, and she wondered what Meria knew of this. She was glad to know she had sprung from love, but reading so made her feel protective of Meria; she had a vague feeling her father had used Meria, in a way. She thought of Baba lying in the dirty street, staring blankly at her. That staring man stuck to the sucking mud was a stranger. That staring man's killer had known a secret of Baba's she could only continuously guess at between her broken bouts of sleep.

Eleanora gingerly turned to the crackling page, and the next entry was dated days later, Baba's penmanship a bit rougher. The words on the page dissipated as she heard her father's voice in her head.

Do you remember the first time you touched me? You ran your hand along my scar, then a scabbing streak on my cheek, and you said, if anything it made me more handsome because before I was too perfect looking. You spoke the way I had only read of characters talking in novels, and it did not hurt that your hands were like ivory silk and your face like that of Titian's Flora.

I bragged to you, shamelessly, that the mark I had left on the man who had given me my scar left him much less attractive, and unable to speak, perhaps ever again. But he deserved it for what he had done to that poor girl, and when I said so you looked so fierce yourself I thought, Here is a girl who does not need my protection.

You put your hand to my cheek now, but your palms have roughened from gathering kindle, and I hate how your fingernails are no longer smooth almonds but have jagged edges from when you put our tent up. Your eyes are softly hooded and your wrists so thin the ouroboros bracelet I had given you had slipped off and gotten lost in a tangle of blankets. You are wearing it again, do not worry. Now I must take care of you and I am glad to, and for all I rebuke myself for the dangerous position I have put you in, I am desperately grateful my mother taught me enough of her healing arts that I can at least ease your pain with ironwort.

You must feel better now, because you were awake long enough to tell me you would rather die than have us discovered. You said it with such venom I could not argue with you, but as I write these words I see that we of course must eventually go back to live amongst other people. Perhaps we will go to Venice yet. I still remember the fairy tales my father would tell me about his childhood there, and I am sure it is the place for us. Yes, living half wild in the forest has been a beguiling adventure. I have felt like Lord Byron, and I enjoyed a freedom I would not have been able to imagine, but I see now we must move on from this and learn to create our own world while moving in everyone else's.

My dearest,

Sometimes I wonder if I have been too selfish, acting with impulse and drunk on your love. Sometimes I feel I ought to have left you alone, let you think that I could not love you, so you might go on living the life you were raised for. But then I know while you would have fought through it, you would have been miserable every day, not so much for the loss of my love, I will not flatter myself, but because you were meant to feel things, and not to waste your life repeating the lives of others, each copy growing fainter and less meaningful like an overused wood block . . .

I must put the pen down. You are waking now, my soul.

Chapter 10

*M*eria looked up from the thin bubbling gruel she stirred over the fire. Though the high voice called again more loudly from the gate, Eleanora did not even look out the window that she lounged near; she simply twisted the silver serpent bracelet she now wore and thumbed a page in the worn leather notebook she cradled.

What time Eleanora wasted staring at paper, like books she left open around the house or strange scribbles she left lying out, rough drawings not even close to the magical images she used to create before Fran was killed. Meria shook her head. She understood Eleanora had been especially close to Fran, maybe even closer than Meria had been to him, and for all of the pain and death the girl had witnessed while working with her father, she had never even known what it meant to have a pet die before now.

And Meria? Before she learned what it meant to stuff her

skirts each new moon, she learned life meant one day her brother might laughingly pull her hair until she wished to strangle him, while the next day she could be wracked with vague guilt and sharp sadness as she placed an apple on his still body, cramped in a shallow grave.

Meria's childhood had been swallowed by a terrible blood feud between her family and another from the neighboring village, a war that she had not understood as a young girl and still was unclear about what had caused it. In imitation of her mother, she had urged her brothers and father and uncles to cleanse their blood. When outside, peeling branches off trees to feed their scrawny goat or gathering kindling, she had been mocked by former playmates for the shame that hung over her family.

After her brothers and uncles were all killed, her father went away to escape the bullet with his name on it. Her mother told her she should be very proud of what her father had done—God knew what pain he must have caused that other family—and when he finally slunk home one night, he was a changed, bitter man who lurked in the cold corners of their hut-like home, avoiding gunfire. Eventually no one, including himself, could stand him being in the house all day. He went out to sit in the sun one morning and was promptly shot.

Her father had been gone so long and returned as such a sour stranger, who no longer pinched her cheeks but slapped them, that it was hard for Meria to wail with the professional mourners at his funeral. The next night Meria and her mother shared a meal of the blood with the family they had been at war with. She stuffed herself until she was sick with white fluffy bread and rich cheese and even a small gulp of raki, merely grateful her father was gone and it was all over.

Even in the difficult months that followed, Meria had trudged on, and it was thanks to her own uncomplaining work and the generosity of neighbors like Bubci that she and her mother lived. And then Fran came into her life. She sensed he had overcome a similar pain, and together they had made a new life for themselves and his baby.

His baby then and a baby now. Eleanora was different, and always had been. For all her outward spirit she was weak in her heart, and Meria felt a slight disloyalty in how Eleanora was less help than a child now. What happened to the girl who was braver than most men, as Fran had boasted? Did her need count for nothing at all with Eleanora? They could use Eleanora's strength more than ever. Her stepdaughter was no longer the girl who had skipped an enticing trip with Baba to stay home and nurse Meria through the nights after she became sick from drinking water right after the rain; no, Eleanora was permanently with Fran in spirit, and only her thinning body listlessly lolled around on Earth. Meria had seen this happen with ancient widows, but how could it happen to a vibrant girl like Eleanora? It pained Meria and left her feeling vaguely jealous and guilty, because as sad as she was, as much as she missed her husband, she knew she would find a way to keep living.

The voices called from outside again.

Meria banged the wooden spoon on the side of the pan, then set it in a bowl. Eleanora still did not look up. Meria glided across the room and out the door without her shawl, opening the ice-crusted gate to two black figures silhouetted against the blinding white snow sparkling under the clear sun. She blinked hard, recognizing Bubci by her plump figure and squeaking girlish voice, but not the younger slouching woman who accompanied her.

Meria forced a smile and ushered the women in, her ears burning as she led them into the house. Hopefully they would not notice how she had ripped the hem of her skirt while foraging the forest for hazelnuts the day before. She had wanted the nuts for food; Eleanora used to love them roasted, though of course Meria would never consider serving such crude fare to guests.

Meria had not seen Bubci since she had proposed Edi as a husband for Eleanora, and her friend looked the same, though her normally puffy cheeks appeared dry and sagging, her looped hair flopping against her temples matted, the whites of her eyes grayer, her whole being seeming as if a fine layer of dust had sifted over her. When she smiled at Meria, there were deep folds around her mouth like the face of a gypsy's puppet. Meria touched her own cheek. Did she look the same? Probably. If freezing winter air dried up the rich, what would it do for one with no protection? Yet somehow Eleanora looked as young as she behaved, always, despite the depression that possessed her, her beauty still breathtaking as she sat staring out the window, leaving Meria the burden of entertaining guests as usual.

The young woman at Bubci's side looked about Eleanora's age, and she was silent, too, but it was a trembling, self-conscious silence, with her slight movements emphasized by the jangling of shining metals: the gold coins woven into the henna-stained hair above her brow, her silver bangle bracelets, and the pouches and charms attached to her heavy studded belt that married women wore. Her lowered eyes seemed to apologize for the noise of her decorations. Even with her head bowed it was clear she was not a pretty girl, but her skin was fair enough, her red-brown hair oiled to a sheen, her manner proper.

She must be the new bride in Bubci's family—Edi's wife.

Meria was grateful she had tidied up the room today, beating floor pillows and dusting, just for something to do since she had fewer chores as the thick of winter settled in. Her guests seated themselves on the plumped floor cushions, their full black skirts crunching, and Meria heard her own forced lighthearted replies to Bubci's rambling gossip as she walked to the back of the room. She lifted the sack of coffee from the carved tree trunk, surprised at its lightness. So what? These were likely the last guests she would receive before spring. It was as good an excuse as any to allow herself the luxury of coffee as strong and as sweet as she used to make it. Later she could casually ask Bubci to loan her some. She poured half of what was left into the copper pot and let a mound of sugar follow. Bubci may prattle about other neighbors, but she would have nothing to say about Meria and Eleanora's situation.

"I was very sorry to hear about your husband's death," Bubci said. "What a good man he was, and what a shame it is you were not able to properly bury the body. You were able to have a wake though?"

Meria shook her head—no one had come, and Eleanora had refused to participate.

"I thought Fran would have preferred to be remembered with a quiet day in his honor," Meria said, not looking up from the pot. "You know how he was a rather private man, with his own . . . unique beliefs."

Yes, that sounded convincing. Bubci had even referred to one of his ideas about the Earth being round as "funny," and in front of Meria, too. No one would suspect she had not been able to afford professional mourners. Eleanora had insisted they save what few coins she had found sewn into the back of a cushion in Fran's study, though Meria doubted they were worth half a sack of cornmeal. Eleanora had so many opinions about money, and yet she never lifted a finger to do actual work now, when Meria needed her most. How much it would mean to Meria if she were able to look up from stripping branches of leaves for the goat, stirring the fire, washing a pot, and see Eleanora enduring beside her instead of lying around, another load to bear. Even that would not be so bad if she could somehow relieve her stepdaughter's oppressive pain. Meria sighed. As she stirred the coffee, she regretted her bangle bracelets were not twinkling on her wrists. She had hidden them days ago in a trunk near the hearth when Eleanora had mentioned how much they might be worth.

"I am sorry I could not attend your son's wedding," Meria said, as she brought Bubci a cup of coffee.

"Beauty and good to you," Bubci said as she accepted it. The woman drank the steaming coffee in one gulp, saying, "Good trails," before she passed the tin cup back.

Meria rinsed it in the pail of water, refilled it with thick coffee, and handed it to the silent new bride before she continued.

"Yes," Meria said, "I wish I could have come to celebrate with your family. But I have not been feeling so well since . . ."

Meria looked down and moved her foot so that her torn hem was tucked beneath.

"I am sure Edi is pleased?" she ventured.

Bubci raised her thin eyebrows, which made her look almost as angry as surprised, since her brows nearly met in the middle above her heavy nose.

"Edi?" Bubci asked. "Oh, Edi, you know he is so hard to please. Meria, do not think me so wicked or wild for saying so, it is a blessing in a way not to have children! Especially as you may marry again yet!"

Meria forced a smile, grabbing the cup from the new bride as an excuse to turn away quickly and hide her tears.

Fran was gone, and there was no one for her to marry even if she wished. As for Eleanora, she had spurned what even she must now recognize as an opportunity. To be married and safe!

Like most villagers, she and Eleanora had not been formally invited to the wedding. The word was spread and entire tribes were welcome. And despite how many must have attended, Meria had not heard any news of the festivities. Few men stopped by looking for Fran anymore. The last visitor had come weeks before, a grizzled bejeweled man who claimed he was sorry to miss Fran but quickly mentioned he was searching for a second wife for himself as his first wife—still living, he groaned, and her family would not take her back!—had borne him six daughters but no sons. He ogled Eleanora so obviously that the girl escaped to her father's study, and even in Meria's growing desperation she would never consider going against God with such bigamy, let alone binding Fran's daughter to such a man. Besides that old goat, for weeks she and Eleanora had only had howling winds for company and snowdrifts piling up and peering at them through the windows.

Meria was not surprised no one came any longer. She had always felt local women were jealous of her success through Fran, and while she understood her stepdaughter, she could see how even Bubci thought Eleanora put on airs. Her friend did not attempt now to even engage the girl in a greeting.

"Yes, Edi, he is the strongest-minded man I know, even more so than his father," Bubci moaned, eyes rolling in a prideful way. "But Edi is as happy as he could be for his brother's marriage."

Meria looked up sharply. Edi? Unmarried still? She thought of that vulgar old man, stuffing a cigarette with Fran's tobacco while he leered at Eleanora. Edi! Handsome and healthy and rich. She still had a chance. Eleanora still had a chance.

Meria studied the new bride with deeper interest. Her dark hair shone with oil, her pale skin had been shielded from the sun, but her complexion's whiteness only made the red veins around her crooked nose stand out. In a few years, after childbirth and being left to work in the fields, she would be a worn-out woman. Behind the new bride, the white sunlight bounced off the sparkling snow and streamed through the window, highlighting the clean lines of Eleanora's face. The girl looked up from her book, and Meria shifted her attention back to her guests.

The new bride's chunky bracelets jangled when she scratched her neck, and as Meria admired the heavy bangles, they slid down to reveal purple and green bruises spread across her wrist.

Meria examined her own torn fingernails. Anything might have happened to the new bride.

She thought to call Eleanora over, then pressed her lips together—who knew what the girl might say?

"Anything else?" Bubci asked, examining her smooth nails. "I am sure you have been buried here, but what else goes on?"

Meria leaned in and dropped her voice. "Oh, not very much. You know how it is, as winter settles in. Our last guest was weeks ago. The head of Nënfushë. He begged for Eleanora as his wife, but I could not bear to have her so far from me. It is selfish of me. I know a woman is nothing if she is not married, and a beautiful daughter is trouble on one's hands. I would like to secure Eleanora a marriage and know she is safe. Only it is hard to make these decisions as a lone woman. Now with Fran gone . . ."

Bubci's rings sparkled as she patted Meria's hand.

"Yes, it is terrible to be without a husband." She crossed herself. "May I never know how terrible."

She stood, and the new bride followed. "Long may you live, Meria. Go on a smooth trail."

Meria echoed her goodbye, and she guided them to the gate. She dashed back in and rubbed her hands near the hearth, where Eleanora tilted the coffeepot over a cup, the pot nearly upside down before a few drops splattered out.

"The one thing that woman is right about is how terrible it is to be without a husband," said Meria, as she delicately stabbed at the baking corn bread with a small knife, satisfied to see the blade came out cleanly. She crossed herself and made the sign of the cross over the loaf before setting it down to cool. "You are much prettier than the new bride and look at all the bracelets they put on her. I am sure they treat her very well."

"I am sure they hardly hit her more than they whip their

horses, though, granted, horses cost more. But maybe they would be kind to me, as I am even prettier than the horses they own, except for that Arabian." Eleanora set the coffeepot down with a clang, walking away. "What would Baba think if he heard your insinuations? I love you, but sometimes you are a fool. A terrible fool."

"I am a fool?" Meria asked, throwing the pot into a bucket of water, her empty hand extended toward Eleanora's retreating back, her thin finger shaking.

"Me?" she screeched, hardly believing that was her own voice, yet continuing, "While you waste your days staring at books, never helping around the house, leaving me to work and worry about food. The way you behave, I mourn not only losing a husband but a daughter! You are no longer here with me. Believe me, I am as sad as you are, but life must go on. You are like a person with a broken head. It was one thing when your father was alive and you worked with him, but that is over and you have no chance at school now, is this not true? I do not even ask you to consider me. I only ask what will you do? Lie around the house while I care for you, as if you were a baby never to grow up, or an old person never to die?"

Meria saw her own shock at her outburst in Eleanora's wide eyes.

Eleanora drew in a shaking, deep breath, and Meria regretted her words when she saw the girl's eyes well up.

"I am sorry, Eleanora, I did not mean—" Meria's quivering hands stretched out for her stepdaughter, but the girl remained planted where she was.

"You blame me, and I blame myself, too. More than you ever will know," Eleanora choked out, attempting to steady her voice. "The reasons why I believe you said those things are wrong. And yet, you said exactly the right things to me."

She twisted away with a hiccuping sob, and her footsteps hammered up the stairs to Fran's study. Meria listened as a chest creaked open, and something like metal balls rolled across the floor.

"Thank you," Eleanora cried down the stairs. "Truly, I thank you."

Meria shook her head, wiping her eyes and sniveling nose on her skirts.

Chapter 11

Meria touched her teardrop in the cornmeal dust lining the bottom of the wooden chest and put her trembling fingertip to her tongue. She missed Fran, more than she had missed her mother, her father, and her brothers combined, when the world had ripped them from her. Her family had been a backdrop of the life she had taken for granted, while Fran was something else, a wizard from another world who had left her lonely for weeks then reappeared with gifts lavish enough for a chief's treasured daughter. For the years she was Fran's wife, she had been a happy fool, never even noticing how this painted chest magically remained full. Then again, why should she have, when she had been endlessly scooping out of it, continuously cooking for his guests, or designing delicate cakes Eleanora described to her? It was all right no matter how many of his friends came to eat with them—the next week the seemingly bottomless chest was heavy and filled to the brim with bright golden cornmeal and surrounded by fresh sacks of sugar and white flour and salt.

As the leaves had turned from yellow-tinged green to amber and red, she had used less cornmeal each day. By the time the black leaves were rotting beneath the snow, she and Eleanora were skipping lunch and skimping on dinner, and yet somehow the chest was empty. Her hunger pangs were sharp enough the other night she had even cooked that small sack of near-rotten rice their stupid neighbor had given to them. Meria had thought Eleanora, with her reputation as a healer, might help this woman's ill daughter, leading to more work until Meria could think of something better. But the woman refused. When Meria told Eleanora, her stepdaughter insisted she would guide the girl through her sickness for free, but the woman had crossed herself and shoved the sack into her arms and fled back to her house.

Eleanora had mentioned maybe going to Shkodra's bazaar to trade some of their belongings for cornmeal and coffee, but after one of their increasing bouts of bickering, she had discovered Eleanora's idea of their belongings extended to Meria's own cherished jewelry but excluded the girl's precious serpent bracelet and books—and she had no right to make a decision like that. Besides, who knew how her trip would go and if she would even return? Meria shivered at the thought of losing Eleanora, too. She would never say so to Eleanora, but it was her last trip there that had left them groping in this empty, new reality. Besides, what would they do after they had stretched their sack of cornmeal into a month's meals of thin gruel? Eleanora thought she was so much cleverer than anyone else, and yet she could never see past her impulses.

If only Meria could go back in time and marry Eleanora to Edi, and then Fran would have never been killed, and Eleanora and Fran could have continued their healing work together. Surely, because of that special circumstance, she and Eleanora would be giggling together as usual, instead of swapping bitter words. She could not help it, when her stepdaughter cried in her sleep, that she now snapped at her to wake up and be quiet. Fran would be so ashamed. But since she could not resurrect her husband, Fran, and the joyous person her stepdaughter used to be, despite all of her prayers, she would at least have Eleanora married to Edi now, and she would be safe. Eleanora would be safe.

Meria crouched near the smoldering fire, mending the torn hem of her skirt with the last of her thread, thinking of having meat again. Imagine if she were taken into Edi's household. That was unlikely; she had never heard of a bride's mother being adopted into the bride's new family, but surely Bubci would not allow her to starve, and Bubci had said, before, that Eleanora would have the freedom to continue her healing work, an unheard-of privilege for a new bride or any wife. Surely they would let her visit Eleanora often.

It was only a matter of finding a time to go speak with Bubci when Eleanora was not around.

In the next few weeks, Eleanora began rising before dawn, and after gulping down a cup of hot water, she left early with Fran's rifle. While Meria scavenged the nearby forest for edible tubers, nuts, anything, she often heard shots fired nearby, though in the evening when Eleanora returned she was silent, even as she let loose her grip on the corners of the skirt she held in her fists as a makeshift bag, dropping chestnuts and bitterroot vegetables onto the floor. Once, Eleanora clomped through the front door in the dying dusk, smiling in a way that shrunk her lips into a red line, saying by way of greeting to Meria, "I almost got it."

Eleanora's face, once the smooth visage of an angel, began to hold a line between her brows, hollows under her eyes, and her full lips were puckered and chapped. Meria mourned the beauty she had once felt jealous of, as it dissolved with Eleanora's good spirits. She thought of the sullen stranger her father had become. She must hurry.

The next gray morning Meria bowed over her already mended skirt, her needle quivering, waiting and watching under her lowered brow for Eleanora to slip out of the house. The girl left without a word. Meria listened for her fading footsteps, and fluffed floor pillows, poured water on the sizzling fire, pacing and rearranging their few pieces of furniture until she felt sure the girl was deep into the forest. Then she took her chance.

Meria had not walked the narrow footpath that led to the center of the village, where Bubci's home lay, since Fran's death, and she felt self-consciously alone. Was that a rustle behind her? She glanced back, nearly tripping on a snow-buried rock. She jogged until she saw the first house of the village, a mere mound of sparkling white with smoke rising from its thatched roof. The fields of corn and wheat were hidden under a pristine, bright white blanket of snow, which smoothly rolled up and covered the stone wall borders of each field. All that remained visible were the stark gray spiky fences of interlaced spears, which were echoed by the gray-and-cream cliffs and purple mountains jutting up and around the plateau of the village. When she reached the extra-tall fence of Bubci's home, she stood still, shivering beneath her heavy shawls.

Suddenly she thought of Fran, arriving at her door with the baby bundled to his back.

Ah, but Eleanora was not a baby now. She had had her chances, she had made her choices, and here they were. She remembered Fran's sad, small smile the second day she had known him. He had tickled Eleanora's pink feet, saying, "She is all I have in the world." She would not let Fran's child starve while she could help it.

Meria stepped up to the gate of interlaced spears, where an elaborately etched brass bell hung, the only one like it Meria had ever seen. Even Fran said he had never heard of such a thing when she described it to him. Her frozen fingers hovered over the bell's braided-leather pull, but suddenly she was ringing the bell as hard as she could, holding her breath.

Perhaps they were not receiving.

She let out a relieved sigh and spun lightly away.

The gate creaked open.

A squat servant drowning in weird white pants as wide as Meria's skirts, with sleeves even wider, stared at her. She recognized his funny round face from when she had come to meet Bubci earlier in the year. She felt he was sneering at her, though his strange accented words were most polite.

"Good day, madam," he murmured.

Meria's nod was a sharp jerk of her chin. She pulled her shawl tighter.

"I have come to see Bubci," she said.

She wondered why her friend would not give him a normal costume. Perhaps she was proud of having a servant all the way from the south, though he was likely here hiding from bad blood.

"Of course, madam," the man said, his clothes swishing as he moved aside. "Does the mistress expect you? I will take you to see the mistress immediately."

He did not wait for her answer, leading Meria through a labyrinth constructed of closely packed, rough stone houses where sprawling generations and extensions of the family lived.

Bubci's two-story home loomed in the center, the largest, and the servant bowed slightly, arm sweeping and swooshing upward though he walked up the wooden stairs first. Meria hesitated—but it would be too peculiar to leave now. She followed him up to the front door, where his knuckles rapped twice.

The new bride opened the door, head bowed, and the servant whispered to her.

The new bride continued to look at the floor, never speaking, as was proper. She merely stepped aside by way of invitation, and Meria entered the large room, slipping off her wet leather sandals near the door. A roaring fire barely contained in an enormous metal bowl suffused a suffocating warmth from the center of the room, and tarnished copper lanterns with fat, oozing candles lay scattered about, though the room was well-enough lit by the sunlight through the narrow windows randomly cut into the walls. Meria almost tripped over one of the many florid rugs scattered about with their corners curling on top of each other, layered under gold-embroidered silk floor cushions. If she could imagine Eleanora in such a setting at all, it would be hopping floor cushion to floor cushion in imitation of a frog jumping stone to stone across a river, then rearranging the whole room: the best rugs would be hung on the wall, lanterns transformed into vessels for floral arrangements, and the pillows grouped into settings for intimate conversations. The room would be transformed into comfortable elegance, with Eleanora sighing contentedly at her work even under the boorish glare of Bubci. Eleanora's spirit would rise again with the distraction of a challenge. Undoubtedly Eleanora's quick wit would cut Bubci's position before the older woman even realized what had happened. Oh, Bubci would finally get what she deserved. Meria giggled behind her hand, quickly quieting herself when Bubci came out from a shadowed corner. Meria smoothed her skirt and nodded to her, offering the traditional greeting of one friendly woman to the other, "Are you tired?"

"Always, always!" Bubci groaned. "New bride! The coffee, please, and make sure it is the way I had to show you how to make it."

Bubci plopped down on two floor cushions squished together, inviting Meria to do the same with a nod and a tight smile that disappeared as she picked something off her dark skirt and flecked it away.

Meria sat across from her, and the new bride arranged a round engraved brass table between them.

"She hardly helps," Bubci said, without lowering her voice, cringing when the table made a slight ping as the top was put in place on the carved and shining wood base.

"And even if she was any good at all"—Bubci paused as she

wiped her hands and dropped the wet silk towel back into the new bride's palms—"I could use another pair of hands in this home. There is always so much to do."

A delicate wooden bowl of cubed cheese appeared on top of the table. Bubci motioned for Meria to eat first, so she picked a dainty piece she chewed slowly, savoring the rich tartness. Bubci's plump fingers danced above the bowl before she plucked the largest piece, which she quickly swallowed, watching the new bride stir the coffee over the fire.

"She is slower than the winter turning into spring," Bubci murmured.

Meria hid her smile with her hand. If her task was going to be easier than she thought, it was because her errand was right, it was meant to be, and she brought goodness to both families.

"I can only imagine how difficult running a household like this must be," Meria said. "In my own home, as you know, it is only Eleanora and me."

Meria made and unmade a fist under the table as she resisted another piece of cheese; her friend must have no hint of her hunger.

"And yet if Eleanora were not worth five women, I do not know what I should do," Meria continued. "I do not mean to boast. You know I am rather fond of the child."

Bubci looked up from the table, now crowded with small dishes of dried fruits and sugared nuts and fried cakes smothered in honey.

"Is it about Eleanora you have come to speak with me?"

"Eleanora? Why, no." Meria lifted her brows. She reached for a sticky hazelnut. "Did you think . . . Oh, I could not bear to part with her, especially with it being the thick of winter now. I came merely to ask if I might borrow some cornmeal."

Bubci's mouth turned down as she bit into a small cake, holding out her free hand until the new bride gave her a fresh towel to wipe her sticky lips with.

"Some cornmeal? Bah!" Bubci sighed. "You could have a cornfield!"

She tossed the cloth on the floor at the new bride's feet.

"I would give you goats, gold, whatever you want. If only you would sell Eleanora to us as Edi's wife. He continues to torment me! His father has told him again and again he makes a fool of himself, seeming almost in love with a woman! That if he had not proven many times over what a man he is, his own father would be ashamed to hear his son harp on and on about a single woman! When there are plenty of other ready women available. Naturally, this only makes Edi more stubborn. It is like when he wanted that Arabian horse, though his father told him a Turkish or Albanian one would be so better suited . . ." Her hands nervously sifted through the sugared nuts.

Meria held her friend's eyes, even as she smoothed her skirt, leaning forward.

"You are wise, Bubci. Besides my selfishness in wanting to keep Eleanora for myself, I fear she may not be suitable as Edi's wife."

"She thinks herself too good for him, does she not?" Bubci's ringed hand shook, and her coffee sloshed over onto the heavy gold embroidery of her black skirt. The new bride came over and dabbed at the blossoming spot with a rag. Bubci pushed the fluttering hand away.

"Oh, no, it is not that," Meria said. "Eleanora, though she would be the perfect wife, I know how helpful she is to me around the house . . . Well, I am afraid sometimes she thinks herself too good for any man."

Bubci put her cup down, crossing her arms.

"Your husband helped this family through sickness many times, he was an honorable man, so God rest his soul." She wagged her finger. "But he put many unnatural ideas into his daughter's pretty head. That said, even she must know this is one of the finest homes in all the mountains."

"I know this." Meria held her palms up. "Everyone knows this. Except Eleanora. She is strong-minded."

"Fortunately for us, women do not do the deciding in such matters. It is bad enough I allow my son to make decisions about such things that are better left to family considerations. But what is, what is. My husband has already given me permission to pay you in Napoleons for Eleanora."

Meria almost choked on her coffee. Gold? Bubci's husband had offered Fran silver coins. Fran! The impressive bargainer. Meria had done better for herself and Eleanora. And might do better still. She took another sip of her oversweet coffee, warmth radiating from her core.

"I tell you, Bubci, as a friend. You have enough worries. I only wish to spare you annoyance." Meria almost laughed, thinking she was not being a hard bargainer, but merely sharing a truth.

"If you wish to spare me annoyance, you will sell us Eleanora." Bubci narrowed her eyes. "I will give you what my husband has offered, plus all of the bracelets and rings I wear now." Bubci tugged on the largest red stone around her doughy finger.

Meria forced herself to pause before responding. "Bubci, I know how generous your offer is, and I will accept it on one condition. You let Eleanora continue her special work in drawing and healing, and allow her to visit me often. It is true she is my stepdaughter, but I have known her since she was a baby. I would worry so much and miss her terribly otherwise."

"Meria! If that is all . . ." Bubci slammed down her cup of coffee, her rings clanging on the table as she pulled them off.

MERIA LEFT BUBCI's home with the bracelets and rings jingling in her pockets, sacks of cornmeal and coffee and butter cradled in her arms. She stopped in the middle of the path and tried on the most dramatic ring, a large black-veined turquoise stone surrounded by tiny sparkling white stones. The little stones had looked like chips of starlight sparking under the candlelight of Bubci's home, but in the pure and piercing sunlight they looked dull and the little turquoise boulder was crude. The ring slipped off her thin finger easily, and she pocketed it. So what? She had plenty of jewelry of her own, sentimental gifts from Fran she would no longer need to consider selling. The daylight revealed Bubci's jewelry's vulgarity, it was true, but she was proud to own it for what it represented: a down payment toward the rich future she had secured for her stepdaughter.

She paused before the gate of her home, gazing at the jewelry overflowing in her palm once more before shoving it in her deep pockets. When she opened the door, she called out Eleanora's name. The girl had not returned yet. She hid the jewelry with her other bracelets in the tree trunk chest that was full again with the sacks of cornmeal and coffee and butter. She swiped at the small tears in her eyes. If only Fran were alive, then everything would be perfect. She crossed herself and knelt. *Please tell my husband that I have done the best a poor woman can for his daughter.*

The house was in shadows when Eleanora slunk through the door. She greeted her stepmother with a kiss on her cheek, her arms full of scrawny root vegetables she set down near the bucket of water. Meria scrubbed them and sliced them thinly before dropping them into a pot of water over the fire, stirring in half the cornmeal and a large chunk of butter. If only she had some salt! It was not much, but they would be eating meat again soon. She wished Fran could know she had made sure his daughter was provided for. She smiled, wiping away her tears impatiently. She must not cry. They had gotten through the worst.

"Where did you go all day?" Meria asked to distract herself from her thoughts of Fran. The last time she had asked Eleanora she had perversely told her unchristian-sounding gibberish about traveling with Hades.

"I flew to Italy," answered Eleanora. "But I could not bear how happy I was so I came back."

"Must you roll your eyes at me?"

Eleanora looked up and laughed. "No, I mustn't. Forgive me. But you know where I go. To the forest. Where else?"

The girl knelt near the front door polishing Fran's gun, with the same pleased grimace Fran had had while attending to the same task.

"I went into the forest," Eleanora repeated. "To shoot at eyes." She raised her hands and squinted as if she were firing an invisible rifle. She held Meria's stare, and then her face relaxed into one of her rare smiles. "I am learning how to hunt."

Learning how to shoot and hunt? Meria cursed under her breath as she dropped the horn spoon into the pot. She fished it out and rinsed it, and dropped it again in the porridge. Did Eleanora meet a man in the forest? If anyone saw Eleanora with a man, they would be ruined. And for what? The girl had never brought home meat. Was she shooting at carrots?

"Learning to shoot a gun? Is someone teaching you?" Meria ventured.

Eleanora looked up with a smirk.

"No, you need not worry. My reputation remains as admirable as ever. I go alone into the forest. I am my own teacher. A sorry one, but my fee is so low even I can afford it."

"Of course, of course you would go alone." Meria let out a large breath, smiling at her stepdaughter until she noticed a scratch on the girl's cheek. "Look at you, you have cut yourself."

She found one of the cleaner rags, dipped it in the pail, and came toward Eleanora.

"You must be more careful."

Fortunately it was shallow; it would heal quickly. Eleanora was still as an obedient child as her stepmother wiped her face, and Meria thought again of cleaning and coddling Eleanora when she was a baby. But she was grown and tough now and no longer needed to be indulged. Fran had been the best man Meria had ever known, but even he had failed his daughter in some ways. Meria had secured Eleanora's future, and that was more than Meria's mother—more than her father!—had ever done for her.

Eleanora rose, stretching her long arms to the ceiling before wrapping them around Meria's neck.

"Shall I put more wood into the fire? Watching the dancing light is at least one luxury we can still afford."

She stared into Meria's eyes and smiled a shadow of her old smile, giving a glimpse of the charm that Fran had boasted entire villages talked about, and why Edi was so eager to own her.

"You look sadder than usual, Meria." Eleanora touched her cheek. "There is still a hole in my heart that is heavier than the piece missing. Are those my own words or am I echoing someone? It does not matter, nothing matters now, but I try to tell myself at least nothing worse may happen than what already has."

Meria turned away, lifting her stepdaughter's arms off her. "Your father always said you were wiser than most men. As for me, I am only upset with myself that I forgot to gather more firewood today."

Eleanora said nothing as she huddled near the small fire, shivering in her thin jacket. Meria thought to offer her one of her own overcoats, but she was wearing all three of them, even the embroidered shawl reserved for festivals. She remembered Fran had a fur coat that must be in his study and was about to recommend that to Eleanora, but she merely pursed her lips.

They ate silently, the largest, richest meal they had had in a long time, and it left Meria nauseated. She stared in her bowl, afraid at any moment Eleanora might ask where she had gotten the fresh butter and cornmeal.

Meria said nothing as Eleanora crawled, shivering, under the blankets right after dinner. She usually did the same, and during these cold nights they pushed their mats together and slept curled next to each other for added warmth, as they had every season, even during summer, when Eleanora was younger. But

Meria stayed up near the fire, darning a skirt of Eleanora's and thinking of what she might use for the girl's wedding clothes. For once those flashy skirts Fran had had her make for Eleanora might be appropriate. She would make the girl whatever she liked.

Chapter 12

The last few days Eleanora had barely been able to drag herself out of sleep in the morning, let alone into the forest to practice with her rifle. She loaded and reloaded the rifle smoothly and automatically, aimed in a blink, but she always missed her shot, and her increasing sense of failure was marked by the growing gaps in the once-full sterling silver box of ammunition. Once, after firing at blankness, she screamed into the forest, and when she saw all the birds she had missed flutter away in fright she laughed bitterly.

What was the point of it all anyway? She had thought she had endured the worst life could hold, and then she had turned to one of the last entries of her father's journal, hidden between two pages stuck together. She wished she had not discovered it.

What was the point of it all?

It was all she could do to keep from screaming that question at Meria, who had begun fussing over her, asking Eleanora if she remembered a certain costume from when she was a baby, coaxing her to drink a foul-smelling brew to bring back color to her cheeks. Her stepmother looked so light again Eleanora had not the heart to tell her the recipe was wrong, and she took a couple of sips in front of her, nodding enthusiastically, before tossing it in the fire when she was not looking. Eleanora was grateful to no longer bicker with her stepmother and relieved she was clearly feeling better, but she did not have the energy to respond with more than a weak smile. Doing almost anything these days felt like lifting the heaviest weight without reason, so in response to her stepmother's repeated offer of a dry cornmeal cake and bitter coffee, she stretched the heavy wool blanket over her head, while Meria continued to cluck concernedly at her. Was she saying it was already the afternoon? Finally Eleanora rose without speaking, the blanket wrapped around her like a hooded cape as she trudged up the stairs to Baba's study.

Eleanora sat in a kneeling position atop the baroque mahogany chest, under the gray window that grew increasingly dim. She had no candle to guide her, but it did not matter that she could no longer read her father's careful cursive in his old leather journal that was cradled in her lap. She knew most every line by heart. He did not begrudge their beaming beautiful baby that the price of her life was her mother's. But Eleanora did. Both parents dead because of her.

She heard a knock, but did not bother to look out the window to the front door below. Let Meria deal with any visitors with their scripted pity barely disguising their curiosity. Let Meria serve them hot water and everyone pretend it was coffee and as if they cared what happened to Meria and Eleanora. Let her stepmother waste the last pinch of the cornmeal on guests who would not care if their hosts starved after they left.

Eleanora reached for a used piece of paper, and in the growing darkness drew two thick eyebrows raised with surprise over wide brown eyes she had already sketched. Or should the brows be slanted down, accusing? She was not sure, and as she pondered this she heard climbing footsteps, the door creaking open. She did not look up. If Meria wanted to ask her to come down, she could. And Eleanora would not.

A throat cleared, deeper than Meria's.

Eleanora stubbornly leaned into her drawing, ignoring the shuffling of feet.

A hairy brown hand snatched the paper out of her own, and she finally looked up, holding back a gasp.

Three men stood near her, and she felt an instant distaste for them, despite the leader's handsomeness. A fair face—a familiar face—even with its arrogant sneer. How was it she assumed he was the leader? She supposed it was his body language—thick arms akimbo, feet wide apart. He was half a head taller than his two brothers, who shared his features but not the shadowy refinement sharpening his nose, plumping his dark lips, enlarging his black eyes.

Who were they and where had they come from?

She hated herself as she smoothed her hair behind her ears and wondered if she had charcoal smudges on her cheeks. Even as she felt her heart pound, she hoped they could not hear it.

"I do not believe we have met," she said, surprised at the smoothness of her voice. "I am Eleanora."

"I am Edi," the leader answered.

Edi! Ah, of course he was. She had seen him in passing long ago, and he was still handsome, and he still knew it. His full lips slid over his pointed teeth into a smile as he stared down at her. She met his dark eyes, unblinking, even as his fingers brushed her palm as he took and crumpled her drawing, tossing it behind him.

She yawned out of nervousness but hoped it looked like confident boredom, and reached for another piece of paper. Anything to give her time to wake from this nightmare. Where was Meria? How had they invaded her father's study?

Edi grabbed her wrist.

She jerked her arm away, biting down her desire to scream, but he held tightly.

"I suppose a gentleman never likes an honor taken from him," Eleanora said, her voice strangely steady while her heartbeat hammered so fast she vaguely felt frightened for it.

"Perhaps"—she forced herself to continue—"I only needed to ask, would you like to hand me a piece of paper?"

"No," he said as he sneered and snatched the pastel from her hand.

She let it go, only so it would not break. He tossed it behind him, chuckling while his brothers echoed the gravelly noise.

"What I would like," Edi stated, sneering, "is for you to put away your childish things now that you are my wife."

"Your wife?" she cried, finally shaken. She could not have heard him correctly, she—

The brothers' thick hands clamped onto her ankles, and her wrists were handcuffed by Edi's strong brown hands. She twisted and tried to kick. They cackled as they carried her downstairs, where Meria sat near the feeble fire, some mending frozen in her hands.

"Meria!" Eleanora screamed. "Help! Please! Do not let them take me! Meria!" She howled until her throat hurt, but her stepmother merely shuddered and crouched lower as if for a closer look at her stitching. Meria's slight back twisted away from the chaotic scene, and in the movement her skirts moved and revealed an open leather pouch of gold coins lying on the floor.

"Is that all I am worth to you, you, you—"

Eleanora jerked her legs as hard as she could, feeling a satisfying crack as her foot connected with one of the brother's chins. He cursed and clutched his face, dropping her leg. She kicked the other brother, gaining a chance to stand and turn and bite Edi's fingers, forcing herself to chomp down despite how disgusting the grinding bone between her teeth was. His free hand grabbed her throat and she slapped at it, choking, desperate to breathe. It was only when her heel hit his groin that his wild grip loosened and she was able to jerk free. Hands tore at her clothes as she dashed upstairs into her father's study, slamming the door behind her and shoving the heavy wooden chest against it. She spun around the dark room.

The banging on the door spurred her heart's frantic beating. She rubbed her sore wrists, her bruised neck. Edi had choked her! She laughed bitterly. If this was what their formal introduction had been, what would he do to her in the dark, months from now, when she was legally his? She feverishly searched the room for a way out. There was only the window, black with night, the shaking door, the books lining the wall. Perhaps she could fight them off with the sharp edge of a book? That was all the stupid tomes were good for. She had a chance against one man, maybe, but one hundred books would not help her against three men. Oh, how her father had filled her head with dreamy lies!

She slumped against the wall, cringing with each shake of the door. She would feel those fists pummel her face and body soon. She had nursed a wife who had been beaten unconscious by her husband, and when she had tried to bandage her broken cheeks, the poor woman had raised her little hands and whimpered.

The door cracked like thunder, and someone hooted before the battering continued. She hugged her knees. Had not Baba loved that carved wooden door? It was an antique from some faraway town, and it did not belong here. Soon it would be splinters.

She felt a pain jutting into her lower back, and she twisted to see what was behind her. Her father's gun. She pulled it into her lap, cradling the heavy wood, rubbing her thumb into its silver. She took a deep breath.

She would shoot herself. A lump rose in her throat, and she swallowed thickly. Why not? She had never believed in heaven, but now the story appealed to her, and she imagined herself finally meeting her mother, and apologizing to both her parents for everything that had happened. She placed the cold rifle between her knees, staring down into the black barrel. Her clumsy shaking hands were fumbling with its mechanisms when the door finally burst open.

Chapter 13

*W*ithout thinking Eleanora pointed the gun at Edi and his brothers.

Edi jeered, "What does a foolish woman know of guns?"

He took slow steps toward her, his arms open and wide as in a dare.

She stood and raised the rifle to her eye, as she did when she went into the forest to practice, centering her aim as Pjetër had taught her.

Eleanora saw her way out.

"What does a woman know of guns?" she repeated. "A woman knows nothing. But a sworn virgin knows as much as any man."

Edi's arms flopped down to his sides, and his brothers backed away.

Eleanora laughed and laughed, and her laughter seemed to disturb the men more than the gun aimed at them. Her escape was stupidly simple.

She lowered the rifle, clutching its smooth shaft with her left hand. She raised her trembling right hand.

"As you three idiots are stupid and mean enough for twelve men, you will make do for the traditional number of witnesses to my vow." She continued in a sarcastic singsong, "I swear to remain a virgin the rest of my life."

And because she knew she was to be respected as a man, but free from any retribution so long as she did not forsake her vow of chastity, she spit at Edi's feet. It was an insult a born man could have been shot for.

"I would swear to turn into a pig, anything rather than marry you!"

Eleanora walked past them, bumping into their shoulders and feeling jittery and high, as if her whole being were vibrating. She dashed down the stairs on shaky legs, to where Meria crouched, the leather pouch pressed to her breast.

Eleanora snatched it away, shaking its gold coins into her palm.

"If I was worth this to you as a woman, what might I be worth to you as a man?" As she cackled and counted the coins, she felt everyone's eyes burning into her. She looked up, then glanced back down at her palm. How many was that again? She folded two coins into her fist.

"I doubt your arithmetic is any good, so I'm afraid you'll have to trust me. This will pay for the door you have broken," Eleanora said. She looked at her stepmother. "My father loved that door."

She scattered the rest of the coins across the floor, satisfied as they rolled around into dark corners.

"If you are so eager for a wife," she said, watching Meria's downcast face, "I am sure there is more than enough there left to pay me for my stepmother. She is older, and unable to bear children, but she may be better for you. She has good experience cooking and cleaning, and she is already broken in. I promise you she will not buck."

Edi's brothers grunted and grinned. Eleanora rubbed her bruised throat, angry warmth spreading throughout her body as she watched tears streak Meria's red cheeks, her thin shoulders convulsing. Eleanora was head of the house now, and her stepmother was merely her property. She could strip the woman naked in front of these animals and Meria would have no recourse.

Edi's brothers bent to grovel for the coins and jewelry on the floor, while Edi stood straight with his arms crossed, his thick neck corded and his handsome face tight as he glared at Eleanora.

She knew tradition bound them to respect her decision; she was now a man in their eyes. She had always thought this tradition one of the most nonsensical. She supposed she was like Nemesis, who transformed into a goose to escape Zeus's advances. What if Edi turned himself into a swan? A high, shaking laugh echoed out of her, and she felt a sudden surge of power as Edi broke eye contact with her, shoving his bloodied knuckles into his pockets. The recognition of her rights—rights her father's protection had fooled her into believing she had—was now really realized by others.

She turned to Edi.

"Unfortunately," Eleanora said, "according to tradition we are not to be enemies but remain respectful neighbors of each other. Still, I must ask you to leave. If you are not going to buy her, I will need to deal with this woman in my house."

Edi shook his head in disbelief and walked toward the front door. His brothers followed.

Eleanora trailed the three men to the gate and watched them mount their horses.

"Long may you live! Go on a smooth trail," she yelled after them. She muttered beneath her breath, half hoping and half horrified they would hear her and turn around. "So smooth, I hope you slide off it into the canyon."

The men's bouncing shadows disappeared down the narrow path. She began to laugh, hysterical giggles gurgling out of her. It was not manly to giggle. The thought made her laugh more. She clapped her hand over her mouth and took a deep breath. As soon as they were gone around the bend, she raced back to the house and dug through a wooden chest in the corner where she kept all of her clothes folded neatly atop Baba's old things. She tossed the clothes all around her—it was now unquestionably Meria's job to silently put away this mess—until she seized what she wanted: a pair of snowy woolen pants of her father's. She threw them in her stepmother's face.

"Make these old things fit me."

Meria did not move as the trousers slapped her face and slipped onto the floor. Her eyes were puffy and pink, and Eleanora felt a twinge of regret at her cruel words until she remembered the living hell her stepmother had sold her into, then left her to fight alone and just barely escape.

"You look sad," Eleanora said, trying to keep her voice light and steady. "As if the one person you had left in the world had betrayed you. As master of the house, I command you—cheer up. Who knows, perhaps now that I am a sworn virgin you'll get your revenge and family honor that you mourn about to anyone who will listen. I'm so sorry I could not do anything before."

She pushed her hair, sticking to her damp forehead, out of her face, tugging its thickness with her fist. Should she cut it? Why bother.

Meria was sobbing, covering her mouth, as if her frail hand could hide such despairing wailing. What had she to cry about, what had she been through tonight compared to Eleanora's betrayal and near death? She rubbed her bruised throat.

"Why do you cry, like you never did before?" Eleanora asked, swallowing the lump in her throat. "Stop crying. There is still a chance I might sell you."

Chapter 14

It was a meditation to be alone in the black-and-white snow-buried forest, free from Meria's smothering silence, her own thoughts, even her own loneliness. Eleanora lost herself in her body, reacting immediately to what it sensed, deciding on its own to step this way, to wait, to dash, or to raise the rifle to her eye and shoot.

Eleanora lived in her father's pants after Meria had tailored them for her days ago, rubbing away imagined spots, brushing them every night, keeping them looking as if they were freshly washed and neatly pressed, though she refused to take them off even while she slept. She stuffed her own frilly blouses into the pants but topped them with Baba's shaggy chestnut fur coat, which she took off only at night, when she insisted Meria wear it if she caught her stepmother shivering. After bundling her thick hair beneath her father's cap, this lithe costume offered a freedom she could not have imagined.

She moved quickly and quietly without folds of rich fabric for bare branches to snag and leave her swearing, knowing her prey had been warned she was coming.

She was silent as a ghost, now.

Near the silver horizon, a sliver of downy gray slipped behind beech trunks; after days of carefully scanning the skeletal forest, she could tell it was a softly moving bird and not merely lacy shadows shifting over the snow. She squinted and smoothly raised her rifle. The bird fluttered, and she adjusted her aim again. And again. Her eyes narrowed into slits.

The bird finally stilled and so did time. The silence in the black-and-white forest seeped through her skin, making her mind as blank as the carpet of snow. The bird's black beady eyes twitched toward her as she shot and kept shooting. The bird was destroyed when she reached it, beige feathers pummeled into the dirty snow, spotted with bright red. Like a white shirt spotted with red. She squeezed her eyes shut to the resurfacing horror and forced herself to remember how hungry she was.

She must go on. Her work with her father had taught her death was a daily occurrence, as much a part of the natural world as the sun slipping away every night. Had she not consoled so many with empty words like that? She reloaded her rifle.

Hours later, she forced herself to remember the gnawing hunger that woke her at night as she stood over a small squealing boar she had shot. Its black-brown eyes stared at nothing. But its legs thrashed and it screamed. It screamed! She clamped her palms over her ears. Perhaps she had just come upon this poor animal; if only she could imagine she had not been the one to cause its torture.

She lifted her rifle. She must shoot it in its head. Anything to make that noise end, that evidence of its suffering.

"I am so sorry," Eleanora whispered.

She shot the beast and tried to console herself with the fact that many boars had killed men and made them suffer, or that every other animal she had eaten in greedy peace had felt the same pain. She focused instead on the ringing in her ears from the shot, letting it wash away the other noise in her mind.

Eleanora dragged the carcass back to her house, keeping her eyes forward, trying to shut out how the bristling warm fur beneath her hands reminded her of her horse. She waved at the window where Meria was, and her stepmother disappeared. Yet the door did not open. Eleanora dragged the body closer, and with shaking fists she banged on the door. Finally Meria appeared, eyes wide.

"I brought back meat for us," Eleanora said.

There was none of the pride she had imagined in her announcement, which had pushed her forward in what she had merely thought of as her practice until now. There was only the soft thump as she dropped the beast's hind legs into the snow.

To clean and dress the animal was the job of a woman, one of many Eleanora had never bothered with. She was relieved to pass the task to Meria as usual, though had her stepmother asked her to help even in the terse, flat voice she used now, Eleanora would have been glad to, despite her growing nausea. But as her stepmother said nothing, she merely brushed past her and sat near the window, trying to follow the trails of individual snowflakes as they fell from the sky to the ground, waiting for it to powder over the slithering red-and-pink path to the door. Meria's sighs and the clanging of pans in the background barely registered.

They ate in a thick silence still cushioned by crashing water-falls, despite so much of the world being frozen. Though the meat was charred and chewy, Eleanora wanted to compliment Meria on her cooking, for the illusion of it being their happy past again, or just to put words in the heavy silent air. But the lie sat on her tongue and she swallowed thickly.

Meria reached for the last lump of meat in the wooden bowl. Eleanora slapped her hand playfully. "No," she said, "that is for the man of the house." She had meant it as a joke, but Meria merely withdrew her sinewy hand and rose from the table.

Eleanora shook her head and flung the meat into the fire, holding back tears.

She lay down on her mat, shoved next to Meria's, which neither of them bothered rolling up during the day anymore.

The next morning, Eleanora held a piece of charcoal she had carved to a tip for drawing. She sat in her usual spot under the window, with a piece of used paper on her lap and an open book on the technique of perspective propped up near her knee.

Eleanora tossed the charcoal onto the ground as Meria passed by. She immediately regretted the childishness of her action, but she stuck her tongue out as her stepmother settled with her back to her in her usual seat near the dark hearth. Meria never asked where she went now; she never asked anything. Eleanora supposed it was her prerogative to unquestioningly do what she pleased, as head of the household. And what a household to lord over—no stores of food, a bony goat, and an old woman perpetually bowed over a gray hearth. An old woman? More like a ghost, trapped in a repetition of the same small movements, even the way her white sleeve floated in the cool air . . .

Eleanora startled suddenly: Meria looked starved. Her stepmother had always been willowy, but now her collarbones cast shadows on her chest. She looked like she was a blink away from death, her breast barely rising as she puffed out shallow white breath.

Why could she see her breath in the house?

Oh, the fire had not been made. Eleanora wanted Meria to address this need, but her stepmother was simply staring into space. Eleanora thought of asking Meria why there was not a fire, but they both knew they had nothing but skinny branches that doubled as something for the goat to nibble on, and in the thick of winter gathering kindling entailed too much risk. They had used close to the last of it to roast the meat last night. Dinner only last night, and Eleanora's stomach was already grumbling.

She drummed her fingers on the floor, then looked at Meria again.

"There is nothing for you to mend?" Eleanora asked.

Meria continued to stare into space before slowly turning to look at Eleanora, her eyebrows barely raised, as if to ask, *What?* This was worse than her weak and random sobbing strewn throughout the day.

"Perhaps the mending could be figurative," Eleanora continued, laughing at her own joke. She nervously picked at a loose thread in her pants. "Well? I am speaking to you."

"Is there something you wish for me to do?" Meria asked.

Eleanora sighed. "No, no, only to continue to give me the silent treatment. I always said I wanted more time to myself. What else is there to do but sit here and stare?"

Meria crouched closer to the cold ashes and stirred them with a stick. She moved slowly, and Eleanora watched as gold bracelets fell out of the sleeves of her dress and slid halfway over her skeletal hands, jangling and catching the light of the cold sun.

Eleanora felt a lump rising in her throat, and to squash it she twisted her own bracelet. "You are wrong," she said, as if Meria had spoken in reply. "There is something to do. I will go to town. To the bazaar. You can no longer stop me."

Meria's pale eyes bulged above her sharp cheekbones. She pulled her sleeve down past her bony knuckles.

When Eleanora was little, she had admired the shiny bracelets just before Baba surprised her stepmother with them. She had twisted and tugged them while Meria held her propped up on her hip. Eleanora swallowed.

"Those bracelets," she said, "can get us through winter."

Meria stared at Eleanora without answering. Her stepdaughter stood, and Meria backed away, wringing her hands.

"And what about your bracelet? Do you not have those gold coins? These are the last things I have that are pretty," Meria protested.

"Good idea." She squeezed the bangle around her own wrist, testing if she could make it bend. She could not. "I suppose a man ought not wear jewelry like this. Anyway, the coins are not enough." Eleanora laughed. Who was Meria to question her?

Her stepmother looked at her sullenly.

"You seemed to think my own life was a fine price to make it through winter," Eleanora went on, unable to help herself. "Well, if you would rather not sell them, I suppose you would look lovely buried in those bracelets."

Meria backed away. "Are you threatening me? You stand there and threaten me? Your father—"

"My father is dead, and unless I sell those bracelets, you'll join him! That is all I meant. And maybe I should let you." Eleanora threw up her hands, the way she had seen her father do a thousand times at patients who substituted his treatments with ridiculous rituals, or at stubborn animals, or at Meria. Eleanora sighed. She held out her hand.

Meria yanked the bracelets off her wrist and dropped them in Eleanora's outstretched palm.

"I have nowhere to wear them anyway," Meria muttered, turning back toward the dead hearth.

"Forgive me for not giving you a wonderful wedding to attend," Eleanora said. She pressed her fingers to her neck, where it was no longer sore but there were green-tinged bruises.

To Eleanora's surprise, Meria chuckled, but her expression was pained.

"Please believe me, I did not know it would be like that. I only wanted for us to be safe."

Later that night they lay close. Meria had pulled apart their mats, as was proper for their new relationship, but they were close enough in the dark Eleanora could easily hear her stepmother's whispered request to go with her to Shkodra.

Her voice was small and shy. "I am afraid you might not return."

"It is better if you stay here, and watch over the goat and keep the fire going," Eleanora said. It would be hard enough to sell the bracelets without Meria demanding an absurd price. Eleanora's price carried no emotional weight except fear they might not live through winter. "I promise to come back to you, Meria."

She woke before dawn, nervous excitement shooting through

her as she flipped the heavy blankets off her. She tried her best not to disturb Meria, but when she looked up from the pewter candlesticks she was wrapping in rags, her stepmother was holding out a cup to her, her lips as straight as her outstretched arm, the way she used to offer coffee to Baba before they left on a long trip.

A trip! Eleanora had not realized how she missed traveling. As she walked through the door, Meria shivering under her shawl, she turned and gave her stepmother a tight hug before she left.

Outside the sun tinted the sky a glowing rose, and the snow sparkled under the clear sky. Eleanora tipped her head back, smiling into the cold air, feeling light despite her bulky leather satchel stuffed with stale corn bread to snack on, the candleholders, and a few other belongings she hoped to sell besides the bracelets.

Her step had a bounce even as her foot sank through the snow, her grin disappearing when her ankle plunged into air.

She grabbed the bare branches of a shrub to keep herself from sliding into the hole in the trail. The smooth white snow had lied, covering empty air that almost swallowed her and cracked her bones. She clung to the bush, despite thorns burning into her palms, finally flinging herself back onto solid ground.

It was only after she had passed through the stone border of her village that she could acknowledge her still-hammering heart, cursing herself for how reckless she had been. But she forgave herself in her excitement, as the trail began its rise into the looming purple mountains. Soon she climbed high enough to feel as though she were walking in the bright blue sky, level with the fiery sun. She walked to the edge of the trail, watching clumps of snow crumble and disappear into the air. Would she fly if she leaped? Her stomach dropped as she gazed into the sky beneath her, and she started hiking again to shake away her impulse.

She was on an adventure, and even if it was not one with her father and Italy was not her destination, it was enough to be free from her home and on her first real trip alone. When she crossed paths with a young girl herding sheep, she called out greetings: "Long may you live! How could you get here?"

"Slowly, slowly, little by little," the girl replied, surprised a stranger was speaking to her, though her eyes were back on a straying goat she chased down from boulders tumbled on top of each other. "Are you an honorable man?"

"Yes, from Arbër. Am I on the right path?" Eleanora asked. "To Shkodra?"

The girl nodded, dashing and clapping at the goat.

"Go on smooth trails!" she yelled.

When Eleanora did not see another person for miles and was surrounded by the sparkling white blanket of the snow, she imagined she stomped on the virgin ground of a new world, completely foreign. Her lips cracked as she grinned into the bright cold morning air.

IN THE GLARING afternoon light, Eleanora peered into a store's square glass window. What a novel way to display an item! She squinted to better see the turquoise-encrusted necklace, but the harsh sunshine made a mirror in which she saw reflections of the townspeople behind her. One frowning, mannish face loomed larger than others, with oily dark hair slipping from under a dented white cap. It was a sun-browned face, scratchy brows sliding down, straining to meet over a freckled sloped nose, which shadowed tan lips. The lips became a thin line as she met those cloudy gray eyes, which then loosened into an O—was that her? Was she seeing herself?

The face scowled back at her. She turned away. Another fact not worth considering. What did her beauty matter? She had never cared much about marriage, and it was no longer an option anyway. Her father had been proud of her looks, but he was gone. School was gone. Italy was an impossibility. She balled her fists to keep from crying. She might try to fool herself that she was on a holiday, but wherever she went she moved within a prison of pure survival. And why even bother with that?

She was not sure, except when she quietly asked herself, something steady within her replied she was not ready to die. She had read many ideas about the afterlife, and did not, in theory, fear death. Perhaps it led to merely a vast emptiness. Then again, she had once been with a patient when he awoke from a coma, begging her to let him return to his dead wife. Baba had even suggested one only died to repeat their life again. When the time was right, she would have peace. Somehow she still had hope, though she was shy to even admit it to herself, that she might contribute to the world with her art. She had much to learn, but if her work would even inspire a single person as so much art had inspired her . . . If she could only make it to Italy! While there was still a chance she might escape this misery, she must try. Perhaps she could still drag Meria out of the hellhole she had thrown herself into when she had betrayed Eleanora. And to do so, she needed food for them both.

She kept walking, her fists jammed into her pockets and the satchel heavy on her back. The slippery cobblestone street curved to the right, and all of a sudden to her left were sun-grayed gondolas docked and bobbing, waiting to sail across the lake that some said was as wide as the sea. Over the deep water, the sky was layered: lighter, darker, grayer blues. Was that sliver of gray-blue above the horizon Italy in the distance? Eleanora squinted. No, only a fuzzy cloud. Lips parted, she stared at the few shuffling passengers shifting parcels and pouches from one hand to the other, preparing to board the rocking boat.

Why not sell their things and flee? With the gold coins she might have enough for a few weeks, until—

She pictured Meria's pitiful, painfully thin figure crouched over the dying fire, drawing figures in the ashes with a stick like a child. Meria had no relatives to turn to, no real friends, only a dangerous pinch of pride that would keep her from begging. Meria had made a terrible mistake, but even so, Eleanora could not leave the woman who had raised her to a slow, sure death. She had promised Meria she would return.

Besides, where would Eleanora go?

She started to brush past the man taking tickets from others, but stopped without thinking to.

"How much does it cost to cross to the other side?" she asked, her hand in her pocket, rubbing the gold coins between her fingers.

He looked her over.

"Can you put a price on freedom, sir?" the man asked, grinning, baring yellow teeth. "It is beautiful to feel you are part of the water, my friend. Show me what you have."

"How much?" Eleanora insisted, even as she opened her palm to show him all of her money.

"Only those coins," he said, pointing at all of her gold ones.

She walked away, head down, scanning the ground, imagining it was sliding beneath her feet and she must step forward to keep up. She had to remind herself that even she recognized a ridiculous price. She had to remind herself that she could not harden her heart enough to betray Meria and leave her to starve. Even if she could, it would only lead to herself starving in an unknown city, one with a shine that would wear off once she realized it was essentially the same as this one. She jammed the coins back into her pocket, still grossly damp from when she had splashed through the river earlier in the morning.

Eleanora moved on, soon flowing with a crowd through canyons created by sooty two-story buildings crammed side by side, facing each other across a narrow alley. She paused when she saw a turbaned, wrinkled man selling cornmeal and coffee and other powders, displayed in open sacks.

Eleanora greeted him. He did not respond.

She pointed to the cornmeal. It was a faded version of the bright golden meal Eleanora was used to, but she asked anyway. "Excuse me, sir, how much does this cost?"

"How much do you want, sir?" he replied, not looking up, as he exchanged a bag for silver coins from another man.

"That same size sack," Eleanora said, pointing to the man's bag. "One of cornmeal, one of coffee."

He prepared the bags, and Eleanora held out a gold coin.

He took the coin without saying anything.

She cleared her throat. "Where is my change, sir?"

He glared at her, and Eleanora stared back, hating the blush she felt creeping up her face. She would not allow him to treat her like this, like a mere mountain woman. She rubbed the butt of her father's rifle. Her rifle. She had come too far for this. He glanced down at her rifle, then he reached into his pocket and handed her five silver coins. She nudged a fellow customer, asking him what the coins were worth.

"You owe me more than this," Eleanora said, blinking back tears of frustration, feeling the other customer's eyes on her.

She had dealt with a sullen man who looked like this before, only then she had clung silently to her father's arm, while Baba stepped in and commanded the situation, smiling and paying easily. Her father had always been so polite.

Suddenly the seller smiled. "You drive a hard bargain. A good trader you are, young man. Long life to you." He handed her two more silver coins.

"Long life to you," Eleanora said with a crisp nod, feeling giddy. Was this what it meant to be a man? What was unjustifiable rudeness from a woman was now admirable aggression? She had been afraid for a moment he might strike her! She shook her head, laughing to herself at her victory. Her full bags were like air in her arms. Though unsure if he had really owed her more money, she had refused to be taken advantage of and had won. She was further elated when the two silver coins bought her oil pastels from a young man selling the same kind her father used to buy for her.

Ensuring the pastels were safely packed in her leather satchel between the cornmeal and coffee, she turned her face up into the bright sunlight—yes, she had some time to wander through town. Eleanora smiled, twisting the serpent bracelet she still wore. She would be able to return Meria's bracelets, too; she had bought them at least a month to enjoy their jewelry, and soon enough it would be spring and perhaps they would finally plant corn and vegetables. Meria had always thought they were silly for having only a small garden of pink rosebushes, and she had been right. Eleanora had traded as well as a man today, especially considering it was her first—

"Watch out!"

An elaborately painted little wooden house on wheels dragged by two shining mares glided by, and the eyes of a woman's lace-covered face peered out from a curtained window.

Eleanora dabbed the sweat on her upper lip with her hand-kerchief, crossing her arms over her matted fur coat. She looked down at her leather sandals dusted with dirt, her white pants stained by river water. What was that woman but a thing kept by a man, dressed and groomed like a handsome horse valued mostly for the steep price paid?

Eleanora flowed back to the center of the cobblestone street with the rest of the crowd. Any jewelry that woman wore was meaningless decoration, not the promise of paper for art, seeds to grow corn that she might trade with neighbors for coffee—independence in other words! Certainly the small bags of corn-meal and coffee were measly compared to how she had shopped with her father, but she had done this on her own.

She straightened her shoulders and ambled on, suddenly finding herself amongst a group of cafés. She backed away from the tables.

I will be back before I am gone, and when I return I have something to give you.

What do you think you are doing?

Where is your father?

Where is your father?

She shook her head violently, and dashed across the street, mumbling an apology when she almost bumped into someone.

She looked up. She stood in front of the heavy dark wooden door of the city office.

She walked on quickly, with no idea of where she was going except that she was desperate to get away. Suddenly her feet spun her around, and she found herself in front of the polished wooden door. She must know, and it was now or never. She smoothed her shirtfront, tightened her rifle across her back, straightened her shoulders, and opened the door, marching to the large dark desk.

"Yes, sir?" said the slumping clerk, still scribbling. "How may I help you today?"

Today? How about how may he have helped her months ago, when she needed it most? But she would not wreck her opportunity to answer the questions she still asked herself between every other thought. She cleared her throat and leaned forward, her moist palms sticking to the glossy wood.

"I must know who killed my father." She braced herself for being brushed off, for the inevitable disappointment of being ignored again. "And I must know why."

The scribe looked up, politely attentive. "Of course. If you would only tell me your father's name, perhaps I can help."

Eleanora recognized him from the day her father was murdered, and as she spoke her father's name, giving specifics about his death, the young scribe must have known who she was. She could not have been her own brother, for what man went without a mustache? And yet apparently she was a man now, feeling she was in a dream as the scribe spoke to her in a reasonable tone. Only in a dream everything unquestioningly made sense and now she felt as if she were the only one who was mad or the only one who was sane. Which was it?

"Yes, sir, I remember your father, Fran," he said.

She wanted to laugh, but she pressed her lips together and nodded as the scribe spoke to her respectfully. She was, after all, a man on a grave task.

"A tragedy indeed," he continued. "Your father had a reputation as a very good man. The man who had killed your father, sir, this man Kol, on the other hand . . . Well, Kol has a temper, it is true, and he has killed many men, but this had been an honor killing done in line with the laws of his people."

He cleared his throat.

"And yours, I believe."

The clerk stroked his mustache, waiting for her to deliberate with him on the moral dilemma of a not-so-good man honorably killing a good man.

"Why was there bad blood between them?" Eleanora asked.

The clerk gave his mustache a tiny twirl and shrugged.

"As I recall, it was something about a woman."

"But who? And what about her?" Eleanora insisted. "You seem sure it was not a mistake. So what had my father done?"

"How can I keep track of such things?" the scribe asked evenly. "You will understand me when I tell you that while, at first, it seems awful we do not keep official records of such things, it later becomes much more useful. That said, this Kol makes quite a bit of trouble, and I can tell you how to find the fellow's home, and you may ask him yourself why he killed your father. This is a man, officially or unofficially, let us say, no one would mind if you made him talk." He looked back down at his papers, raising an eyebrow. "Or if you made him never talk again."

ELEANORA STOOD IN front of the crooked door of a boxy one-story house of rough-stacked stone and a red-tiled roof, crammed between two other homes hiding behind smooth high walls, a block away from an encroaching field that marked the end of the residential neighborhood and led the way into the mountains.

Would Kol be home? Likely no one would answer the door.

She sucked in a deep breath. She had come so far. She could not turn back now.

"Oh, master of the house!" she shouted, more loudly than she would have if she were not so afraid.

No one answered. She forced herself to knock, pounding the door so that it rattled with her heart.

Chapter 15

The door cracked open, revealing a sliver of the length of a short dark man with bare feet and a crooked greasy mustache.

"What do you want?" he asked, training his squinty dark eyes on a muddy smudge on the black braiding of his white pants, and rubbing at it with his hairy thumb.

Eleanora could smell the raki on his breath, though she stood a foot or so away.

"I am looking for Kol," she said, feeling unsure of herself.

She curled and uncurled her fingers, then shoved them in her jacket pockets to keep from fidgeting. She had been told he was middle-aged and lived in a home like this near the edge of town. She half hoped she had the wrong house.

"Oh? Kol, you say?" He crossed and uncrossed his thick arms over his stained shirt, then began picking at his dirty nails. "And why would you be looking for this man?"

"I wish only to ask him questions," Eleanora said, rubbing together the coins in her pocket.

"About?" He still did not look at her.

"This man Kol killed my father," she blurted.

Eleanora peered past him; strewn on the packed-dirt floor were a crumpled black vest and white hat.

"Really?" He raised his tangled eyebrows, looking at her like he finally saw her. "And who would your father be?"

Eleanora felt her cheeks warm. Was she at the wrong house? How many men could this Kol have killed?

"My father's name was Fran."

"Fran? Ah, Fran!" He sighed. His black-edged nail traced an invisible line down the side of his face. "With the scar down his cheek?"

Eleanora nodded and kept nodding nervously. She put her curled fingers to her lips to stop her head from jerking.

"Yes, I knew him." He smiled, looking her over. "I wish your father were still alive."

Despite her growing unease, Eleanora automatically smiled in reply. "Yes, Baba—"

"Yes, oh, yes, your baba, how cute. Yes, if only he were still alive." His lips crawled farther up and over his yellow teeth in a grin that left his eyes nearly shut as his head tilted to the side. "Yes, I wish he were still alive. So I could have the pleasure of killing him again."

Eleanora suddenly saw only his disgusting mouth; if only she could shatter his disgusting mouth. She reached for the rifle strapped to her back, but before she could grab it he yanked her into the house, kicking the door shut with his foot and pinning her arms against the rough wall.

"You want to avenge your baba's death, eh?" He searched her face. "Is that why you became a sworn virgin? Before you became one, you must have been rather good-looking."

He pressed himself against her, and Eleanora kneed him in the groin, gaining the space to kick him again and again.

He collapsed into a howling heap, his white knuckles clutching his head and covering his face as she struggled to get at his awful mouth.

"Please, please stop!" he cried.

She shuffled backward, shaking her head. What was she doing here? He raised his eyes to her, and pity washed over her. He smiled thinly, and then she saw his hand was on his tarnished pistol, pointed at her. She grappled with her rifle, her hands automatically seeking their positions, her finger on the trigger.

A gunshot exploded.

Chapter 16

Kol lay writing on the floor, not still as Eleanora's father had lain, though Kol was also on his back and the whites of his eyes were terribly bright against the dirt floor. The blood blossomed through the white of his shirt, and Eleanora pressed her shaking hand to her own chest as if to stop the flow of his blood. How could she have shot someone? She irrationally wished she had also put a bullet through her own chest. She knelt beside him as he cried, panted, begged. "Do not leave me here to die slowly. End it now. Please."

She stared. It took all she had not to lie beside him, to be limp and unconscious as fear and pity for a hurting animal flooded her. The man who had murdered her father dissolved into a small being, whimpering and bleeding to death, and with her training she saw no matter what she tried he would die in hours. She had dreamed she would be happy at the death of her father's killer, but instead she felt a nauseating wave of guilt and stabbing regret at having killed someone.

"The pain," Kol gasped. "Just end it now. Please."

Eleanora stood and pointed her gun at his head. He closed his eyes. Hearing nothing, he stared up at her again.

"I cannot," she sobbed. "I am sorry. I am so sorry. Why did you do it?"

He became still, staring off beyond Eleanora, and she saw the same scene, months ago, only flooded with sunlight. She squeezed her eyes shut. *You should not have to see something like this*, she heard a voice tell her. She squealed as she felt something tickle her ankle. She opened her eyes—it was his hand, too weak to grip, just a rasping grasp. She hated him again, as much as she had when he was merely an idea that kept her up at night, hated him for putting her here again, making pain and guilt flood throughout her again.

"Why?" she cried. "I only wanted to ask you why."

She pointed her gun at his head again.

"Tell me why!"

His pale lips parted, but instead of begging, blood bubbled out. Eleanora watched, unable to move.

The door groaned open.

She slammed the door closed and bolted it with shaking hands, standing with her back against it and panting until a man's deep voice protested from the other side. Eleanora jolted away from the door, while Kol's eyes brightened with hope, his chin twitching toward the door that began to shake as fists pounded against it.

Eleanora whipped her head back and forth. There! A small glassless window. Did it face the alley between the houses? She dashed to it, holding back a scream as Kol's hand grazed her foot, fighting to pull herself through as the man outside continued to batter the door, sounding as if he threw his whole body against it. She hissed with the effort of pulling herself up and through the tight window. Her rifle crossed the opening like a toggle in a buttonhole, holding her to the wall. She twisted the gun and fell to the ground on all fours as she heard the door crash open and a man scream.

She sprinted as fast as she could toward the swaying field. She was sure she heard feet falling behind her, but was too frightened to look back.

She ran through the meadow, tall grass whipping her face, agony clenching her chest, her feet becoming clumsy and heavy, her satchel an impossible weight. She ran, until she was lost in a grove of bronze-branched trees, until it was quiet except for the rasping breath tearing through her, until she would collapse and die if she took another step. She stopped, her hands on her knees, her head bent over her waist, her gulps for air panicked and painful.

Underneath her galloping breath she thought she heard distant footsteps, but when she held her breath she heard only her hammering heart.

Chapter 17

It was dark when Eleanora reached the river, her legs leaden and trembling. The rolling water was flinty, its depths disguised in the half moon. The last time she had approached the river from this point she was well rested in summer sunlight, and the river had nearly killed her then. At morning, when she had crossed, she had slipped into the current many times, her leg getting caught between two rocks. Luckily another hiker had been near and had helped her. What might the river do to her now, when she was alone in the dark? To try to cross was to drown.

She paced the shore in spite of her tired legs; to wait at the river felt like death, too. Earlier she was certain she heard a stranger's footfalls behind her, and she climbed the mountain trail faster than a goat being chased. She reached a large boulder and crouched behind it, looking back, seeing no one. She had laughed at herself then, remembering the scowling man's face she had seen reflected in the store window in Shkodra this afternoon. Ages ago, but perhaps *he* was following her.

She began to laugh again, unable to stop, trying to smother her hysterical giggling with her hand clamped over her mouth. She should not laugh at that man. After all, he had killed Kol, only hours ago. She screamed into her hand and made herself keep walking. She could not think of this now, though beneath her guilt was a vague satisfaction from the punishment she had meted out.

She hugged her arms to her chest, though it was not so cold at the base of the mountains; her panting breath was invisible. She still had her fur coat from the walk during the snowy morning. She passed the shallow cave carved out of the boulder near the shore. It was empty when she had seen it in the daytime. Should she enter? She threw a rock in. She had no way to make a fire, and she cursed herself for not bringing her father's lighter. No, she had lost it in this river, with her horse, the day—

She could not think of that now. She sat down, then let herself collapse onto her back, her satchel a lumpy pillow, and tried to pinpoint stars in the sky. Was that Queen Cassiopeia, admiring her beauty in a hand mirror as she sat on her throne? Eleanora traced the constellation's zigzag shape with her quivering finger. As a child, she had imagined snatching the queen's mirror out of her hand, but now it looked so far away. And she was so tired . . .

THE HARSH SUN woke Eleanora from a nightmare, her face hot and sweaty. She rubbed at her forehead with her handkerchief, closing her eyes. Oh, Baba knew what she had done, he knew, and while he had been able to forgive her for leaving him, he could never forgive her for murdering someone. Not saving someone's life was a sort of sin, and to take one, to intentionally steal one, was inconceivable. And she had done both. She shook her head till her cap fell off, then rose, punching the dust off her hat before she pulled it back on. She stretched her aching back until a lower muscle sent a spasm of pain through her. Her hands on her knees, she looked up. The river was opaque but without depth, its gray-green water sliding across the smooth rocks paving the riverbed.

Still, when she tried to cross, she nearly slipped a few times, finally falling flat onto her back. She tried to ignore the throbbing pain and be grateful she had not risked cracking her head last night. The wet cold seeped through her pants, reaching above her sash, making the cloth sticky. Perhaps she could lie in the grass and let the sun dry her.

She heard a stick crack behind her. She grabbed her gun and spun.

A boar with thick twisting tusks watched her from across the river. She laughed at her thumping heart, but its wide-eyed stare reminded her of another's and she quickly turned away. Her pants slapped and stuck to each other as she walked as fast as she could, refusing to run, but also refusing to look back, no matter what she heard. The longer she stared straight ahead, the more she felt that someone's eyes bore into her back. What had happened to the brave, ruthless man she imagined herself to be? She was a baby again, tangled up in skirts and swaddling, sure something hid in the dark, but so long as she would not look, its existence was somehow less and it could not threaten her.

She pushed herself forward, her stomach growling. She thought of Pjetër's house, but she was far from there and would be in her own home soon enough, with Meria cooking. But no. Home no longer meant shelter and safety; it meant the responsibility of survival. To think she had worried about not having a certain shade of pastel only moons ago.

She had returned with a package of pastels, small sacks of cornmeal and coffee, and silver coins. Or had she lost these while running? She patted her pockets. Empty? She shook the contents of her satchel onto the ground. Two sacks tumbled out, her box of pastels exploded onto the ground, silver coins now buried in the brush, along with Meria's bracelets. Her mouth dry, she let out a huge breath. She still had these things, at least. And her rifle.

ELEANORA WAS SHAKING with hunger when she saw her home's fence. She twisted around to reassure herself no one followed her, and dashed to her gate, slamming it closed behind her. She checked three times to make sure it was bolted before she staggered into her house.

Meria rose from the dead hearth, her eyes nearly as wide as their sockets.

"Eleanora?" Meria said, her arms outstretched, shaking like skeletal branches in the winter wind. "You returned. I thought maybe you would . . . I am so relieved to see you again." Meria waited for Eleanora to speak, fingering her collar. "But why have you come back so soon? Did you even go? What did you bring us?"

Eleanora stood there, stupidly opening and closing her mouth, struggling to find the right words. "What did I bring us?" she echoed. Should she tell Meria what she had done? What Meria had said she wanted? What Eleanora had wanted, too, but realized she had never admitted to herself? But now that it was done, she felt a sly pride creeping up. She had punished the man who murdered her father and brought them so much pain. Family honor was ruined by a murder and restored by another. Was that justice? Eleanora laughed.

Meria backed away, fiddling with a cold pot hanging over the ashes.

"My bracelets, they were worth a lot for us, at least?" Meria asked. "Well? What did you bring back?"

"I have brought back what I could," Eleanora said, setting down her satchel finally, pretending to rummage through it so she might hide her face. What would Meria say when she knew?

"Eleanora, did something happen?" Meria asked, her thin lips turning down in concern. "Are you well? You know you can tell me."

Eleanora stepped toward her. So she would understand after all.

Meria looked her over, her gaze pausing at the top of her shirt. She tut-tutted absentmindedly. "You have a stain."

Eleanora looked down to see a rusted-red spot on her shirt. Did Meria already know? She felt like she was dreaming again, with characters that accepted everyone else's actions as a matter of course. Eleanora need only say the words, a mere formality, before she could crawl into Meria's arms like when she was a baby. Her stepmother's relief that Baba's murderer had been punished would erase the growing guilt about what she had done, and if someone came for her, she knew Meria would protect her.

"It looks like blood. And the last good shirt you have," Meria rattled on. "Eleanora, why do you not say anything? Where do you expect to get another one like this? You like to make decisions by yourself, you want to be in charge of this household, and yet—"

Eleanora slapped Meria, watching her stepmother's oversize head rock back in slow motion.

What a satisfying crack.

The blooming red spot on Meria's pallid face made her look alive. Eleanora felt at last she was not dreaming. Everything became frighteningly real. She had committed an unthinkable crime. Someone would come for her. Baba had always said murder was evil, no matter if the Council of Elders called it honorable, no matter if the world blessed it as war.

"You hit me?" Meria whispered, touching her tear-streaked cheek, and Eleanora became ashamed even as she still burned with frustration about the unfairness of it all.

"My father never hit me," Meria wailed. "Your father never hit me! And you dare hit me? When I treated you as if you were my own child. I took your vow more seriously than you, and respect you as the head of this house. When I think of everything, everything I have done for you. I—"

"Everything you have done for me?" Eleanora spit, angry at the tears rushing up. Her fists rubbed her eyes roughly. "And to think of how much more you would have done for me had I let you."

How dare this stupid woman make her feel like this. Eleanora knew she was not a bad person, but at this moment she could not even explain to herself how things had come to this.

This seething ghost with tangled pale hair covering her pasty face, shaking in front of her, was a stranger. She was not her beautiful stepmother who had raised her. And what did she owe this woman, who had tried to trade her for trinkets to an evil man who would have happily bruised and broken her? To this ungrateful woman she had kept fed, whose honor she had protected?

Eleanora dug through her satchel. She hurled the precious bracelets and sacks of cornmeal and coffee at Meria's feet and stumbled out the door.

Outside the gate, Eleanora forced herself to take deep, slow breaths to calm her hiccuping sobs. She must not rush, she had nowhere and no one to go to. She had an eternity. Or did she? What if someone was already coming for her? Someone who knew what she had done? She swallowed hard, to stop a growing nausea. She must be calm. When she got back to town, she would buy some beautiful white bread before she figured out how to get away to Italy. Perhaps she could sneak onto one of those boats, lie low so no one could see her, absolutely no one, until the gondola bumped into the dock and she rose into the morning light, an unknown person with a new life before her.

Her clumsy feet crunched into the icy dirt of the path, each step beating earth into earth as a thousand footsteps had done before her and would continue to do, until the rain washed it all away and everyone started again. This would be the last time her feet trod here. She kicked a clump of snow.

The path began to narrow, leaving room for one as it curved down and around the slope. She froze at the sharp corner. The red-orange sun had sunk level with the trail, a burning back-drop to the black, featureless silhouette of a giant man in the distance who lurched forward, toward her.

Eleanora's legs tightened, ready to bolt, but there was no-where to go. She looked frantically around: to her right, silvery shrubs hid a steep fall into the valley where the river ran, and to her left was the steep climb into cliffs.

"He is only another traveler, he is only another traveler," she chanted in a whisper, until something inside her told her to hold her breath and be utterly still. Though her knees felt like jelly, she stood like a statue, watching the shadow man stagger to-ward her. Sometimes his movements seemed sped up or slowed down; it was hard to tell with the sun so bright behind him. Her eyes watered from the sunlight, and she felt dizzy and again like she was in a nightmare. She ought to run before he caught her—who knew when someone would shake her awake?—but her body was paralyzed, as in a dream when her conscious mind might command one thing but the unconscious narrative over-rode it.

Surely the shadow man was only another hiker, headed deeper into the mountains beyond her house. Her house? Meria could have it. Eleanora stepped forward. She was leaving, and she could not afford to be afraid anymore.

He took his time hobbling toward her.

She forced herself to look him in his narrowed eyes, shout-ing, "Long may you live! Are you an honorable man?"

He muttered something indiscernible, but she felt she under-stood him. He was saying that he knew—he knew what she had done—all the while his left leg dragging, pants torn, exposing a gash in his leg with its skin curled back, revealing bloodied muscle. His wound would not stop him. He had been sent to find her.

Eleanora held back a cry, taking gulping breaths to keep quiet. There was nowhere to go as he stumbled toward her, and as he came closer she was hypnotized by his fair face, startlingly handsome even while wrenched in pain. He closed in on her, mumbling unintelligible accusations, suddenly collapsing on top of her, dragging her down.

She fell backward onto the cold, wet ground, her head against the edge of the path that crumbled into a cliff, the icy earth collapsing beneath her. She struggled to wriggle out from under him, and her panic dissipated despite the danger of the two of them rolling off into the valley's chasm, for now that he was so near she realized the man was merely sick and delirious. He was only sick.

She twisted her body free from his. As she was gasping, squatting near his head, he opened his blue eyes and weakly smiled at her.

"Are you a fairy?" he mumbled, his full pink lips twisting as he gasped in agony, his torn, bloody leg kicking. She put out her hand and he seized it, squeezing her knuckles white.

"I wish I could become one, but I am not." Her father had always called her his mountain fairy. She looked at the man's beautiful face. His blond eyebrows were thick and straight, his nose narrow and noble, turning down at the tip over his pillow lips. The lines framing his mouth made her think he had smiled often for many years. He might be as old as her father, as old as the man she had left lying . . . She shook her head and stood. She would not think of him now. She could not undo what she had done, but she could save this man.

"You must let me help you," she said. She grunted as she tried to pull the stranger up, nearly collapsing under his deadweight before he was standing again, limping. When he tried to walk, their lack of rhythm made their lurching progress nearly worse than her just dragging him back to her home.

Meria did not look up as Eleanora jerked open the front door. Her eyes were puffy and bloodshot, but she said nothing as her stepdaughter pulled the stranger onto the floor mats.

"He is very ill," Eleanora said, between panting breaths. "His leg is torn, perhaps broken or infected."

Meria wrinkled the red tip of her nose, but she walked over and peered at his leg, smoothing dirt off a cushion farthest from the stranger. He had become suddenly still.

"Do what you wish, so long as you stay out of my way," Eleanora said. "I mean to save him."

"Perhaps I could get dung from a neighbor's dog," Meria offered, "to mix with raki to cure the wound."

Eleanora shook her head. That old supposed cure-all was worse than doing nothing.

"Wash his wound with raki and give him some to drink," Eleanora ordered.

She ran upstairs to her father's study, scanning the shelves for a thick medical book Baba had shown her many times, saying she must reference it if he ever were ill. Her fingers danced over the various gilded and leather book spines. She had not had the chance to use it to help him, but she would use the book now. There! She snatched it from the shelf, flipping through it as she dashed downstairs.

The stranger shivered, and as Eleanora put her hand to his forehead to check for a fever, he held her eyes.

"I cannot blame her," he mumbled. "What creature would not want to protect her babies?"

"Of course," she said, in her most soothing tone. He was delirious. Eleanora inspected his jagged, deep wound. *Ah!* Perhaps it was from an animal, some beast protecting its brood. She searched his pain-wrenched face again.

Meria knelt and offered her a wet rag.

"Did you boil the water first?" Eleanora asked.

Before Meria could say she had not, her stepdaughter was out the door scavenging for more firewood.

Chapter 18

*E*leanora climbed the stairs slowly and silently, balancing on her tiptoes as she clasped the medical book under her left arm, cradled a bowl of boiled water in one hand, and in her other clenched a needle and thread she had waved through the fire and dipped in boiling water. She paused just before the landing, which often creaked unless she avoided its bowed middle. She told herself she was being careful not to wake the stranger. But really, she did not want him to know she was coming so she might have the chance to turn around and run away from the house and never come back.

But why?

She did not know, but she knew she could not be at fault for another death, and to leave him would be to leave him to die. In Meria's hands, in any villager's incapable hands. She had seen her father unable to save men from lesser wounds after they had been bled or had been fed dogs' feces mixed with raki.

She sighed, standing outside the closed door, tempted to let the slippery bowl drop from her hand and run. How strange. She had begun observing herself as if she were a separate person, and she often found herself as amusing as she had found other villagers when traveling with her father.

She sighed dejectedly, then straightened her shoulders. With her jutting elbow she nudged the cracked wooden door.

It swung open in the dark silence of the room.

The man lay in the back as she and Meria had arranged him, atop two mats with extra pillows, under a heavy woolen blanket to smother his shivers. Eleanora had left him a knotted rag to seize in his pain. He was still now.

She knelt to set the bowl at his feet. The bowl almost clattered onto the floor as she shifted her hold on the needle. She sucked in her breath to keep from swearing. She lit the half-melted candle. She had not allowed herself to read or draw with its light no matter how long a sleepless night might seem; she had never known why she was saving it. Perhaps for him.

She had forgotten the raki.

She tiptoed downstairs, barely noticing Meria's tense shadow, and slunk back up with the near-empty bottle. She felt foolish that they had wasted it on curious casual guests, but did not regret her own secret sips when Meria was not looking. She took a gulp now. The man's breathing was shallow and slow. She lifted the bottom corner of his blanket. Even under the clean rags she had thickly bandaged his leg with, she could see the calf was swollen to almost twice the size of the other leg. She carefully touched one of the specks of red that had seeped through the white rags. He did not flinch. She was relieved he might sleep while she worked.

Meria had offered to help, but Eleanora told her she would be a distraction if anything, though, really, she was afraid of her possible criticism. This would be the first sewing Eleanora had ever done, and the first healing she had practiced on her own. After moving the man into her father's room and bandaging his leg, she had spent hours studying the book's illustrations for stitching a wound. She tried to remember the details of when, long ago, Baba had done this for a young boy—an only son well worth the expense, the boy's father had murmured as he handed Baba gold. The boy had been injured by falling through a tree he had climbed, seeking leafy branches to feed his family's goats. The boy had healed quickly as if by magic, someone later told Baba, left with a thin pink streak of a scar—another miracle by Baba.

Eleanora yawned nervously and brushed her hair out of her eyes. Her hands hovered above the man's bandaged leg. She began to unwrap it, shuddering as she inspected the ripped skin—even worse than that little boy's, and he had needed a bone set, too. Blistering at the edges and showing scarlet muscle underneath, the wound was like a little crimson canyon carved through his calf. She looked at the numbered illustrations in the medical journal again: one, a black-and-white forearm sliced through; two, stitches made to draw and hold the skin together for the fastest healing; three, the wound embroidered and closed. Eleanora leaned close and admired the artist's skill. If only the work was really as clear and simple as the illustrations. She looked back at the man's chest, slowly rising and falling almost imperceptibly in the shadows.

She took a deep breath, steadying the eye of the needle in

the quivering candlelight, pinching the near-invisible thread. It took her three tries to get the thread through. She cleansed his wound again, and his leg convulsed.

The man's head lifted.

"Who are you? What do you think you are doing?" he asked, his gravelly voice stern.

Eleanora's cheeks burned. What was she doing? Why was she even here? She ought to be gone by now. She would leave when she finished. She cleared her throat.

"I am Eleanora. The daughter of a doctor. I am cleansing your wound," she said, using her most soothing voice, reserved for work like this. Baba had always praised her for her voice becoming calmer the more hysterical a patient might become. "And then I will sew it up. It will heal as if it had never happened."

"I never heard of anyone doing such a thing."

"My father was a great healer," she said. "He did this before, and saved legs and arms this way."

His head dropped back, the air swooshing out of the pillow. "You brought me here. Why did you bring me here?" he asked.

"I saw that you were in pain, that you were suffering." Eleanora tiptoed over to his head and crouched. She put her hand on his forehead, the sticky skin hotter than the water in the bowl. "I only wanted to help," she said, but despite her effort her cooing, in-control voice had transformed into something begging and desperate. "I keep trying to do what is right, and yet . . ."

He seemed not to notice the change. "Well, if you say what you do has been done before by other men."

She searched his handsome face. His blond brows were drawn

together, a lock of ivory hair was matted with sweat, and beads of moisture dotted his scalp. He blinked, and for a moment she saw how clear his blue eyes were. When his eyes closed again, she allowed herself to study his face. He was beautiful, even in his pain. His eyes shot open, his pink-red lips clenching into a straight line. He grabbed her hand, crushing her fingers, but she would not cry out if he did not. His grip loosened, and he smiled weakly at her.

"The pain," he gasped. "Just end it now. Please."

She winced at his words. She had heard that phrase somewhere before, long ago. She shook her head and shuffled back to his leg. She pinched the needle between her fingers, the candle-light making it gleam. She drew a deep breath and began.

With a strange fascination, she watched the shining needle push against the skin, creating a dent of resistance, until the skin gave way and the needle tunneled in, finally sliding through to the wound's opening and piercing through the other side of skin, bridging the two sides of the wound together. She knotted the thread twice, so that the skin closed at the top.

The man sucked his breath in and pounded his fist against the floor.

Eleanora looked up, and he met her eyes and jerked his chin, nodding for her to go on, his head rolling back as he gasped. Eleanora wove her way back to the other side, and through again, again, and again, gingerly tightening the thread so the gash shrunk into an angry red streak down his calf. She tied the thread, and a deep sigh escaped her. She had not realized she was holding her breath.

Even if she was able to get fresh olive oil and proper herbs to make a healing ointment for his wound, it would leave a scar, but what sort of pain did not? Baba had had a theory that all pain left a scar, hidden in the flesh even if one could not see it.

She wrapped his leg with fresh rags and then gathered the bowl, book, and needle, careful to be quiet. He seemed to be sleeping again, perhaps passed out from the pain.

She stepped out of the room, and from the dark floated a ragged, deep voice. "Thank you, fairy."

ELEANORA SMILED AT the gray ceiling as she woke. She had saved him, and she had done it on her own. Was this the ecstatic pride her father had felt, after nights of being unable to sleep, as his brain raced around about what he would do if there was an infection, how he might have bandaged the wound differently, if it were better to use the exactly right herbs or none at all? She sat up, tossing the heavy blankets from her. Was Cheremi—he had whispered his name to her on the third day—awake yet? Did he want anything? It was too hard for him to walk down the stairs, so these last few days Eleanora went to him, cleansing and dressing his wound, swapping his blanket for a freshly brushed one, bringing him meticulously arranged little dishes. Some were only corn bread and broth, though she tried her best to get him stewed meat, spending hours hunting in the forest, dragging home a boar, a chamois, or a hare as fast as she could, tapping her foot as Meria stirred a simmering pot filled with herbs Eleanora had found.

She pretended not to see the looks Meria gave her when she dashed upstairs, balancing the twigs in the crook of her arm, dishes in her hand, clutching blankets and towels to her chest. She pretended not to see the disapproving glances, though she found a perverse satisfaction in annoying her stepmother. Had she not returned and continued to provide for the thankless woman? How many more sacrifices need she make, how many more ridiculous vows must she take? Was she the reigning head of the household or not?

She was merely following tradition as decreed; as head of the household she was host, and she performed her duties well, making an honored guest of Cheremi. If only she were really a man, then she would promise her daughter to Cheremi, with his beautiful looks and his beautiful manners, like a hero out of one of the Italian novels she no longer bothered with lately.

If Eleanora noticed Cheremi wince when she spooned the stew into his mouth, she insisted on making him wait as she blew over the meat to cool it. She fed fragrant sprays of pine to the smoldering fire contained in an iron bowl at his feet. Sometimes she dared herself to touch the glowing bowl, testing if she could do so without burning her fingers. And while she did these little tasks, Cheremi told her about his travels, his wandering for work as a guide to foreigners who wished to explore the country.

Eleanora felt, while he spoke, as if she were meeting her father again, only as an awed stranger, who appreciated his charms more than a familiar family member ever could.

"Have you ever been to Kopek?" Cheremi asked her, the pillow rustling as he turned his head toward her.

"No, I have not yet," Eleanora said, her voice barely above a whisper. "I have been to a village I heard was like Kopek, though." She shied from looking up, embarrassed of how greasy her hair must be, and of the smudges from hunting she likely had on her face. Instead she watched her trembling hands pour boiled water into a bowl half filled with raki, imagining the little ripples were flowing to the smooth rhythm of Cheremi's voice. He had the same urbane accent that her father had had, which she had never been conscious of Baba having until now, when she heard it roll from this strange man's red lips. She had never heard a voice so musical.

"Have you?" he asked. "You have traveled almost as much as me, I think. Nonetheless, you must see Kopek one day," he said.

She felt his eyes on her, even as she bit her lower lip and focused on not overfilling the bowl. She folded the blanket back from his feet up to midthigh, unwrapping the damp rags around his wound. His wounded calf was less swollen; soon it would be as lithely muscular as the other. She glanced higher up where his thighs joined, wondering if he would look the same as what she had seen in her father's medical books. She nudged the blanket a little higher, then tugged it down, embarrassed by her crude curiosity.

"The city has the most beautiful women," he continued. "So beautiful, the jealous men keep them hidden in their houses so no one can ever see."

Eleanora swirled a clean rag into the bowl of raki and water. She smiled at the story as she washed his wound. "If you or anyone else has not seen these women, how do you know it is true? Besides, most of what we hide is out of embarrassment, not pride."

Cheremi laughed, and Eleanora looked away so he would not see her blush. "You may be too clever for me, though I might have guessed that by the magic you performed on my leg."

"I am only grateful that I could help you," she said. "And that you turned out not to be a bore."

Cheremi laughed again.

"And grateful that perhaps," she said, "you will tell me one more story."

"Let me try to remember what I have told you before," Cheremi replied, his long fingers drumming his chin as he stared at the ceiling. "So I do not repeat one to you."

"Why should I mind if you did?" she said. It was easier to speak normally without his eyes on her. "Stories are never the same even when repeated. If only by virtue of how one responds to the story. It is never the same."

"Yes, I suppose you are right," he said, chuckling in wonder. "Has anyone ever told you that you are too young to be so wise?"

"I have been told I am too clever, but never that I am too wise. But tell me again about the strange waters you tasted. You described something out of a fairy tale, and I am still not sure if I believe you."

And so he told her, again, about sipping the uniquely flavored springs of Bulqize, a city far south, and sneaking through the castle of Ali Pasha, even farther away along the coast. Or he could have told her again how all the glass of her house reminded him of the city of a thousand windows in Berat, which reflected all the light shimmering off the river that bordered the town. He had gone to Berat after a man in Telepene had told him he must see it. Eleanora tried to imagine herself roaming so freely, spurred from one city to another on a whim to experience some novelty.

As much as she liked to hear about the curious beauty of the places he had been, she loved to watch his dark-pink lips move. If she had the right pastels or pots of paint, she would put them to paper. She was glad she did not. To paint him would require her to stop looking at him. Was this how da Vinci had felt when he painted *La Gioconda*? How he must tear himself away from her in order to properly pay homage to her? Was this the secret vexation of an artist and his muse?

When she gazed at the fine lines of his face, a frustrated energy burned through her body; his beauty almost hurt her. Of course she must meet a man like Cheremi when he was forbidden to her by a stupid tradition she barely believed in, and, more important, when she must flee this place soon. Perhaps that was best—she wished she could not look at him every day. She might grow used to his profile soon, and to be senseless to that seemed so blasphemous, so ugly an idea that she'd rather she were blind instead, or that she were staring at an empty floor in her father's study. Anything but to grow numb to this. Though she shivered when she thought of what her life might be like if he had not stumbled into it—hopeless and lonely, lonelier than she had allowed herself to realize. Her father gone, trapped in the house with two people she hardly knew anymore: Meria, who had betrayed her, now nothing to her but a frowning mouth she must feed, and herself, who had committed that unbelievable crime in the city.

Someone would come for her for what she had done. She was grateful to have a friend, even if she did not deserve him.

She squeezed her eyes shut, and took a deep breath. She slowly opened her eyes again, watching Cheremi's pale full lashes tremble as he slept. Like a budding leaf in a spring breeze. Suddenly he was staring back at her. She looked down at the freshly folded blanket in her hands, and her feet carried her to the foot of his mat. She straightened a corner of the blanket already on top of him, feeling the warm wool in her hand, watching it move against his toes.

"Forgive me," she stammered. Her cheeks flushed, the burn flooding her face as she wished it away.

"What have I to forgive you for?" Cheremi yawned, covering his mouth with the back of his palm. "For making me feel guilty for what good care you take of me?"

She dropped the folded blanket on the floor. How clumsy of her. What had she brought it for anyway? She could not take the blanket off his body, sworn virgin or not, now that he was well enough to do it on his own. He would think her strange.

"I am sure you would do the same for me," she said. "I am only sorry I woke you. You had a smile on your face, as if you were having a good dream."

"I believe I am still having it. You look like something out of a dream, with those flowers tangled in your hair." He laughed, struggling to sit up. She wanted to rush to him and help him, to pull up a pillow, but her feet were planted in the floor.

She fingered the dried blossom she had tucked behind her ear. Did he remember he had called her a fairy, a spirit of the woods? But how could he? He had been delirious then; it was obvious now, to see how far-seeing his clear blue eyes were today.

"This? I suppose wearing flowers is an old habit, from when I was another person." She tossed a flower at him, missing his lap, feeling flustered and foolish. He would think her strange. She, who had prided herself on her controlled calm while she nursed cursing patients. "I will bring soup to you," she said. A random, idiotic comment, but he did not seem to notice.

Meria had been cooking the bone broth since the morning,

based on Baba's restorative recipe that Eleanora had dictated to her. Meria always asked if Cheremi liked what she had made, but never asked him herself, insisting Eleanora bring food up to him, as she was the man of the house. The man! That was like Meria, to be so proper, though Eleanora felt something like envy in her stepmother's trailing eyes whenever Eleanora floated up the stairs.

Eleanora walked toward the door. She forced herself to turn and face him.

"May I bring you anything else?" she asked. Oh, her voice sounded so stupid and stiff. What was wrong with her? She was equal to any man, but behaved like a shy, sheepish girl.

"No, what else could you possibly bring me?" he asked. "You save my life, and then treat me like a king." He twirled the flower between his long fingers, and then flung it back at her feet. "I am forever in your debt. Thank you, and not only for the soup."

He smiled as he stretched his arms above his head. "You have the strength of a mountain fairy to have brought me back here."

Her coiled fingers rose over her mouth and she rushed to the door, closing it without answering, standing for a moment with her hand on the knob before she dashed downstairs.

ONE MORNING ELEANORA returned from wandering in the woods, which remained sparkling white but now echoed with the crackling of ice and dripping of melting snow. She had come upon a spray of yellow flowers on an otherwise bare-branched dogwood tree, and now she clutched the bunch of blossoms to her chest as she walked through the front door, humming.

"It feels too early in the season for such beautiful flowers!"

Meria exclaimed, her voice artificially light, her face beaming when she glanced up at her stepdaughter as she walked in. Eleanora startled for a moment—Meria's was the radiant, beautiful face she had known as a baby. Then it vanished in shadows, as she bent over the hearth, stirring a small pot, though a ghost of it showed as she looked up frequently to share a smile with Cheremi. He sat nearby on the floor, leaning against a wall, his chin resting on his good leg as he petted the goat and fed it dry branches.

"Yes, too early, or maybe too late," Eleanora said, her good spirits suddenly deflated. She dropped the branches on the floor, shooing the curious goat away. She clanged pans in the wooden chest as she searched for the mahogany vase Baba had carved for her floral arrangements. She wanted to show it to Cheremi, since he had admired one of her still-life pictures that featured the vase. Eleanora's stomach rumbled at the rich smell of meat. She felt a jealous twinge: Where had it come from? Who had gotten it for Cheremi?

"What are you two cooking?" Eleanora asked, forcing the question to sound casual.

Cheremi looked at Meria with the same shadow of a smile he had often shared with Eleanora, and she felt irrationally as if she could cry.

"Well?" she asked.

"I know I have been under strict orders from my miraculous healer to rest, but I sneaked out while you were away," he said, teasing the goat with a twig and laughing when the beast suddenly clamped down on the crunchy leaf. "More dishonorable than that, I kidnapped your priceless gun and took the life of an innocent hare."

"I hope it was not the hare of a powerful clan," Eleanora managed to jest. What a moronic joke. Cheremi did not laugh, and she pretended absolute focus on filling the vase with water. "You know I would have gotten a hare had you told me you wanted one." She fanned out the blossoms, comforted by the velvety petals between her fingers. She snapped one in two. "You ought to rest more. Perhaps it is too hard on your leg for you to come downstairs."

"Perhaps, perhaps not. You do too much for me, and a man begins to feel it," he said. He shrugged, pushed himself up, and walked over, barely limping. He carefully lowered himself next to Eleanora on a floor pillow. She put the vase on the floor, moving the floral arrangement so it was not too close to the hearth's heat. But what did it matter? How long could it last anyway?

"What beautiful flowers," Cheremi said, fingering the broken blossom. "How did you dream up the idea to arrange them like so? I have only ever seen something like this in a large city, in Tirana I think it was." He leaned closer. "Is that not the same vase from your pictures?"

Before Eleanora could answer yes, Meria interrupted to say that it was time for dinner, and she hoped they would like it.

When fresh cornmeal appeared days later, Cheremi explained he had traded some of his tobacco with their neighbors. Eleanora hoped he still had plenty for himself, and if he did not, she would offer him the coins she had saved to buy more. His clove-heavy cigarettes shared the scent of the exotic bazaars he described to her at night, and out of that fragrant smoke she imagined translucent houses made entirely of glass—while the same smoke also screened visions of women and men who ran away for romance.

Baba had always told her if she must marry at all she must marry for love, laughing loudly when Meria hinted about Eleanora wedding a rich widower she had heard of, waving her words away when she referred to a patient Baba had brought home—or dismissing her disgustedly when she mentioned Edi. More than once Fran had argued, to the outraged exclamations of his audience, that more families ought to allow their daughters to choose their husbands, but even if Meria was near him serving food as he insisted this, he never looked at her while he said such things.

What had Baba felt about his wife? Had he always sensed the weakness Meria had revealed when she tried to sell out her stepdaughter?

Eleanora was unsure, though as she remembered it now she thought it must be connected with Baba's leather notebook. *My soul . . .* She had never had a chance to ask Baba, but perhaps she could ask Cheremi. He would understand.

Cheremi could understand almost anything, and she took to consulting him for things perhaps she already knew. If she did know, she let herself forget, because he spoke each day with more strength and surety, his charming voice with its smooth accent became her gracious guide—like Baba's had been. She was skeptical at first when Cheremi advised her which woods to hunt in, but he turned out to be right. She was grateful to have someone to tell her what to do since her whole world had changed so much since Baba was—

He was vanished, painlessly. That was all. The suffering man on the street who had choked on his own blood—she could not think of that now. And what had followed that tragedy had been a series of mad accidents; she could even begin to excuse Meria's betrayal. Her stepmother had been foolish and desperate, and could she judge so harshly after the unbelievable thing she had done in Shkodra? Whatever absurd vow Eleanora had made, she and her stepmother had been two women lost and alone until Cheremi arrived. Sometimes while doing housework or hunting, she spoke to Cheremi in her mind, confessing to him all she had endured before he had come into their lives, her buried-deep terror that the family of the man who killed Baba was hunting her, too, especially after what she had done. But even with her most articulate inner voice, her words were like vague etchings unsuccessfully illustrating unbelievable events, happenings incredible to her even now as she lived their aftermath. How did one successfully describe a dream, even when memories of it intruded on one's daily reality? What was it that Marsilio Ficino had written? "The soul exists partly in eternity and partly in time." But had not Ficino also commanded, "Live in the present. Live now. Be happy." She meant to do that and to be as good a person as she could, better than she had been before. She would force herself to forgive her stepmother. Maybe she could even begin to forgive herself for what she had done. When she reread Petrarch's sonnets in the spare hours she had now that Cheremi provided some food for them, she felt a new depth of understanding for his platonic love for Laura.

Meria began to sweep the house daily again, polishing old copper, one afternoon hanging rugs and blankets and clothing to freshen in the late-winter sunshine. The rainbow of skirts and pants shimmered in the sun and wind. How pretty her old blouses and embroidered skirts and pantalets looked! But those were no longer for her. Her thoughts of her wasted womanhood faded with the afternoon light, until later in the evening she felt

a twinge when Cheremi looked up at the swishing of Meria's
dress as she glided by him, settling near the fire to mend his
socks.

The next morning Eleanora woke before the others, slipped
outside, shivering as she grabbed her stiff cold skirts and darted
back inside, the door closing without a squeak, thanks to her
carefulness and Cheremi's oiling of the hinges the other day.
She wrapped her ruby silk skirt over Baba's pants. Even over
the bulk of the trousers the skirt fit looser around her hips and
waist. How skinny she must be! But it brought back a more
restrained, graceful way of walking, her hips swaying while her
upper body was still, not like when her whole body bent and
leaped and crept in the forest. She dug through her old chest
and found a fresh blouse and wrapped her hair in a matching
wrinkled red scarf she had gotten from outside. That should
please Meria, as lately Eleanora had not even bothered wearing
her father's old cap. She had just let her freshly washed hair lie
about her shoulders. She wished she had the looking glass to see
herself in, but she had insisted on giving it to a neighbor who
had given them eggs. What did that matter, when later her own
desire was reflected in Cheremi's blue eyes, which lit up as she
brought him coffee that morning, and followed her as he said
goodbye when he left for the village to look for work.

Eleanora stood watching as the door shut behind Cheremi,
then sat near Meria at her stepmother's usual place near the
hearth.

"Are all your pants so dirty?" Meria asked in a lowered tone,
her eyes on her weaving. "If there is a stain you only need let me
know. I managed to get out the one that was on your old shirt."

"That was an accident. The result of an accident. Why must

you pester me about that, again and again? It was ages ago," Eleanora said, stiffening.

"Pester you? I asked you once or twice. It looked like blood, that is all, and I only wondered how that happened while you were marketing, in the city."

"Wonder until eternity. When I was your daughter, perhaps I might have told you, but, thanks to your matchmaking, now I am the man of the house. And you, you are merely . . ." Eleanora trailed off. What if Cheremi could see her bickering with Meria? She would not be petty. She made her voice bright. "Though I need not tell you, I am now spotless. My pants are not dirty in the least," Eleanora said, turning to look at Meria's frowning face. She lifted the hem, covering her face with the red silk. "I wear the pants still. They are only clothes, Meria. Costumes we wear, for whatever reason." She lowered her skirt, her smiling face dipped below her stepmother's, trying to break her concentration. "Besides, I know no law that a sworn virgin must dress like a man. Unless Lekë has spoken to you specially?"

Meria laughed bitterly. "Lekë has already spoken, and you know what he has said about vows like yours. We all know the law." Her eyes remained on her spindle. "Why switch back to wearing your skirts now?"

"Why not?" Eleanora said. "Spring is around the corner, and I feel hopeful that when the snow melts a suitor will come and take you off my hands. Then I can go back to being a careless girl."

"You know you can never go back," Meria said, picking at a tangled thread. "I am not as stupid as you believe."

"I might say the same to you," Eleanora retorted, rising and walking away to pet the goat. "Remember who is the master of this house," she said, wagging her finger in the beast's face.

Meria did not look up, her spindle continuing to whir.

The sun had set by the time Cheremi returned home, his eyes downcast while he sat in a corner smoking. Meria asked him how his day's work had been, and he replied, in a shorter manner than usual, that it had been work.

Earlier in the day, Eleanora had begun drawing his face from memory, partly as exercise and escape, but also in avoidance of her stepmother and helping her with any chores. If Meria wanted to make a point about her stepdaughter's position, she had made it, and Eleanora would be a lazy lord, as was her right.

Eleanora observed Cheremi under her lashes as she sketched with the stub of charcoal. When she glanced up he met her eyes. He scooted closer.

She curled the paper away from him so he could not see her drawing, but he leaned near.

"Who is that handsome youth you are dreaming up? Should I be jealous?" He squinted. "Or is that what I look like to you?"

Eleanora giggled.

"Are you to tell me this you I know is not you at all? Well, this is you, to me, as close as I can make it out," she said, studying her drawing. "I try and I try, but I cannot quite get your eyes."

His face was near hers as he examined her drawing. He looked up at her. "You already have them."

Eleanora jerked her chin down, staring at the paper trembling in her hands, her face burning. She could not believe she was so flustered. She had the cliché hammering heart of a foolish girl in a romance novel, when she was this man's equal, this man's savior. Thankfully it was dim where she sat; the fire created as much shadow as light, which was what had inspired her drawing. She liked how it obscured parts of Cheremi's face, smoothing his chiseled beauty. It was like the charcoal in her hand, not letting him be seen as he was, but as an exaggerated version that highlighted the real man.

Cheremi now left every dawn, sometimes returning in a few hours, sometimes returning after she lay down for the night, imagining she had only dreamed him. She still hunted and foraged in the forest, but with the cornmeal and eggs and cheese he irregularly brought back, there was not as much pressure to provide. Oftentimes she caught herself walking in the woods, rubbing her thumb into the polished wood of her rifle, snapping bare branches, talking to Cheremi in her mind.

If it were not for Baba, she would say, *I would not be an artist. He was an artist himself, in his own way, his work had so much imagination and he helped so many people and it is terrible he is gone. If it were not for him, I would not have been able to save you. I blame myself for being here while he is not. I do not let my stepmother talk about my father, I cannot bear it. I hate how he is gone, and I refuse to believe it most times, though I feel grateful he is not here to know what I did to that man. No, I cannot tell you what happened, you would not believe it. I barely do. But I can think of him neither, nor how his family might come for me. When such thoughts arise I drown them. Sometimes I am afraid that will become a reflex, and I am fearful I may become numb to everything without noticing. You see, I have had to shield myself from feeling anything.*

Until now. And it frightened her, when she finally admitted to herself how much she cared for Cheremi. But Baba had often gone out of his way to check in on patients whose lives he had saved, and perhaps this was how he had felt. Surely her feelings were just that, compounded by the intense loneliness Cheremi had relieved. And it did not help that he was like Titian's Adonis come to life. She wondered if Cheremi had ever seen a book with Titian's paintings.

She wondered where Cheremi had come from but resisted asking, even as she mocked her superstitious belief that doing so might suddenly spur his return home. At some point she must leave, to cross the sea. Italy and her dream of becoming an artist still haunted her, and when she roamed the woods looking for fire kindling and hoping for flowers, she sometimes imagined herself in Italy, painting, and her teacher asking her whose face kept appearing in her work. *Oh,* she would murmur, *I never noticed how often I return to his face, but it is a man I knew once.* It would be difficult to leave Cheremi, and in her conversations in her mind with him she admitted this to him, and when she imagined his wet eyes as his palm held her cheek, her stomach tingled.

But he would never. He must have noticed her unusual authority at home, due to the stupid promise she had made. And surely he had a betrothed, a wife, perhaps even children to return to.

Oh, how she hoped he had no one, sadly sympathizing with him left alone in the world, but smiling secretly to herself: that would make them even more alike, then.

He never spoke of his family, Meria had noted, brows cocked meaningfully. Eleanora ignored her idle talk. Meria was a silly woman, and Eleanora often imagined telling Cheremi how she no longer blamed her stepmother for trying to sell her, as Meria could not help her foolish desperation.

And sometimes Cheremi would argue with her, that what her stepmother had done was unforgivable, and, how he wished she had not been forced to take a vow, because now he could never ask for her—and Eleanora would cut him off with shy embarrassment, and say, her voice full of sympathy, that her stepmother had only been trying to survive, and, in her own ignorant way, protect Eleanora.

What could a woman like Meria know of Cheremi?

Nothing.

What did Eleanora know?

She knew as often as he was in a teasing mood that took nothing seriously, he was melancholy, smoking silently after he returned from his visits to the village. She knew how quickly he appreciated a picture of hers, admiring the placement of a shadow no one had ever noticed before. She knew how he had traveled far away for his work, seemingly searching for something, but perhaps just enjoying exploring. Eleanora planned to travel so far, so frequently, people would wonder the same about her.

Soon, soon.

Wind whooshed down the chimney, making the fire roar and ash fly through the beams of sunlight. With the days warming and Cheremi's help around the house, there was always enough kindling now, and the fire burned bright even in the afternoon. She put down the short pastel she had been pinching, stretching her arms above her head, comforted by the whir of Meria's spindle and the smell of buttery corn bread mingling with the clove-laden smoke of Cheremi's cigarette. What a relief it was to take warmth for granted, and to have an hour or so to enjoy a book or to draw again. If that was all she had to be grateful to Cheremi for, it was more than enough. Who had saved whom?

"How is it I deserve this?" Cheremi asked. He tossed his unfinished cigarette in the fire. "The answer is, I do not. I remembered some work I must finish in the village. Eleanora, may I borrow your rifle?"

"Of course. But what does one need a gun for to thatch a roof?"

He lips twisted into a smile that did not reach his eyes. "That job is finished. But I told the man I would help him hunt a jackal he says threatens his chickens." He shrugged. He rose easily, hardly using his hands now.

"We will wait to have dinner until you return," Eleanora said, rising.

"I may be late, so please go ahead without me. But I will return tonight," he said.

"Go on smooth trails," Meria said.

He laced on his leather sandals, grabbed Eleanora's rifle, and gently shut the front door.

Night fell fast after he left, the wind howling and shaking the windows, and still he did not return. Meria stayed up after she and Eleanora shared a small portion of the dinner prepared. Meria finally took the coffee off the fire after the water had boiled away. She did not offer to make any for her stepdaughter, and Eleanora did not mind; what remained was Cheremi's. Cheremi! Unprotected from the supposed spirits roaming and whistling through the trees, their cries sharp enough to distract from the constant rushing of the waterfalls. She did not know what was worse: that he might be lost in the woods, or that he might be comfortable and unconcerned near another home's hearth.

By the third night he was gone, Meria and Eleanora had nothing but sour cheese for dinner, which they shared while huddled near the low fire. That would be all they would have for a while, Eleanora thought, looking at the empty peg where her rifle usually hung.

"I will go into the village and ask about Cheremi," she said, getting up. "Perhaps at least I can find my gun."

Meria looked at her. "Why do I not go instead?"

"You? But I am the supposed man of the house."

"Yes, I know, but you were my stepdaughter not too long ago and believe me when I say it matters how things look."

"Right now it looks as if neither he nor my gun will return. So let me go."

She walked into the village, asking a few men who were reluctant to talk to her if they knew where Cheremi had gone.

"Cheremi? The city man, sure." They raised their brows at each other, looking over her jumbled costume of her father's cap and her old skirts. They had last seen Cheremi a few days ago, carrying a Mauser that looked like her father's. A beautiful gun. Lots of sterling silver. Expensive. "Where had your father gotten that rifle?"

"Who cares where he may have gotten it. Do you know where Cheremi was going?"

"No, no, I could not say," one man said, scratching his scalp. "If he up and left, he is not your responsibility, no one would blame you if something happens to him. Why do you care so much?" He winked at the other man.

"Why do you?" Eleanora retorted.

Cheremi had disappeared forever. Hiking home, she almost hoped she would discover his body at the bottom of a small ravine edged with dripping ice. Anything rather than endlessly wondering what had happened to him. Somehow it would be worse to lose him to other people, lose his stories to them, when they would not appreciate them, when they would probably interpret them as idle chat from a man looking for random work. And then perhaps he would become only that, living some-where else, and her time with him would mean nothing.

Perhaps he had never really been here. It was easy to imagine in the days that followed as Meria slipped back into silence, as Eleanora returned to her lonely walks in the thawing, crackling woods, her mood swings between panic and lethargy driven by hunger, as she scanned the melting ground for anything re-motely edible, scoured her mind for what was left in the house to trade for a handful of cornmeal or rice or beans. She would take Meria's bracelets from her, and give her stepmother another reason to hate her. It was time to kill the little goat. It would look at her with its little black eyes and bleat and not know, and she would not even be able to use the gun to make it painless. Eleanora began to cry, roughly wiping her running nose and stopping almost as quickly. No one cared or could comfort her.

She cracked off half of a budding branch. She was just be-yond the sight of the trail that could lead her out of the village forever. What if she finally did so? She did not have the coins, but she could go back for them. Be quiet. It would be easier not to say anything to Meria. Her stepmother would not want to go with her. She would only try to dissuade her, to break her resolve, to remind her of everything that might go wrong. Meria was half dead already, and the rest of her simmered with resentment. Would it be so cruel to stop keeping alive something that was not? Maybe it was the honorable thing to do: to relieve something of its suffering.

The pain. Just end it now. Please . . .

She did not deserve someone like Cheremi. Perhaps he was gone because he had somehow found out she had let her father die, and that other terrible thing she had done.

She stopped on the trail, her head tipped up as she blinked back the wetness welling up behind her lids. She would not cry. Her nose tingled with the effort, then it passed, and she could open her eyes again. A tear trickled down her cheek, and she rubbed it away. None of this mattered. Nothing mattered. Except leaving. She marched on, her eyes glued to her feet: one step in front of the other. That was all it would take for her to leave, to fly away to Italy, reclaim her dreams, start a new life. So she walked, seeing each grain of dirty snow.

Suddenly two hands clamped the back of her arms.

She screamed. They had found her! They knew, they knew.

Before she could kick, the hands spun her and she faced a baffled Cheremi.

"How could I know coming up behind you would frighten you so? A stupid joke, but you see now it is only me, you . . . Hush, hush . . ."

She clutched and clung to him, burying her face in his wool coat, which became warm and wet beneath her cheek.

Chapter 19

Cheremi held her tightly, his hand cradling her head against his hard chest, and she could smell the earth and water and cloves of his cigarettes through the cold rough wool that covered him. The scent of security, of Baba.

She inhaled more deeply, her heaving, hiccuping breath slowing. She opened her mouth to ask him where he had gone, but something like a wail escaped and he shushed her like a baby, smoothing her hair, his lips pressed to the top of her head. He tilted her chin up, but Eleanora kept her eyes lowered, watching her tapping foot grind the dirt into the melting snow, suddenly embarrassed for him to see her so weak, with a sniffling nose like a child's.

His rough thumbs wiped away her tears.

"Were you crying for me?" he asked, his face serious but his voice teasing.

He did not allow her to answer, he simply spun her and held

her shoulders, so they were walking back to the house—their home—as if he had been gone for the day and she merely met him at the fence after work, as if this were a routine they took for granted.

Eleanora stopped before the closed gate and slowly turned to face him, still staring at the half-thawed ground.

She cleared her throat. "You left me." Why was it so hard to demand the explanation she deserved? "I thought you were gone, maybe forever. You . . ."

He said nothing, and she laughed nervously.

"Where were you?" she asked. "Where did you go?"

He smiled at her. She could feel it even though she could not bear to look up, and she watched his hands inch toward hers in the air below their waists.

"I went away, searching for something I could not find," he said, his curling fingertips brushing the inside of her palms. "And then I came back. I always meant to come back to you."

"But why?" she asked.

"Why did I mean to come back to you? Or why did I come back?" His voice still held a smile, knowing that was not what she asked. "Well, for one, I had to return your gun to you. Whatever could be said of my past, of myself, I would never act that dishonorably. But what does any of it matter, when I found you waiting for me?"

Eleanora's heart pounded between her ears; she hoped he could not hear it. She watched as his hands stroked hers again.

"Better than waiting for me," he said, "I saw you coming to look for me, to meet me."

Eleanora was about to protest that she was actually leaving—

and he might leave with her, too—but he said it so persuasively it became her truth as his arm encircled her, pushing open the gate behind her. If he had not held her, she would have fallen backward, and she was startled back into reality. She followed him to the house.

"Cheremi!" Meria gasped. Her shining eyes narrowed when she saw Eleanora close behind him. "Glory to your feet! Glory to the trails that brought you!"

Cheremi grinned. "Glory to your cooking."

"Glory to your stepdaughter," Eleanora muttered, feeling jealous, "who you told not to look for him."

Meria ignored her, already rummaging in the chest for a pot. Like a magician, Cheremi had produced a sack of beans and rice.

"Eleanora never spoke of it," Meria said, stirring the fire so it began to blaze. "But I know she was so worried about you. You are like a father to her."

She hates me, Eleanora felt in a flash. *If she only knew how he held my hands* . . . Then Eleanora remembered he had only petted her palms, he had stroked her fingers, he had held the air between their hands. He had shown her the affection of a cousin, a brother, a father. She watched as Cheremi grinned at Meria, teasing her about how she rinsed each grain of rice. It was meaningless. She kicked at an upturned corner of the rug, realizing she still wore her shoes. Meria was merely annoyed at the cold mud that she had tracked in. She walked back to the front door and slipped off her sandals, glancing at Meria as she passed her.

"It is so good to have a man in the house again," Meria whispered.

Eleanora laughed. Was she a man or a woman to the world? Had she not sacrificed enough, bargained her pleasure for power?

"What about tradition? All I have done for you?" Eleanora asked. "Do I not count?"

Meria said nothing, stirring the simmering pot.

The next night, Eleanora sat a cushion away from Cheremi, while Meria baked corn bread and fried eggs Cheremi had brought home with him. The smoke of his cigarette mingled with the smoke that escaped the hearth's fire, and the two curled together in the air and melted into the blackness of the ceiling.

Eleanora sat, silent, cradling an open book of Petrarch's poems. She had to turn the pages back every minute or so to review the meaning of a sentence that slipped out of her grasp. She would meet Cheremi's eyes occasionally over her book, and in the soft light of the fire the furrows between his brows and the starburst of wrinkles when he smiled were blurred, and he looked as young as a man could without being a boy.

Cheremi shut his eyes as he sucked on his cigarette, its embers burning brighter.

"I adore the smell of cloves," Eleanora said, sighing. "Do those taste as good as I imagine?"

The smoke escaped his upturned lips. "I cannot say. By now I know your imagination is quite strong. Do women smoke in the mountains?"

"Of course. It is one of the many things that women do, but we all pretend they do not and that a good one would never want to," Eleanora said. "That said, I have never tried it."

"But she may try it. She is a sworn virgin, did you not know?" Meria's toneless voice was as soft as usual, but Eleanora felt her question echo across the room, her words punctuated by a crackling of the fire.

Cheremi took it like an easy joke, like he took everything, smiling and amused. Eleanora was glad he could not see how her ears burned. She shut the book with a snap, then senselessly opened it again to have something to look at.

"Meria mentioned you had taken a vow before," he said, eyes twinkling in the dark. "But naturally I did not want to believe such a thing."

"Yes, it is true I am a sworn virgin. How did you never guess, given the privileges afforded to me in my home? I am a veritable lord, I am worse than Caligula," Eleanora said sarcastically. She had gone too far. She did not want Cheremi to see her this way. She lightened her voice. "I am a sworn virgin. So let me try your cigarette."

He passed her the cone-shaped cigarette and leaned farther back in the cushion he had propped up against the wall. Eleanora pinched the cigarette between her fingers and sucked. Her throat was on fire. She tried to smother her cough, but the effort made her shake and she ended up hawking harder. She covered her mouth and shook her head, passing the cigarette back to him.

Cheremi chuckled, then leaned closer and held the cigarette to her lips.

"Now again," he said. "Only this time very, very slowly."

Eleanora took a steady breath and felt the cloves disappear into her chest like air, then float back up and rest on the tip of her tongue, before the smoke slipped from her mouth like fragranced breath. She licked her lips. She had tasted, shared the air from his mouth.

Cheremi smiled and put the cigarette back to his lips.

"You remind me of someone I knew long ago," Cheremi had said, his words reverberating in Eleanora's mind as she stared at her father's leather journal.

She sat on the wooden chest under the front window, rereading the last line of Baba's last letter, its ink smeared by long-dried drops. Tears? The blurred words were still legible.

> *I wish you could see this child of ours. She has my eyes, and I can only hope she will have half the bravery you showed your last days. Smiling through your pain. Asking about the baby. Always reassuring me you felt fine, and how happy you were with your little family. You swore you regretted nothing. You are stronger than any man I have ever known.*

The first time she read this passage she had wept with relief: she had killed her mother, but no one blamed her for it. What had happened to Baba, what she had done in Shkodra to that man—who deserved it, by anyone's measure, she tried to tell herself—may be different. But this at least was plain and clean. Her mother had loved her for the short time she had known her, and regretted nothing. She could have recited the entry to herself by now, but rereading it was more soothing than a lullaby, than the peaceful silence blanketing the house.

Eleanora and Cheremi were alone that afternoon while Meria was out gathering firewood, or was it water—who cared? They were alone. Cheremi sat across the room from her, leaning against the wall facing the front door, a fuzzy beam of sunlight ending at his outstretched feet.

She heard his voice in her head again, though his pink-red

lips were still as he flipped through a heavy book full of illustrations of ancient symbols and their explanations, its blue
cloth cover embossed with a gilded serpent biting its own
tail. She twirled the snake bracelet on her wrist. Her mother's
bracelet.

She reminded him of someone he knew long ago. He had
said so in a whisper torn from his throat. She glanced at him
across the room.

She wished she could put the journal in his lap, so he could
read one of the most moving love stories she had ever read.
Purer than Paolo and Francesca. But she knew he could not
read, like most other men, and a shyness held her back from
openly speaking of Baba and his love for her mother. She could
hardly bear to speak of her father to Meria, after all that had
happened, and often stories of her father lay in her closed mouth.
He was so much a part of who she was, and Cheremi would
have admired her father, she was sure. She tipped her head back
and blinked away tears threatening to spill out. She did not
want to disturb the day's tranquility, so perhaps it was better
to simply not speak of Baba. In her mind she saw the clumps
of dirt thudding onto Baba's rough pine coffin, the gravedigger
pausing to scratch his thigh, yawning. She dabbed the wet inner
corners of her eyes. Cheremi must not see her like this. She took
a deep breath. Besides, her tears would ruin her father's letters.
She slammed closed the leather journal and blurted, "Who do
I remind you of?"

Cheremi looked up, startled, his blue eyes naked for a
second—angry, ashamed?—and then his lids half closed as his
slow-growing grin returned.

"You remind me of a girl I knew long ago," he said. "So long ago, in the ancient days when gods roamed the earth . . . and when I was about your age."

She tried to laugh, and it came out a little choked. "Was that really so long ago?" she asked. "Where is this girl now?" She hoped she was ancient and gnarled. Buried and gone, even.

"No one knows where she is," he said. "She disappeared into the air."

He closed the book in his lap and squinted at her.

"But maybe you do not remind me of her. Perhaps I like your face so much I replaced hers with yours in my memories. I do remember she was very beautiful."

Eleanora tugged at the scarlet sash she wore over her father's pants, mesmerized by the unraveling ends of it, hoping he could not see how her face burned.

"Very beautiful, but also very wild. She never would have blushed like that," he continued. "But perhaps she should have."

Cheremi pushed himself up and walked out the front door, taking the rifle with him. Before he closed the door behind him, he turned and winked at her.

Eleanora tossed the leather journal across the floor and stood up, then sat down again. He was a man, and perhaps she was his equal—but she was equally his windup toy.

He still teasingly smiled at her, the same way he did at Meria, but since stroking her palms the day they had found each other on the trail, his occasional squeeze of her shoulder, his pats on her hand had disappeared.

What did it matter? She felt the air between them as if it were water they swam in together; she might move her arm to touch her chest and the movement might ripple all the way to him. She touched him without touching him, and she felt him do the same to her.

Had her father written something similar to her mother in his journal? She stretched her fingertips, stroking the worn leather cover of his journal. No matter how many times she read his letters, it was extraordinary to think of Baba as young and in love. She knew he had loved her, his work, good books and fine food, and many little things that made up life, yet he had watched the world with an amused indifference. How had such passion run beneath such coolness? Perhaps it was due to the death of her mother. Had Baba not told her sometimes people could no longer feel anything where a thick scar grew? How did she think the death of her father would affect her?

She shook her head and stood.

Eleanora counted her breaths before she followed Cheremi out the door, as she had each afternoon since he had returned. Fifty breaths if they were alone, one hundred and fifty if Meria was also in the room.

Each inhale passed with a thousand thoughts between them. Would she find Cheremi silently smoking near the trail? Would she have to wander around the woods and pretend to be pursuing something besides him? A few days ago she had met Cheremi in the forest beneath their home. Before she had said hello, she dropped her handful of kindling and grabbed the rifle from his hands to shoot and kill a boar he had not seen. He had praised her shooting. He had eaten little of dinner that night.

Eleanora put her lips to the window and blew her breath against it, tracing concentric circles in the steam.

No, she told herself, *an extra-long exhale could not count as two.*

It took an eternity until she reached her fiftieth breath. She kicked the leather journal out of the way before she walked out the door.

Cheremi leaned against the fence, smoking, staring out across the valley made invisible by a flood of shadows, from mountain peaks like islands emerging through waves of clouds. Eleanora imagined their wet patch of land was a boat with only room for the two of them, floating through the sky. She stood next to Cheremi and crossed her arms against the frozen air, and he put the cigarette to her lips. She avoided meeting his eyes, though she was sure they rested on her pursed lips. She took a slow suck, enjoying the scented smoke wafting out of her mouth. Eleanora lifted the cigarette from his hand, half afraid and hoping her fingers might brush his.

"If you could go anywhere," Eleanora said, "where would you wish to go that you have not been?"

She took another slow drag and passed the cigarette. The clouds drifted slowly beneath them, and she closed her eyes. Let him say Italy, and they could float across to the country now.

"Oh, I do not know where I will go next," Cheremi said, tucking the cigarette in a corner of his mouth. She wondered if he tasted her lips on it.

"I have been nearly everywhere," he said.

"You have even been here, now," she said with a forced laugh. "You have seen so much." She sounded wistful, toeing the thawing ground. "More than I have."

"One day I will show it all to you," he replied, tossing the unfinished cigarette and grinding it out with his heel. "It is the least I can do after you saved my life."

She wanted to say he had done the same for her, but her

mouth was dry, and instead she stood still. When she felt the weight of his gaze shift to the empty footpath in front of them, she let herself look at him.

She almost wished she had not.

The clouds rolled away from the lowering sun, and a harsh light washed over his face, his eyes lost in the shadow of the cliff of his brow, his pores deep and dotted even around the crow's-feet at the corners of his eyes. White hair sparkled through his fair mustache, deep parentheses framed his smile, and light red threads trailed the whites of his eyes. But they led to clear blue-gray irises, and the strong profile of his nose echoed the majestic lines of the mountains beyond his face. And while he shared some of the signs of age she had sometimes recognized in Baba, she also saw the same proud masculinity she had admired in her father's face, youthfulness in the burnt red in his lips. She looked down at the melting ground.

LATER THAT NIGHT, she thought how she might go to Cheremi while the three of them lay on the main floor. He no longer slept in her father's study since returning from those three missing days. She might move closer to him in the dark, to feel the heat radiating from him—no, not even from him, but from the cushions his body had warmed. She might move closer to him to feel his breath—no, just the air his breath had moved to kiss her cheeks. She might, but instead she lay still under her blanket wondering if he woke sometimes during the night, too. Nightmares still stirred her in the middle of the night, but she went back to sleep more quickly, feeling safer with Cheremi nearby. Still, she shied from even looking at him in the dark. Her gaze might wake him. She considered how easy it would be to reach out her hand to touch the corner of the blanket on top of him, and the next morning she thought maybe she had, but as she blinked at the dawning sun she was sure she dreamed it all.

She rose, standing on the balls of her feet so as not to make a sound. She stretched her arms above her head, observing the steady rhythm of Cheremi's rising and falling barrel chest, and Meria's delicate breath as she lay on her side. The coins remained hidden in her father's study. She would sneak up to the room and open the chest so slowly it would not creak, then tiptoe out the front door. Today was the day she would finally leave this house and go on to what she dreamed of before Cheremi; she would take the first steps in a journey that would lead her farther than he had even traveled, farther than her father had even yearned for her.

But by sunset that was a mere dream, too.

She had spent the day unsuccessfully hunting, and Cheremi had come back from repairing a wall in the village. He probably knew the villagers better than she did. She smiled, her chin perched on her folded hands as she faced him, while Meria hung in the background with her spindle.

Cheremi leaned forward, and Eleanora somehow sensed he was going to tell her this story again, even before the words came out of his lovely lips.

"He was a curious man, curious about ancient castles," Cheremi said. "Some said he was the king of England, and it is possible, as he was only interested in royal ruins."

Cheremi lifted his eyebrows.

"Who can account for foreigners' tastes? Always obsessed with half-forgotten histories."

"A half-forgotten history is the best sort of history," Eleanora said. She recognized his tale and hoped he further embellished it as he repeated himself. "You can make it into the tidiest explanation for why things exist as they do. Isn't it the most convenient way to justify the near future?"

"Are you reading from a book I cannot see?" Cheremi asked, his eyes twinkling. "You speak like a wise chief from some story. You are much too young to be so intelligent."

Meria coughed in the background, her hands suddenly fluttering between them, setting up the table for dinner. Eleanora and Cheremi leaned back without acknowledging her.

"My king of England," Cheremi continued, "though, was not so wise. Only young. The supposed ruins he was excited about, which to me looked like large broken stones stuck in the ground, were guarded by a tribe convinced treasure was beneath the stones, buried there by years and magic. The tribe threatened to take the Englishman's Kodak and arrest him."

Cheremi paused to suck on his cigarette. Eleanora had heard of Kodaks and how they captured images sharper than any pen and paper, but she was embarrassed to ask him how they worked. It must seem so obvious to him.

"I swore to them he was merely curious whether the sight was Illyrian—who even knows what that means? I only know the word because he repeated it often enough—and that any harm that came to the English king would have to be taken up with my tribe and all of England."

Cheremi laughed, somewhat bitterly, sucking on his cigarette.

"As if England or my tribe would care. But they left us alone then. The foreigner and I left, nonetheless, after he sneakily pointed his Kodak at the ruins. I coughed to hide the noise of its clicking. When we camped for the night, I unpacked our corn cakes. The foreigner bit into one of the cakes, baked before we left for the trip, and spit something out. It was a gold coin, with the profile of a man etched on it. The foreigner knew this face and said it was the king he looked for. He packed it away carefully. The next morning, though, he could not find the coin."

Eleanora smiled into her weak coffee. Had it been an engraved silver ring last time, discovered at the bottom of a leather satchel? Eleanora felt a jealous pang. How many days and nights had the foreigner spent alone with Cheremi? Who knew the other places the foreigner must have seen.

"It was such a curious land," Cheremi said. "It would make your Italy feel familiar."

"Have you been there?" Eleanora asked.

She had asked him before, but she hoped his answer would change from a simple "no" to a declaration he wanted to go there—with her.

Before he could answer, Meria stood between them with a bowl of water and red-and-white linens to wipe their hands with before dinner. She shuffled the low wooden table into place, setting atop it carved wooden bowls of goat's yogurt and small pieces of corn bread. Meria no longer shared meals with Cheremi and Eleanora, instead waiting near the hearth until they were finished, eating whatever was left, as women did in more conservative households. Though Eleanora was happy to eat alone with Cheremi, she found Meria's hovering distracting, feeling some sort of judgment by her hanging back, an oblique reminder that Eleanora might be left alone with an unrelated man only because she was a sworn virgin, and, according to society, as blameless and boring as any other man.

What did anything matter when Cheremi was across from her, asking her if after dinner she would read "those songs" to him? Eleanora did her best to translate her favorite Italian sonnets, sometimes improvising her own rhymes as she read aloud.

Let society make her into some sort of a sexless man. Had Petrarch needed any more from Laura than to see the wind in her golden hair, and wish to be that air? Now that Cheremi had lightened Eleanora's daily load, she had a hidden stash of drawings of him, each image inspired by a heightened emotionalism she had never known she could achieve.

Meria had laid out all three beds and was asleep when Cheremi and Eleanora crawled under their blankets. Eleanora pulled hers up to her chin, wondering if he noticed she had nudged her mat a speck closer to his. She did not deserve a happiness like this, considering what she had done, but maybe it was because of what she had been through she could appreciate this, she . . .

She was running out of the forest, chased by a nameless someone she could not see even when she looked back. But she felt the person was right to chase her, all the way into the river, the river running slowly backward upstream. Cheremi was at her side now and looked at her and smiled, wiping away blood on the corner of his mouth, and she knit her fingers together with his. He led her toward the river to cross. She did not want to cross it, yet she could not let go of his hand. She must keep him near and safe. A tree fell in front of them, and another, until the whole forest was falling, and she did not know how they would escape it . . .

Eleanora stirred, blinking awake into a gray daybreak, realizing Meria was dropping firewood into the hearth, each piece crashing into the other with a crackling thud.

She turned away from the noise, from the window's growing glow, and saw her hand cradled in Cheremi's. Eleanora left her hand there but rolled onto her back, her loose hand covering a dawning smile, when she saw Meria staring at her as she let more kindling fall from her arms into the growing flames. Eleanora's heart leaped into her mouth, but she kept herself still so she would not disturb her hand in Cheremi's and possibly wake him.

She knew she had fallen back asleep only when she woke up again to the sun hot on her face, alone on the floor mats.

Cheremi was already up, hunting or looking for another odd job. Meria wished her a good morning as she passed her a cup of coffee, and by the afternoon her memory of holding Cheremi's hand was like one of the cottony clouds she watched stream by the window: as bright as it was quickly gone.

Eleanora spent her day wandering through the thawing forest, listening for Cheremi's steps between the dripping of melting snow and the crackling of branches that were beginning to bud. Maybe he was in the village, helping to thatch the roof that had collapsed earlier in the winter. But had he not said that work was done? Eleanora hummed to herself as she gathered roots she thought Meria might use to thicken a stew. She would not rush to the fence. She made herself wait until the sun began to set.

With her leather satchel hanging from her shoulder, she wiped her hands and cleaned the dirt from her fingernails on the underside of her red sash as she strolled toward her home's fence. Cheremi was not there. Should she have hurried? Had she missed him? Was he already inside with Meria? Eleanora put her hand to the gate, turning to see the sky becoming a burnished gold.

Cheremi walked toward her, a shadow. Without greeting each other, they leaned against the cold fence, staring across the canyon gaping beyond the trail, the silhouettes of mountains staggered upon each other. She let her hand nearer Cheremi dangle outside the fuzzy warmth of the brown fur coat her other hand nestled into. Her bent fingers hung, hopeful. He squeezed her hand, and she felt a tingling rise from the bottom of her belly, her throat, warming her entire body, highlighting a hollow hunger.

The sun sank level to their feet. Eleanora let her hand hang where Cheremi had left it, while she tilted her head back and watched the night bleed into the sky, chasing the shrinking sun. She had been lonely. Baba had left her, and who had been her friend besides him? She had thought her stepmother was, but Meria had shown her true colors. She had Cheremi now, but he had a life beyond the village to return to. She shoved her other hand into her vest, clenching and unclenching her fingers as her tingling hand lost its burning numbness.

She had always been rather lonely, except when she was with Baba or her books or her drawings, and realized her dreams of escaping to Italy were dreams of escaping this loneliness for a world populated with people who appreciated her, whom she might make laugh and laugh with her. People who would recognize her talents as an artist and whose own predilections would inspire her evolution. Oh, but it was so much more than that: she would belong to them.

In her mind she heard herself sharing this with Cheremi as

they leaned against the cold fence, her tilted head taking in the emerging stars. She would never be able to capture nature's seamless transition into night, even with the right paints. The sun burned in the sky even as white stars began to twinkle, like moth holes in blue velvet.

"Do you believe spinning around those stars might be other worlds?" Eleanora asked. "Perhaps with other versions of us, making variations on our same decisions? Or are they doing the same things, having this same conversation now?"

He was silent.

"Maybe I will shout my question," she rambled on, "and see what my echo answers."

"What does it matter, when you and I are here?" Cheremi said.

The burning end of his cigarette pointed out beyond the trail, taking the place of the vanished sun in the inky blue-black sky.

Cheremi tucked the cigarette into a corner of her mouth, smiling without looking at her. He felt like the beginning of belonging, of her dreamworld. Just his coming from beyond the mountains reminded her of life outside this small, circumscribed place.

As Eleanora passed the cigarette back to Cheremi, she looked away from the twinkling sky to his face. His perfect profile seemed a natural layer on top of the shadowed landscape behind him.

He turned toward her. She forced herself to meet his eyes, and she felt her lips mirror his slow smile. He would not break the gaze, and finally she looked down at her sash, twisted between her fingers.

Why did he stay when his leg was healed? What about his adventures as a guide, or whatever had pulled him away from her for those three nights? She dared not ask him in case he began to wonder himself.

"Do you know how beautiful you are?" Cheremi asked.

He reached over and stroked her cheek. Eleanora froze and held her breath. Nothing could ever happen between them; it was as Meria said. Surely Cheremi realized that himself, which was why he allowed himself to make love to her like this. Or maybe he was teasing her again.

"Yes, you look like that girl I knew when I was becoming a man. Or perhaps"—he smiled—"perhaps it is she who looked like you."

Eleanora looked at him sharply. Who kept sliding between them? A ghost? Or a living woman who had left him? But who could leave him when he was more beautiful than anything she had seen in a picture?

For all she knew, this girl was a sister who had been married off. Eleanora sighed.

"Oh, and you sigh like she did, too!" Cheremi laughed. "Will you run away from me, as well?"

Had he seen through her intentions to leave him and the village? What else might he know? She thought of the man she had left lying on the floor in Shkodra. No, no one knew about that. Cheremi could never know about that. Her hand inched toward his across the fence, and he grabbed it.

"No," Cheremi said, his eyes narrowing, "I would not let you leave without me this time."

Eleanora held her breath.

"Will you go with me, then?" she asked.

Cheremi's eyes cleared. He swung her hand lightly as if she were a friendly child.

"Of course. Only where are we going?" he asked.

It would not matter what she said in this game of teasing, and so she told him the truth. "To Italy, that is where I want to go most."

"As far as that?" he asked. "And what is there?"

A life for living, her heart said, while her lips let slip, "Only you and me."

"And perhaps hundreds of hundreds of Italians?" And he laughed and dropped the unfinished cigarette onto the ground and stomped it out.

Eleanora stared at the sky, a twinkling blackness that must stretch across the sea over to Venice.

What would it matter who else was there, so long as it was not she, the one I remind you of?

 *Chapter 20*

*E*leanora nudged open the door to her father's study, admiring the seamless way Cheremi had mended it back together. As if nothing had happened. It was silent as she pushed the door open wider. She told herself she was searching for a book, an Italian translation of the play *Ghosts* by Henrik Ibsen, though she really hoped to find Cheremi, whom she had not seen all day. He had not met her at the fence, though she had waited until stars began seeping into the sky.

Might he have left again? How could he without telling her? No, no. He was near. She sensed it.

By the time she had come home, leaving the carcass of a hare outside, the table was set for dinner, but she did not greet Meria's silent shadow near the hearth, instead stomping straight up the stairs.

When Eleanora gently shut the study door behind her, she was not surprised to hear a movement in the dark room.

"Is that you, Cheremi? I was looking for something," she said. "Only a book, by Henrik Ibsen."

She had practiced pronouncing the author's name in her mind should she find Cheremi, feeling a shy pride as she finally said it smoothly aloud. Cheremi often admired her ability to read, laughingly admitting he could not even recognize the languages books were in.

He rose from the corner, his back to her as he faced the night-black window.

"Of course," he said, his voice flat. His hand wiped his cheeks and flopped down to his side. "Please"—he steadied his cracking voice—"Please, go ahead."

"Are you all right?" she asked. She rushed toward him, stopping before his back, unsure of what to do.

"Yes," he said sharply. "I am fine."

Clearly he was not. He had never spoken so shortly to her and she could not bear it. She took a tiny step forward. Her hand lifted; she saw it floating across the infinite space between them. Dare she? She watched her fingers suddenly graze his slumped shoulder.

He spun at her light touch, and she saw his eyes were small and bloodshot—he had been crying! Had she ever seen a man cry? Never, except once her father had cried, and he explained he was reading a love story; Meria looked annoyed and yet almost ready to cry herself. But her father had smiled through his tears, while Cheremi's face was fallen and forlorn. Her father—

Oh, Baba, Baba.

Eleanora stood there, her fingernails reflexively digging into her palms, close to crying herself. She had been able to bear the pain of others in her medical work only in order to lift some of the suffering. To stand here dumb, unable to help Cheremi, was worse than the agony she had endured after her father had died. Died, died, died. She could not always pretend Baba was somehow merely gone. He was dead. And perhaps it was best, considering what she had done, who she had become, that her father was dead. Dead. Dead, dying alone in the dirty street, choking on his own blood. He had told her once, long ago, as they struggled to save another man on his deathbed, that that would be the worst way to go. Her father would have had enough time to know he was dying, alone, abandoned by her.

Eleanora sobbed, stumbling into Cheremi with outstretched arms, clutching him to her as he wept into her shoulder. She stroked his head, cooing at him between her tears, and as he began to lean into her, she panicked she might collapse onto the floor under his heavy weight. But suddenly he was holding her instead. His sobs ran dry, and his ragged breathing smoothed. All she felt was his hot, moist breath on her neck and his thick arms tight around her—and the pinch of guilt: she was glad for whatever caused his pain, because it had brought him into her arms.

Her body loosened against the length of his, while his arms pulled her in, his hands running up and down her back, pressing her to him. While one hand held her back, his other trickled up and down her spine. His breath had grown ragged again, only this time it tickled her ear and gave her chicken skin the length of her body, commanding her to grind against him.

What could she do but respond to his touch? When the weight of his head lifted from her shoulder and his face was far enough from hers that she could see the blue of his eyes flickering across her own, she closed her eyes and tasted his forceful kiss. She echoed how he bit her lips, opening her mouth to the thrust of his tongue and feeling his tongue with her own, as he had just taught her. Without warning her pants were pooled around her ankles on the floor, his greedy hands searching between her thighs. She felt a pleasure she had never imagined, never read about in books, and then the ecstasy vanished—

What if Meria heard them? What about her vow?

But he was in control now, nothing else mattered, and she lost herself in response to him as he laid her down on the floor pillows, all the while his mouth locked to hers. When he slid into her, she was pierced with euphoria and fear, and wondered about this miracle Cheremi taught her. Was this the supposed suffering she had been warned against, another chore to endure as a wife, an activity to avoid at all costs as an unmarried woman? She gasped—she had never experienced a purer pleasure. She wrapped her legs around Cheremi's waist, and his thrusts grew more urgent until he gasped and collapsed onto her, his breath in her ear again, his damp head heavy on her shoulder. Eleanora lay there, warmth washing through her, with a small smile of disbelief.

Cheremi's weight almost smothered her, but shallow breaths were enough so long as she did not wake him. She stroked his head, watching the bright light of the moon. That he should lie there, after this had happened to her, added to her astonishment. She thought all the secrets of the human body had been exposed to her. Was this so natural? It must be, which added to the surprise of it: that a part of her should not be so surprised at all.

She thought of Meria's whispers to wives with sidelong glances to make sure she heard just enough, and she realized she was supposed to feel bored and ashamed about what had led to this man's stomach sticking to hers, his heart beating on top of hers. She should feel guilty for breaking her vow, for surely this counted as much against her as marrying someone would. But she could not; instead she beamed back at the moon shining through the window. The waterfalls sounded sharper, crashed louder, and there was a beauty in their cacophony. The falls' noise seemed to blend with the hushed giggling of men; perhaps the world was chuckling with her about this blissful rite revealed to her. She continued to pet Cheremi, listening to his deep breaths blend with the quiet roar of the waterfalls and its strange snickering.

Cheremi's eyelashes fluttered. He searched her face, kissing her smile before he rolled onto his side, his leaden arm flattening the white shirt scrunched around her chest. He pulled her on top of him, and she felt like her stomach balanced against the slope of a mountain, but she held her head above his and looked into his sleepy eyes.

"I came here searching for someone," he said, "and I found you instead." His eyes flickered over her face. "But maybe you were who I was looking for all this time. You remind me so much of another I looked for, nearly forever . . ."

He turned his face from her.

She touched his cheek; she must distract him from that pain again. That long-lost girl could no longer be a threat, with this new power she held over him.

"Who were you looking for . . . my soul?" she asked.

Her father had often called her that, and she knew what he meant now, but beyond.

"That girl, she is surely gone by now," he said. He twisted her hair around his finger, tugging so it almost hurt, but she could not bear to ask him to stop.

"The one who I searched for, the person I came here for . . ." His voice cracked and he let go of her hair. "I came here looking for the man who killed my brother."

Eleanora froze, pressing her cheek against his chest so he could not see her wide eyes, so her head could not shake in denial. She remembered those cracking footsteps she had imagined following her into the forest as she hiked home from Shkodra. She squeezed her eyes shut and saw the blood pooling on the earth floor, she heard the thudding footsteps behind her again as she ran until she thought her chest would burst.

She hoped Cheremi could not feel her heart pounding. It was just her remembering imaginings, after all.

"I see now," he said, "that I was meant to find you."

Eleanora's breath caught in her throat. Did she hear a door open and close quietly in the distance? No, it was only a coincidence. It was all only a coincidence. A sound like creeping feet creaked toward the door.

Eleanora jumped up and pulled on her pants, but Cheremi was still on the floor as the door burst open.

Chapter 21

$\mathcal{E}$di stood with his feet planted wide in the doorway, stroking his thick black mustache, dark eyes flat and unblinking as he watched Cheremi dress, announcing to the air, "I always knew she was a woman without shame."

Edi's full lips curled up and over his glinting teeth as he watched Eleanora frantically shove her shirt into her pants.

"Of course," Edi continued, "you would disgrace yourself with a man old enough to be your father. He loved you too much."

Edi leaned back against the door frame, revealing his two leering brothers crowded behind him. The white moonlight slid off the etched silver of Edi's and his brothers' pistols, and Eleanora cursed herself for leaving her rifle downstairs. Edi met Eleanora's eyes and wrinkled his nose. "I always wondered about your father and you."

Cheremi rushed at Edi, his fist cracking against Edi's jaw before his brothers tackled the man and held him to the floor.

Cheremi only stopped writhing when he realized he could not escape.

Edi rubbed his chin, smirking as he winced.

"When I kill you, I will clear my family's blood," Edi said, "and unfortunately I will also have cleared dishonor from your family. It is amazing that two worthless lives could do so much."

Edi walked over to Eleanora.

"For a dirty, dishonorable man, you are still rather beautiful."

He traced her bottom lip with his rough thumb, his fist suddenly smashing against her mouth.

"Ah," Edi said, "those lips are even more like a blossoming rose now."

Eleanora struggled to stay standing as she felt her head rock and hot blood trickle down her chin. She would stand and take more, only she could not allow anything to happen to Cheremi.

Edi grinned and crossed his arms.

"There is that strength of yours I heard about and always admired. I wanted you very much. Though I see now you would have made a terrible wife. You could use a little humility."

Eleanora heard Cheremi's curse cut short as he lost his breath when bone met bone behind her, and someone swore, muttering, "Stop struggling."

She tilted her head back and rapidly blinked away the growing tears. She must save Cheremi. Edi uncrossed his arms, watching her, his smile wavering. She let herself cry.

"I am so sorry," she whimpered, really to Cheremi, but while looking at Edi.

Seeing Edi's face soften, she forced the words out of her dry mouth.

"You are right," she choked out. "I have brought shame to your family and mine, by breaking my vow."

The words were bitter, but no more than the metallic-tasting blood in her mouth. She knelt, her trembling hands pressed together in front of her.

"Please," she begged, "let me say goodbye to my stepmother, and then . . ."

She hiccuped as if terrified at what might follow, a fear not so difficult to pretend.

Edi crossed his arms and nodded his assent.

Eleanora's knees trembled as she rose and rushed out the door, Edi's gaze heavy on her as she pressed her fists against her thighs, shrinking from brushing against him. She nearly stumbled down the stairs, her legs like jelly. She had bought a little time, but what to do with it? Her feverish gaze darted back upstairs. Edi watched her. She ducked deeper into the main room so she could not see him anymore.

Meria stooped near the hearth with mending in her hands. As she came closer, Meria continued to stare at her frozen hands, but Eleanora could see her eyes were heavy and wet. Her stepmother's lips twitched, but still she did not look up.

"Meria!" Eleanora bent to whisper into Meria's ear, but she shrank from Eleanora's touch. She lowered her voice and spoke frantically. "Edi will say nothing if you move. Hurry. Go get my gun."

Meria raised her hand as if to shield herself. "What? Your gun? I can do no such thing. It goes against all honor, all code."

Meria's shaking hand picked up her heavy brass scissors to

snip a loose thread, clenching the mending to her chest. The fire crackled.

"I did not know anything like this would happen," Meria rambled, "but I refuse to go against all order, against accepted laws. I am so sorry. I did not know he would come like this. I thought, if anything, the elders would meet, perhaps the chief would banish you."

"Banish me?" Eleanora echoed, kneeling at her lap, twisting her stepmother's thick skirts in her fists. Cold shot through her core. "Did you tell Edi I broke my vow?"

Meria set down the scissors, and her hands fluttered to her throat.

"No, I would never. I only mentioned to his mother," Meria said, her eyes squeezed shut as she spoke. "We were speaking as friends. She asked me why I looked so sad. I told her, I said, I was afraid you brought shame to us, that maybe you had dishonored your vow . . . She had already heard how you went into the village, you never go into the village, and you went to look for him. It looked bad. So bad! Perhaps I should not have said anything, but Edi had already heard about that, and I tried to warn you. You go against what everyone else believes, you break your promises. You risk my honor, my life! You risked Cheremi's life! You cannot say I did not warn you."

A log thumped as it shifted in the fire.

"Warn me! Warn me about what? For having a friend? What could you tell anyone," Eleanora wondered aloud, "when nothing had happened until tonight?"

Meria looked up, her dark eyes gleaming. "You see then, I was right. I—"

"I see that you are wrong," Eleanora stammered, "and you are a wicked, weak woman who clings to superficial honor to justify your evilness. You always blamed me for my father's death," Eleanora said, jabbing her finger in Meria's shocked face. "Do not deny it, when I felt it to my bones! But it was you, you and everyone like you who killed him. I kept you alive while you prayed for my death. You may keep praying that I be killed, but even if I were gone, what would a man like Cheremi want with a shell of a woman like you?"

Eleanora knocked Meria's needles out of her hands, and while her stepmother automatically reached down to pick them up, Eleanora grabbed the scissors. She slipped them into her pants' pocket, partly to restrain herself from jabbing her stepmother with them.

Eleanora took slow, shaking steps back to Edi, her head hanging, feeling him track her from above.

She took a deep breath on the last step before the landing.

She stepped up, kicking him behind the knees so his legs buckled; her elbow crooked beneath his chin and her other hand held the open scissor blades against his neck. She grappled with him so they faced his brothers, who held down a bloodied Cheremi. She gripped the scissors so tightly she could no longer feel her fingers, but when Edi squirmed and pulled at her arm, she swallowed hard and pressed the blade into his throat until blood trickled down his white shirt. It was nothing worse than when performing a difficult operation with Baba. That was all. She swallowed hard, and stared at his brothers, one younger and smaller with a wolf's triangular face, the other with a square head, and both with wide eyes.

"Give me your guns," she ordered.

They looked to Edi.

Eleanora gritted her teeth as she pressed the blade deeper into his sticky skin, fighting down her growing nausea. His chin touched her fist as he jerked a nod. His brothers were on each side of Cheremi, gripping him by the armpits. They used their free hands to slide their guns across the floor to her feet. In any other moment, Eleanora would have shrunk from the chance of the weapons accidentally going off, but she felt a jittery confidence with this man's life in her hands.

She bent to pick up the guns while still holding the scissors to Edi's throat, but he reached for his own gun, twisting away, his fingers forcing her head upward. She bit his hand, bit through the disgusting crunch and an animal yowl, not stopping until she was able to see the floor again. She groveled for a gun, aimed it at Edi, and pulled the trigger hard.

An explosion filled her head, and Edi crumpled to the ground, howling.

She picked up the other pistol from the floor and stood with a gun quivering in each hand. Edi's brothers glanced at each other, stepping toward her. She closed her eyes as she pulled both triggers, the recoil from the double blast shoving her backward, the explosion filling her head, and as she stumbled onto the floor the brothers fell backward. A sharp ringing buzzed between her ears, while they lay silent.

Only Edi's mouth still moved as he struggled to sit up near her, his thick blood pooling on the floor. She scooted away from the oozing redness.

"You stupid whore," Edi sputtered, blood dribbling down his chin. "My family will come for you. Shooting is too good a death for you. Your father, your father deserved—"

Still slouching, Eleanora raised her shaking hand and shot Edi in the chest.

Eleanora gripped the sides of her head as if that could stop the wild ringing hollowing it out. She stared at the blackened hole in the middle of Edi's white shirt. Who had she become that shooting him had been a thoughtless reflex? She, who had cried when she had seen a man shoot an injured donkey. *He meant to do worse to you. You had to defend yourself. Even with Kol*—she shook her head violently, becoming dizzy and nauseated, her hand slapped over her mouth in case she retched.

She heard a groan and cocked her gun at the back corner of the room. It was only Cheremi, rising from the floor, the back of his hand smearing blood from his nose across his frightened face. He blinked rapidly as he looked at her.

"What did they do to you?" she asked. "Are you all right?"

He nodded, staring at her, not coming any closer.

"We must leave this place," she said.

Cheremi shuffled toward the door, but Eleanora paused.

"There might be money in their pockets," she murmured to herself. She paused, something tickling her chin. She scratched and looked at her bloodied nails. Ah, yes, Edi had hit her. Her lips throbbed, but she continued to whisper to herself. "Money, money. It would be useful."

She patted the still-warm pockets and found silver pieces and ammunition, cigarettes and matches, an amulet. She carefully put the amulet back into its pocket. Everything else she stuffed into her pockets. She tugged belt holsters out from under the bodies and layered them onto her waist, but even the bulk of her pockets could not keep them from sliding down her narrow hips and crashing onto the floor. She flinched at the noise, looking up to see Cheremi staring at her with wide eyes. He averted his gaze, turning away, but not before she could see he was shaking his head, and this disturbed her more than the ugly ruined bodies staining the floor.

Eleanora brushed past Cheremi, trying to ignore how he shuddered away from her. She stumbled down the stairs to the dark room where Meria crouched, her face in her palms, though her skeletal fingers revealed her gape. She gasped and shuffled away, but Eleanora stumbled toward her stepmother and tore her hands from her face, and clutched at the writhing woman. Even as Meria tried to squirm out of her grasp, Eleanora pressed herself against Meria, feeling her bloodied blouse stick to the other woman's bony chest. Eleanora put her wet hand into her stepmother's hair, tugging her head close.

"You killed me, you killed me," Eleanora stammered, crying into Meria's shoulder. "I died, your daughter died the moment you sold her out. And now your master is dead, too." She choked on her sobbing laughter, wrecked with sadness. "Are you happy, Meria? I am dead, dead to you. Dead to myself. Though you are also a ghost, a flimsy, see-through ghost."

Meria weakly fought Eleanora's grasp, and Eleanora let her push away. The light from the fire flickered over her stepmother, and Eleanora felt a small satisfaction with the dark splotches staining her stepmother's dress. At least there was that. Other people would know her guilt. Eleanora roughly rubbed her eyes, spinning away, feeling completely alone in the dark space, her hands held out to grasp at anything, but even Cheremi was far, far away, his hand on the door, his head down, as he clumsily hopped on one foot, trying to pull on a leather sandal.

She gazed at Cheremi, but even after he had both shoes on he did not look up. She thought she had known what it was to be alone before, but it was nothing, nothing compared to the loss of intimacies she had only imagined until hours ago. If he had ever felt anything for her it was because he had not known her. She had not even known herself.

There was a rustle behind her.

She whipped around. It was only Meria, who had sat back down near the dying hearth, mending held against her crumpled chest.

"I know you always gossiped behind my back about my lack of religion," Eleanora said. "For all your crossing yourself, we shall see each other in hell after all. Thanks be to your stupid god my father never saw what you made of us. He—"

"Eleanora, it is over," Cheremi interjected. "Come. We will change quickly and leave."

It was not over, but any anxiety was washed over with a wave of warmth—they would leave together, after all. "Change? For what? They are only clothes." Had she not heard something like that before, in a dream? "No, no, we have too little time as it is," she said, her voice strangely steady again.

"At least we will wash our faces, our hands?" He looked at his stained palms before he wiped them on his white pants, leaving red smears.

"No, I wish her to remember me like this."

She grabbed her rifle and left the door open to the cold night.

"I always wanted to go beyond here," she whispered to herself.

She walked out without looking back. She could not hear him, but she knew Cheremi followed her.

Chapter 22

Cheremi followed Eleanora as she dashed down the only path through and out of the village, the path from which he had staggered into her life. She wondered if it was worth reminding him as they darted between the dark houses, watching for shifting shadows, only slowing when they had sprinted beyond the stone boundary to recklessly slide down the dim trail to the bottom of the black valley. But he must feel it as surely as she did, as surely as she felt the rocks burrowing into her shoes and grinding into her heels, as surely as she felt the full moon glare onto her, exposing them to whoever may already be hunting them. She was sure he felt it was fate. A lump rose in her throat, and she shook her head, almost tumbling head over feet on the rocky trail as she did so. She told herself that was why she did not remind him—it was not because she did not want him to think about the tragedy that had brought him to her. She was not afraid of that; it was impossible it was the same man.

When they reached the rushing river, the moon had hidden behind clouds, and the near-invisible water gurgled in the dark. She slung her rifle across her shoulders without stopping, stomping into the freezing current, welcoming its sting. She squatted in the river, letting it rush over her and hoping it would wash the blood away, though why it mattered now she could not say. She did not turn when she heard Cheremi sloshing behind her. She tried to wave him off when he tugged her hand, and she almost lost her balance. Her teeth chattering, he pulled her across the water and they crawled to shore.

The old boulder overshadowed the rocky shore, as it had months ago, a thousand years ago, as it would a thousand years from now, and Eleanora, suddenly exhausted, led Cheremi to its shallow cave. He gathered driftwood along the way, making a tidy pile of it just inside the cave's entrance where Eleanora crouched. She patted her pockets and tossed him the damp box of matches. Some of the wood must have been waterlogged from the river; the flames kept sizzling out. Shivering, Eleanora stirred the fire until it blazed.

She looked at Cheremi from under her lashes, patting the cold stone floor next to her. He sat near her, staring at the fire. As she let herself lean against him, she recalled the meeting of their bodies only hours ago, and she timidly put her arm around his shoulders, with the dawning understanding of how she might lead his body to respond to her touch. As her hands began to trickle down his shirt to the waist of his pants, he seized her wrists, glaring into her eyes as he pushed her onto the rough ground.

It was only reflex that kept her head from slamming onto the stony floor. She might not have minded, as he lowered himself upon her, keeping her hands pinned above her head. Pleasure pierced her, and as he bent his head to her shoulder, his bristling breath shot goose pimples from her earlobe to her toes. When her body began to warm to his, he groaned and collapsed on top of her, breath heaving into her neck, rolling over to his back, his eyes closed and his breath slowing. She would risk her life a hundred times to know she had the power to make him feel that.

Cheremi's face was smooth with sleep. His strong profile was that of a young Adonis in the soft light. She rubbed her thumb in the hollow where his ribs joined. She could no longer fight her heavy lids. She would rest, only for a moment; she would be more vigilant if she did, if . . .

She jerked awake. Had she heard a step crunch in the sand? A twig cracked in the distance. She must listen for Edi's family, she must . . .

What about Cheremi's brother?

Her eyes shot open, slightly stinging in the smoke.

Was Kol's body still bleeding on the floor of his home in Shkodra?

Her pulse beat between her ears.

It did not matter if it did. It was impossible it was the same man. It was a funny coincidence. Cheremi's brother was not Kol, but the victim of a man like Kol, making Cheremi a victim of random violence like herself whom she must protect, she must stay awake and listen for Edi's family, she must . . .

Lips pressed to her forehead.

Where was she?

The weird murky light burned her eyes. She touched her throbbing lips and cried out at the pain. Sunlight crept into the claustrophobic cave, making dawn feel like shrinking twilight, while finding Cheremi's smiling face looming over hers added to her sense of surreality.

Oh, yes.

She turned on her side, bringing her knees to her chest. The fire was dead, but its stale smoke was trapped in the cave. "Good morning, my soul," Cheremi said. "When you are ready, we will leave." He went outside.

Eleanora rose. Her back ached, her jaw was sore, but she could get through anything, so long as Cheremi spoke to her so gently. She followed him out, one foot outside the cave when she thought to scatter ashes and burned sticks with her foot, so their trail would not be so obvious if Edi's family tracked them.

They started on the trail, and to distract herself from memories of the other times she had climbed the same stair-like rocky path, and the other people she had been then, she admired Cheremi's straight back as he ascended. He pulled himself atop a man-size boulder, holding out his hand to help her. In her mind she saw through his shirt, to the lines of the muscles that she had caressed only hours ago. Her throat was too thick for her to speak, and so she merely scrambled up on her own, suddenly unable to look at him.

He wiped his palm on his pant leg. "We are almost there, my soul."

She was endlessly on the edge of asking Cheremi where he was leading them, but she was terrified what he might see on her face if he said they would go to Shkodra, to a small home on the edge of a field. But then, if he asked why she looked so, she could say she was frightened Edi's family might find them, and she thought they should go farther south or leave the country.

She tripped on a small stone, nodding she was fine when

Cheremi's concerned face looked down from above. She would hate to lie to him. She was quiet and uncomplaining despite her exhaustion as she followed him down the familiar path toward Shkodra. Who was she this time? She shrugged away her worries, desperately hoping she and Cheremi would branch off the beaten trail. She twisted her bracelet nervously.

They never did.

Chapter 23

Cheremi stood in front of the squat house, as Eleanora had so many months ago, a lifetime ago. Only where her hesitating hand had hovered there now hung, behind Cheremi's trembling fist, a torn and bloodied shirt nailed to the cracked wooden door, a reminder of a death yet to be avenged. An announcement of shame.

A door creaked.

Eleanora held back a scream. It was only the gate next door. She crossed her arms tightly and stared at the ground. What if she looked up to see Kol slouching against the frame, shirtless and scowling and picking his dirty nails, demanding to know what they wanted. He might point at Eleanora, blood dribbling out of his filthy mouth. "Brother, how could you bring such a coward here? A woman without shame, who could not even finish her job and put me out of my misery. She tried to kill me, did you know?"

And Cheremi, what would he do? Would it be any better if

instead Kol were still lying on the floor, silent except for the soft gurgling from his throat?

In her mind she raced to Lake Shkodra and jumped in, but she forced herself to stand planted there, tugging on her serpent bracelet and cursing when she pulled it off and it bounced on the dirt. She picked it up, keeping crouched longer than necessary, feeling as if she might take off and run.

"This is where my brother and I lived," Cheremi said, his bowed head buried in his hands. "Where I found him, killed."

I know, I know, Eleanora almost admitted. Her heart pounded between her ears—the words had been on the tip of her tongue. Her hand clamped over her mouth, to stop the rising, rambling defense of herself. *But do you know how he started it? He killed my father, and then he tried to kill me.*

Tears of frustration brimmed behind her eyes. She must blink them back. She dug her fingernails into her palms, drawing slivers of blood. She took a deep breath.

"To murder a man in his own house . . ." Cheremi said. "To violate the sanctity of a home and tradition. Who would dare . . ."

He choked on his words, leaning his forehead against the rusty-bloodied shirt.

Eleanora imagined herself splashing in the lake, her hands hoping for a hold, water slipping through her fingers. She could not swim, but if she sank it would not matter. She wanted to hang on to Cheremi's shoulders.

To comfort him? Or keep herself from drowning?

Her hand floated over his bent back, but before she could touch him, he stepped forward and lifted the door dangling from its rusting iron hinge. He must have broken it while struggling to get in to save Kol. And how could he have fixed it before he took off to chase her?

He stepped inside the dark house.

The patch of sunlight shining through the doorway illuminated the dust floating through the small room's musty air. Eleanora followed Cheremi, scanning the packed dirt floor. Kol's body had been removed and the floor cleaned. But was that a shadow of a stain?

Eleanora squeezed her eyes shut, then allowed herself to look around. She must pretend she had not seen this space before. Ashes in a fire pit dug into the center of the floor, a few flattened floor pillows around it. A small folded wooden table leaned against the wall to her left, and on the back wall she faced there was a hollowed tree trunk holding a dented copper kettle and cups, and two small wooden chests in opposing dim corners.

Was the house really so little?

That day it had been big and black, the length between where she had stood over Kol's body and the small window as long as a field. She sat on the chest farthest from the window she had crawled out of. Cheremi pulled a shirt and pants out of the other chest, leaving his bloodstained clothes on the floor. As he dressed, he told her he was going to ask the neighbors for news of his brother's murder. He reached back into the chest, pulling out a tarnished pistol that he slipped into his sash.

"My soul, do not cry so. You are safe here, with me. We will be all right," he said, kissing the top of her bowed head. "I am grateful you are here to face this with me."

Eleanora nodded, her head bobbing long after the door closed, until her palms slammed against her ears and she screamed into her knees.

She was sitting in the dark when Cheremi returned with coffee, cornmeal, eggs, firewood, and little news.

"No one saw who might have done it?" she ventured, feeling guilty when she heard how high and innocent her voice sounded. But she had to know. "No one knows why it might have happened?"

"No one knows anything," he said. "None of the men would talk to me. They passed raki behind my back, they even handed me coffee under their thighs because I have yet to avenge my brother's death. Like a fool I drank it, and nearly choked on the bullet they had placed in the cup. Such shame."

"Shame!" Eleanora exclaimed. "My soul, the only shame is in someone treating a friend like that!" She wanted to ramble on, perhaps her reasoning would soothe him—and also keep him from saying anything more than no one knew anything about his brother's death. "What foolish ideas they carry on about honor. It is one thing to hear such things said by old men in the mountains, but I thought town folk might be more evolved. Who knows what might have happened to your brother, who he may have—"

"Honor is honor," he interrupted, sighing. "But you are a woman, and even the most intelligent woman like you cannot understand what a man's honor is to him."

So her making love with him had stripped her of her wisdom? When he had once called her the cleverest person he knew! She snorted, but when she glanced at him, she was grateful he had not heard. The pain on his beautiful face rebuked her, and she stroked his cheek as he continued.

"What else was said, my soul?" she asked.

"Marni, one of our cousins, told the men I had been away in

the mountains for work, that my brother's death was a shock to me. I did not try to explain I had been searching the mountains for his killer. Marni took me to his home and told me he had reported the murder to the officials, who did not care much, of course. A troublemaker, they said. As if it were Kol's fault. Then he had Kol buried and . . ."

His stiff expression gradually crumpled, but he did not cry. He covered his face with his hands and finally sobbed. He wiped his palms on his pants, his face composed again. Nothing he said meant anything to her. All she cared about was the agony in his face. She gingerly put her arms around him.

"What will you do now? We won't stay here tomorrow?"

"Of course we will stay here tomorrow, and until the next day. Tomorrow, alone, I . . . I could not find his grave in the dark. Tomorrow I will go again."

Eleanora wondered if Kol's grave was near her father's. Likely there was only one cemetery in the city, the one with long swaying shoots of grass between the tall crooked columns of the gravestones. That day she had gone to bury Baba, the man had shooed with his rusty shovel an impish boy who watched while his oxen grazed. She did not want to see that again, though she hoped an ox would trample, more than trample over Kol's grave. He had caused all of this. To think of that wretch near Baba.

She would do anything Cheremi asked—anything!—but she would not go to the grave.

"Do not look so sad, my soul," Cheremi said, his thumb rubbing her cheek. "I will find my brother's killer. We will not live in disgrace for long. There is nothing for you to do but let me take care of this, and I will."

He patted her tightening fist, and it irritated her how his large palm covered her whole hand. Nothing for her to do? When she had saved him? When long before he knew she existed, she had done what he could not. She had had her revenge.

And for what? She never felt the ugly waste of it more than when she sat here, holding Cheremi's hand and yet completely alone. She was the only one who could give him the revenge he wanted. She moved closer to him, leaning into his side, trying not to cry.

Eleanora noticed she was shivering. She patted her pockets, finding the stolen matches in the dirty stiff pants she still had not changed from. She struck one, another, but her shaking hands could not light the kindling Cheremi had dropped in the hearth. Starting the fire was another bit of woman's work she had never learned; Meria had always tended the hearth.

Cheremi sighed and grabbed the matches out of her hand and lit the fire. He found a small pan in one of the dim corners, and after a pronounced pause began frying eggs for dinner. Eleanora set up the small table, and found crumpled red-and-white-striped linens smashed against the wall. She dropped the towels on the table. She had not known how stained and filthy her hands were.

"Where is the water?" Eleanora asked—another thing Meria had always done. Even in an unknown place her stepmother would have silently, expertly brought back a pail of completely still well or spring water.

Without saying anything, Cheremi dropped the pan on the table and left the house with a bucket. He returned ten minutes later and set the sloshing pail near the table.

"Thank you," Eleanora said, her eyes on the floor where

the water had slopped out of the bucket. The dark spot almost looked like—she shook her head.

She dipped the linens in the water and offered one to Cheremi, who wiped his hands quickly. Eleanora was surprised by the towel's chill, and then realized that Meria had always heated the water before dipping the towels in. Eleanora would do that next time.

But how many next times could there be? How many miserable meals would they eat in this sad room?

She picked at the fried fringe of the rubbery eggs, the small piece burning down her throat. She was afraid to ask for a cup of water.

"When might we leave this place?" she ventured. "Edi's family must already be searching for us. I believe his family has ties to this town."

"My soul, do you forget I have ties to this town, too?" Cheremi said, eating the last of the eggs. "I cannot just run away from cleansing my blood. I could go as far as your Italy, or anywhere else, and my shame would follow me. I am not a coward. I would rather be dead."

"Rather be dead!" she echoed. "What is more cowardly? Leaving behind these, these mistakes, or letting everyone else's mindless beliefs decide your life for you?" Eleanora asked. Her hand inched over the table toward his. "We still have time to escape, to leave all this. We should leave, and we should leave soon. You should ask officials tomorrow for news of your brother, and then—"

"And then? What else should I do?" Cheremi asked, crossing his arms. "Tell me. Do you think you are head of every house you sleep in?"

Eleanora bit her bottom lip. His face looked ancient and lined in his anger. Who was this old, hard stranger across from her? This was not her grateful friend whose life she had saved twice. What if he knew what she had done? He would reach across the table, big hands clamping onto her throat, and what of it? She deserved it. She would only be sad she had put him in that position.

She tried to hide her face as she began to cry.

Cheremi rushed over, holding her, rocking her, hushing her.

"My soul, my fairy," he cooed, and kept cooing, until her hiccuping sobs slowed and smoothed. "You have been braver than any man, what you did last night. Do not think I do not know I owe you my life, twice over. Let us rest, my soul."

She wriggled so he could press her even tighter against his chest.

When he loosened his grip, Eleanora got up and put the table away. Cheremi pulled a blanket out of the chest that kept his clothes, then sat back down and stared into the flames.

She sighed. Was he waiting for her to make their bed for the night?

She shook her head, relieved he had not heard her. When she asked him where the bedding was, he pointed to the chest he had taken his clothing out of. She unfolded the dank reed mats and thick wool bedding, fluffed the red wool pillows, covered the bed with a thick felt blanket, then lay down. Cheremi joined her. Staring at the black ceiling, she stroked his head until he slept. She was so tired, and yet she was afraid of what she might dream of in this room, what she might cry out in her sleep.

The next morning she woke to Cheremi sitting around barely glowing embers, watching her.

What had she confessed in her dreams?

He drummed his fingers.

"The fire is nearly out, my soul," he said, with exaggerated patience that showed he had none.

It was only after Eleanora's failed attempts to start the fire that Cheremi impatiently took over, though he waited for her to make the coffee. He told her he would be back by sunset, and that she should of course use some of the cornmeal to bake bread for their dinner.

She watched him walk out the door, dawn bursting through behind him. After he lifted the door back into place, the room was blacker than before. In the empty space her thoughts raced. Most of them were petty, including her irritation that he expected her to keep the fire, make him coffee, bake him bread. When he was in her home, she had treated him like a king, and now he treated her like any other new bride. Was that her relation to him now? If it was, then perhaps she could tell him the truth. But if legal servitude was the price of his forgiveness, and not simply his love for her, as she was . . . But who she was these days did not bear such close inspection, now, did it?

She tossed the cheap tin across the room, feeling foolish as she knew she would pick it up. She washed it, along with the other dishes from last night, beating the dust from the bedding, folding and refolding the blankets, wondering what else she could do to stop the voice in her head from taunting her that she was no better than people like Edi and his brothers, people who were surely looking for her, hours away from finding her, finding Cheremi, who was looking for her.

Was she to go mad on top of everything else?

She shot up from her seat, dizzy as she looked around the dim room.

There! A broom in the corner near the window. Sweeping the beaten earth floor took no time at all, and she was left with a small dust pile she did not know what to do with. She was afraid if she lifted the broken door she would not be able to put it back. Finally she tossed the dirt out the window, smiling when she noticed a lone olive tree not so far away, its branches tinged with green. At least spring would come sooner here than in the mountains.

She paced around the small house, bored but not tempted to venture outside. She felt Cheremi would prefer her here, safe, though she felt insecure with the door half off its hinges.

A gate slammed outside and she jumped, nervously laughing at herself. What was there to worry about? Cheremi had not found her out yet.

She collapsed into a slump on the same chest in the corner she had sat on yesterday—the one Cheremi had not opened—bringing up her knees to her chest, hugging herself and rocking. There were, of course, no books in the house. No paper or pastels. She thought of her sunny home in the mountains, her seat at the window, wondered what Meria was doing. No, no, she could not think of her. She would cry.

To distract herself she jumped up and cracked open the heavy top of the wooden chest. In its darkness, before she even pulled out the cloth, she felt heavily embroidered folds of fabric.

Woman's clothing in the home of two bachelors?

She felt a pang of jealousy, numbed only when she smelled how musty the stiff garments were. Perhaps the clothes belonged to a dead mother, or a sister who had been married off and would rather leave these pretty things than have them destroyed by her mother-in-law's embroidering and dying them to match the costume of her husband's tribe. Eleanora pulled out a creamy skirt, and tarnished silver chandelier earrings and bangle bracelets tumbled from its folds, jangling on the floor. She ripped off her dirty clothes and slipped on the skirt and the bracelets. She was a new woman in this dress, disappearing under thick piles of skirts and a headscarf. The skirt fit her nearly perfectly. She was putting her hands through the sleeves of a blouse when the door was lifted from the hinges it dangled on.

Eleanora backed away, gasping.

A black silhouette stood against the arched opening to the sunny street.

"What are you doing? Where did those clothes come from?" Cheremi's voice asked.

It was impossible to see his expression, but his voice was sharp and shaking.

"I only opened your chest," Eleanora said. She turned her back to Cheremi, to the breeze from the open doorway, as she hurried to finish dressing before someone saw her from the street.

"My own clothes were so dirty, I needed to change, so I thought—"

"I had forgotten those were here," Cheremi said.

He arranged the door back in its place, and as Eleanora's eyes readjusted to the house's dim light, she saw how he still stared at her.

He put his hands around her waist, holding her at arm's length to gaze at her.

Her belly warmed with a shy pride, and she forced herself to look up and smile into Cheremi's eyes. But he was looking beyond her.

"Oh," she said, sighing. "Is it only that I remind you of someone again?"

"Yes," Cheremi answered without smiling. He fingered a loose tendril of her hair, and he stroked her ear. "You are missing a flower here, but you still remind me of a beautiful mountain man I used to know."

Eleanora broke into hysterical giggles, and Cheremi turned her around and pulled her backside against him, hugging her close and kissing her neck as it vibrated with laughter.

DAYS LATER, ELEANORA fingered the same skirts, now lying on the floor near her and Cheremi, who breathed deeply next to her. Without looking she knew he slept peacefully, though at night he often cried out while she lay awake in the dark, her ears straining for strange noises.

Were those footsteps outside the door? No, no. Just someone passing in the night.

She let go of her breath, petting his smooth shaved head.

Was it better the clothes belonged to the same lost love he said she reminded him of, or another woman altogether?

If it were one lost love, it showed Cheremi's loyalty, his being capable of deep love, but perhaps then his love was already spent and an ideal imprinted on his mind. And then if there were two or more women, perhaps what he felt with her, those shivers she seemed to give him, were more due to her being a kind of creature he liked, and not any unique feeling she herself inspired.

Oh, how she hoped he had had a sister.

But she was sure she reminded him of that other woman. He could not be so cheap in his affections; she could not believe that. And yet, to be merely a mirror of someone he had already loved was unbearable. To be loved because of some coincidental resemblance to another woman who had held his heart after all these years . . .

She rolled onto her side to watch Cheremi as he slept.

What did this matter, when he lay here with her now? Or when they would be together in Italy, or some other country? Surely they would go any day now.

Cheremi rolled over and kissed her mouth, twirling a tendril of her hair as he opened his sleepy eyes.

"It is so hard to leave you," he said, smiling, the last shards of the sunset striking his teeth white.

Eleanora smiled back at him, until she realized what his compliment implied. He was going again, and she did not have to ask why. She knew he went to search for his brother's killer, speaking with men in cafés, sometimes at night, and surely during the day, between the odd jobs he did, repairing wheels on carriages and carts, delivering firewood.

Men who knew of Kol's unavenged murder refused to deal with Cheremi, but there was still work to be done with the hotel owners, or the odd foreigner who had heard about how he had led other explorations into the mountains. Some of these foreigners had offered him rich payments to guide them through the mountains, but Cheremi turned these offers down, though he would sometimes take the men to the village at the foot of the mountains, earning a small fee for that and from the other guide he handed them off to. Those trips might have been lucrative, but he could not leave Eleanora, Cheremi would say, smiling. When she offered to go with him—anything to escape this house, to get away—he said it was impossible.

"Impossible?" she had asked. "As your wife, I could travel with you as you work. For a fee, perhaps I could provide sketches as well to the foreigners! How is that?"

"You are very clever," he had answered, tweaking her chin. "But you know what I must do. I must find him first."

And she had no answer for that, because he would never find him. The person he searched for no longer existed. How could his brother's killer be this delicate woman who fit into his arms, bangle bracelets jangling when she tugged his earlobe, silver earrings tangled in the hair he pulled? When she looked at Cheremi now, she thought with sadness about this pain that had happened to him before their life together had begun. But she had endured a similar pain . . .

One night as they lay together, hours before dawn, Cheremi spoke into the darkness.

"I came very close to catching him," he said.

Eleanora stiffened in his arms, glad he held her from behind, unable to see her face. "But I thought you did not ever see this man."

"I did, and I did not. You see, I had been gone many months for work, and came home to see my brother . . . left to die, in his own home."

Eleanora squeezed her eyes shut, but then she saw Kol lying on the same floor as she, his own eyes open and accusing. Her eyes shot open, and she searched the dim room for anything else to focus on.

"His killer was just running out of the house," Cheremi continued, "frightened because he heard me. In a look, I could see nothing was left to be done for my brother, and I took after his killer. I was so close I could almost touch his shirt."

His shirt? But he had worn my father's fur coat.

She pressed her lips together.

She absentmindedly stroked his head. She might tell Cheremi everything would be okay, that he would catch the killer, but then she did not want to encourage him. And if she opened her mouth, the words might tumble out: he already had caught the killer he sought.

Oh, yes, that killer lay in Cheremi's arms, experiencing a little death each night and glorious rebirth in the morning, transformed into another person.

Her caressing fingers paused. To think Cheremi mourned the man who had killed her father without reason. Whose side would Cheremi take if he knew Kol had tried to kill her? Kol had brought his death upon himself. But what did it matter? Kol, Baba, they were both dead now. Had she not learned, from an ancient book of arithmetic, that two negatives canceled each other out? She and Cheremi were left with zeros, little loops of eternity, radiating rings. Eleanora held her ringless left hand above her face, trying to see it in the dark. But then it was the right hand that had pulled the trigger.

"Ah," Cheremi said, sighing, "but someone is no longer listening to me. You are so intelligent, and yet I cannot forget this is men's talk, and it is a credit to you as a woman that it bores you." He twisted and tugged at her hair. "How could a woman understand the shame a man feels when his honor is gone and his neighbors pretend not to see him?"

Eleanora almost laughed. She wished this conversation meant nothing to her.

"If they do not see you, why must you see them? And in such a fine light?" she asked.

"You speak like out of those books of songs you used to read me." Cheremi kissed her forehead, then sat up. "I know you are frightened. But even if we went to your pretty Italy, I would still have to search for him."

Eleanora raised herself on her elbows, looking out the small window. The sky was lightening, transforming from black to gray so seamlessly Eleanora could not pinpoint when the change had begun.

"Why?" she asked.

"Why must anyone do anything? Except make me coffee."

He laughed and chucked her chin, waiting on her to stir the fire, brew his coffee, so he could gulp it down and leave. She told him to be careful. When the door shut she let herself scream into the pillow.

After that each evening dully doubled upon itself.

Was it one or one thousand nights that followed?

Eleanora counted out on her hands. Probably ten. Each day had been spent scrubbing the floor, fluffing bedding, brewing coffee, polishing their few cups and dishes . . . In between her chores she peered out the window and watched the silvery green leaves increasingly blur the branches of the lone tree, though sometimes she would suddenly duck, even while she laughed at her absurd terror of a gun being shoved in her face. One of the few variations in her day—besides what little figures she might draw with a stick of charcoal and paper Cheremi had brought her one day—was whether or not she succeeded in not crying that day, or not burning the corn bread. She tried to successfully bake out of a masculine desire to prove herself, and Cheremi laughingly applauded her efforts, though he also began bringing home loaves of brown bread.

When she could stop comparing each task she performed to how excellently Meria would have completed it, the novelty of keeping house brought her a little amusement and pride in making Cheremi's life more comfortable, until enjoyment faded with routine and the realization she merely discharged duties expected of her.

She had an irrational hope her stepmother might knock on their door, and an often paralyzing fear of Edi's family discovering her and Cheremi. She had no idea what she would do in either case, but both her hope and her fear were replaced by dread nothing would spur her and Cheremi to leave Shkodra. She discovered the little residential part of town she saw during her duties was not more than a cramped, crowded version of her village: houses were surrounded by tall stone walls instead of wooden fences, small plots of grass fields and olive groves rolled in the distance instead of swaying corn and wheat fields, passing men pretended she did not exist as more than a moving picture for them to appraise.

Besides her fast walks to fetch water from the well and gather fallen branches and clumps of hay for the fire, she was confined to the small house, first out of her fear of Edi's family finding her, and, later, because of what seemed to her to be worse: plain habit, which she tried to disguise to herself as considerate concern of Cheremi's disapproval if she explored the city alone.

She could not bear to upset him. Being in his arms held both a dreamy ecstasy of novels she had devoured and the grounding comfort she had missed since her father had left her. Sometimes when even that ecstasy escaped her in her worries, she felt pleasure giving him pleasure, and while he lifted her own loneliness, she felt she did the same for him. And after what had happened to his brother, she could not bear to leave him further alone.

"To see a world in a grain of sand, to see . . . the curve of infinity in an eyelash," Eleanora muttered to herself, chuckling as she scratched the dull charcoal into the paper, tracing the finger-size eyelash she had drawn in the morning.

She had never noticed before how often reading books had filled her hours. Or when she had to hunt, or when she traveled with Baba, or had Meria to giggle with . . .

But those days were over.

She looked up from her drawing. She ought to wash the dishes from last night. She looked at the eye staring back at her, tore it in two, and threw it in the hearth. She had stopped showing her drawings to Cheremi, afraid the eyes might look too familiar to him. She shook the thought from her mind.

What was there to hide?

She did not show him the pictures because he would merely be bored to see another set of those endless eyes she drew.

Eleanora stood. She wrapped a scarf around her head, took the key out of Cheremi's chest—she now thought of the chest full of the woman's clothes as hers—locked the front door Cheremi had repaired last week, and left.

Though she had seen a limited stretch of street when she fetched water and firewood, it was not until she had wandered onto a cobblestone road that she remembered the vibrant city she had admired that first morning she had walked through Shkodra with her father, and she begrudged Cheremi for keeping her from this.

But what could he know?

Perhaps, despite the time he had spent with her in her little village, he took all of this for granted. Surely he was only trying to protect her.

She walked outside with her head held down, but soon the activity of the city drew her out and her eyes wandered freely. After months of eating mostly corn bread and coffee, it was a thrill to see a rainbow of fruits and vegetables, baked goods that were clever pieces of sculpture. Had she ever known these things existed? That one might just buy them, eat them in a few bites for no reason except for the expected pleasure of doing so? That seemed like something worth striving for, to be able to take such pleasures for granted, but then if she did, would she remember how she had yearned to be able to do so, or would endless cups of coffee with so much sugar she could smell its sweetness give her as much pleasure as the watered-down brew she drank now?

Before she could even figure out how she might taste such delights as the market offered, she became frightened there was an even greater one she took for granted. She rushed home to be there before Cheremi arrived, to make coffee and pour lumpy batter into a pan, and to watch him move about the room, while she crouched near the fire.

"You make things too hot for me," Cheremi said, wincing and almost spilling the cup as he handed it back to her.

She carefully dabbed his shirt with a wet rag. Cheremi's

roughness made her want to cry. She felt like crying about her wanting to cry. What a weak woman she had become.

"I am very sorry," she muttered, dumping the cup in the pail of clean water. "How was your day?" she asked, trying to make her voice even.

He did not answer.

She asked again.

"My day?" Cheremi said, drumming his fingers on the table. "My day was the same as the day before, and the day before that. I have nothing new to report."

She thought how she might tell him about that day she had searched for answers to what had happened to her father, but her heart beat fast with panic at what she almost revealed. Luckily the fire was small, and he could not see how her hand trembled as she poured him fresh coffee.

She did not mention Italy the rest of the night.

Chapter 24

The alleys of Shkodra were like the labyrinths in ancient myths Eleanora had read, and she gasped and laughed at herself when she imagined for a moment that the bearded man behind a cart was a centaur.

Two-story buildings, crammed side by side in two seamless walls facing each other, created a canyon in which a river of townspeople streamed through. Wide enough for two people, one current of traffic flowed toward the city's center, the other out, and opposing sides shouted greetings over merchants' chants.

Three days had passed since Eleanora had wandered beyond her neighborhood, each day a dull echo of the last. She had begun to resent her hours were spent only waiting for Cheremi to return home, and her resentment frightened her more than any fear of exposing herself to Edi's family or Cheremi's irritation. She had stood in front of her wooden chest, clothing heaped around her feet, debating a white headscarf over an ivory one. She chose the ivory one, which matched her full embroidered skirt and was so long it almost dragged on the ground. She touched her earlobes to make sure both earrings were on, locked the front door, and decided to find the city's famous library.

Eleanora stared everywhere, only looking down as she stumbled on the uneven, slippery cobblestones lining the narrow alleys she found herself in. She passed a triangular square where women veiled in white huddled together, fingertips dyed red, offering homespun goods to the highest bidders. The youngest woman, her kohl-rimmed eyes flashing, snapped at an older man in a foreign tongue. He chuckled and slid her three more coins, and Eleanora laughed, turning her head to see another member of the small audience also smiling, though he would not meet her eyes.

She looked at the tip of her worn leather sandals, then smoothed her stiff skirt, enjoying the feel of the richness of the gold embroidery even as she worried her costume was not correct.

What did it matter?

The point was to find the library. She continued down the alley, realizing no other woman lifted her head except to speak in low tones with another. Eleanora held her head higher. No matter what other women did, she must find someone to ask for directions to the library. She approached a reedy man standing in front of a store with red clay pottery tumbling out. Though he had no other customers, he took a few moments before he acknowledged her. And how might he help her? She told him she wanted to find the library.

"The library of Bushati?" He raised his thin brows. "You are lost, I presume? If you continue down this main street, through the big arch, you will come upon a mosque with a courtyard with a cypress tree in it. The Sultan's Cypress."

"No, not the Sultan's Cypress," Eleanora said, perversely enjoying his discomfort. "I want to go to the library. To read books."

He stared at her, knitting his skinny brows together, as if she spoke a foreign tongue. A smile softened his face, which Eleanora mirrored, though it did not reach her eyes. He spoke as if to an invisible man next to him.

"So she goes to have books read to her. Perhaps religious texts."

"No," Eleanora insisted. "I go to read novels. Alone. By myself."

He smiled, and his eyes shifted side to side as he looked to see if anyone else heard this absurd conversation.

"Of course." He rubbed the back of his scrawny neck. "Well, long may you live."

Eleanora echoed his goodbye and continued down the street. She would go to the stupid cypress and find the library herself. She wove through crowds, walking under a large, crumbling arch that marked the entry to the heart of the market. Traffic slowed to a trickle. Women covered in lace and gold embroidery strolled behind tall men, some leading gleaming horses, all pausing before storefronts. There were brass-studded leather belts the wives in Eleanora's village would wear, mountains of snow-white caps for men, and short stiff vests. In a rainbow of rolls of shining silks, Eleanora recognized a bright blue wool that reminded her of fabric her father had bought her long ago. She walked faster.

Where was that stupid cypress?

Before she saw any tree she came upon an open square, weeds sprouting between rows of large cobblestones leading to a free-standing two-story white building with a red-tiled roof and small windows.

Eleanora tapped the shoulder of a lone man who crossed her path. He shrank from her touch, but nodded. "Yes, that is the library. But women—"

"Women are not allowed?"

"Well, actually, I do not know."

"I will find out then. Thank you for your help," Eleanora said crisply.

She stood at the foot of the shallow stairs, waiting as two talking men brushed past her before she entered.

The library's long white walls were lined with manuscripts and books, and perpendicular floor-to-ceiling shelves stuffed with scrolls. The shelves seemed to go on forever within the large room, and she could not see where it ended. She inhaled parchment- and ink-scented air. The library was like her father's study's bookshelf multiplied by infinity, and in its center was a wide wooden table that men sat at. A young bearded man studied silently, one arranged a stack of manuscripts, and three men argued, hands flying, hissing about Constantinople. An older man came to quiet them.

There was an official arrogance in the way the older man waved away the men's whispered apologies. Before he disappeared, Eleanora asked him where she might find novels by Sami Frashëri.

The older man narrowed his eyes.

"Which book?"

"Any," said Eleanora, "but I especially like *The Love Between Talat and Fitnat*."

His face softened, and his spotted hand flew to his heart.

"It is one of my favorites, too. Have you read *The Given Word of Trust*?"

"No, but if you would be so good as to show me where it is . . ."

She followed his weaving walk through a maze of manuscripts, until he stopped so abruptly in front of a shelf of newer looking books she almost bumped into him. His fingers danced over their leather bindings. He plucked one out of the row, and presented it to her with both hands. She thanked him, and he nodded in reply, with a small smile. As he whisked around the corner of the shelves, she grabbed another book by the same author, the one she had already read.

She found a seat alone at the long table, humming beneath her breath as she ran her fingers over the books' embossed leather. The binding creaked as she opened the novel the librarian had recommended. She inhaled the delicious smell before she began to read. The Turkish words on the page dissolved as images arose in her head. The story was about a father and a son. It became clear the father would be forced to shoot his son to keep his given word and honor.

She slammed the book shut and settled down with the familiar novel instead.

"Excuse me," the librarian said. "Excuse me. It is closing time."

The rudeness of being ripped from a dream!

"Please, oh, please," she begged. "If you could only give me another moment to finish the story."

But the librarian wagged his finger and made sure she left with the few scholarly men who had lingered.

Out in the dusk and dusty courtyard, Eleanora felt disoriented, as if she had awoken late from a nap. She should go back through the large arch, then to the bazaar. But how would she get there? The stalls had closed and she was left with unmarked, endless walls.

She began walking anyway, relieved when she found herself under the crumbling arch. She must make a few turns off the main street into the alleys to cross the field between the bazaar and her neighborhood, but she could not remember which turns to take. Shkodra was a new city at night, and the few glaring gas lanterns on the fronts of night-blackened buildings confused her more than they helped her, making her blind when she turned back to the darkness flooding the narrow streets.

She turned down a street. A dead end, with a lump of laundry in the dark. Strange. She stood still. The lump was a crumpled man. She choked her scream, afraid her voice might stir the body, or worse, find it did not move, and bolted back to the main street, from where she turned down another alley, walking until she knew she had gone farther than it would have taken to find her house. She laughed at herself. She was searching again for a house she would now rather run from, but where else could she go? Wherever Cheremi was, was her home.

Meanwhile, he waited for her. She remembered how she had waited for him at her home for those long five days, and she thought it was fitting. She was angry, and she had not known it then. She finally ran across the field, grasses whipping her thighs, and saw the house. She knocked on the door and stood trembling in the chill as Cheremi opened the door, standing aside to let her walk in.

The hearth was black and cold.

"Thank god you are alive! Where have you been?" he demanded, remaining standing, so far from her.

"I only went to the library," Eleanora replied, trying to keep her answer light, as if she were a few minutes late from a normal errand.

He crossed his arms, the hard stranger again, planted far away from her.

"I only went for a moment, to read a story that reminded me of us, and everything was fine, only in the night I got lost, but I am here now." Her voice trailed off weakly.

"You risked bringing attention to us," he said, "because you wanted to go look at books? To look at a book you have already seen, too?"

Eleanora stared at him. She had expected angry concern, to explain what had kept her out so late, to hear how dangerous it was to be lost at night, but this? She stood there, digging her fingernails into her palms, blinking back tears.

"And what do you do each day?" she asked, unable to look at him. "At least I am in a disguise, no longer a sworn virgin, whereas you, you get to go out every day amongst people who know you and where you live, and you tell every stranger you meet who you are—"

"I get to go out every day?" he interrupted. "I go out to work for us. I go out and deal with my shame. I have cups passed behind my back, while I try to clear our disgrace. And you? You cannot stand being bored. You would rather not work, so you go out to look at books all day. Now everyone in the town will know about you."

Cheremi paced, his face red.

"The mountain woman who goes to the library. Do you not think people will talk?"

Eleanora was stunned.

Do you not think people will talk?

It was something Meria would say to her or to her father, and she and Baba would look at each other and try not to laugh.

"Of course, I think people will talk," she snapped. "I think people will talk about you, 'Cheremi returned from Arbër,' and I think Edi's family will hear."

He stood near the door, his arms crossed and his eyes looking past her, and her stomach sank as she felt the infinite distance between them. What was life without his heart pumping steadily into her ear? Who else did she have?

"I am sorry," she said, not meaning it nor caring.

She repeated over and over she was sorry, stumbling into his arms, feeling it was an unbearable eternity until finally he was holding her again.

It was only later, in the dark with his deep regular breathing and his heavy hand on top of her stomach, that she realized what bothered her more than his hypocrisy of going out in the open every day: he did not remember she had been a man who had saved his life. Twice. Yes, he earned food and firewood for them, but he unnecessarily did so in a city so dangerous for them both. But she would not share her frustration with him, for fear her saying so would make him shift his body away from hers, and so she told herself it was not worth thinking of.

She woke up alone in the cool dawn. Cheremi had left. Cold smoke rose from the hearth, and she imagined crawling out from under her blanket to the small pile of firewood many times before she opened her eyes and did so. She dropped the sticks into the dying hearth, gently nudging the wood until the little licks of fire grew. Slowly the flames became large enough for her to make coffee, and as she sipped her stinging hot cup, she wondered who had handed Cheremi his coffee this morning.

Had he gone to a café? Had other fingers brushed his when the cup was passed? She thought she had seen a woman working in a café yesterday. Her mind began to tingle awake with the coffee. She bit her lip until it hurt. He had left early because he was still angry with her. And how would he feel if he knew what else she had done?

She put down her unfinished cup and began dressing. She would have chased around town for him and begged him to come back—until she remembered this had started with her leaving their home. She sat back down on the bedding, hugging her knees. What if he went missing again, like he had in her village?

She felt a pierce of panic and walked over to the small window that framed the lone olive tree with full silvery-green branches. What would life look like without Cheremi? She found a scrap of paper and drew his face for hours, trying to capture the gold-white curl of his mustache, the hollow beneath his cheeks, the pillow of his upper lip. She was struggling with his eyes when the door opened to bright sunshine. Cheremi closed the door. He had that shadow of a smile on his face as he walked toward Eleanora.

She jumped up and clutched him, warmth washing over

her. She inhaled his scent. She kissed both of his cheeks and searched his eyes, smiling.

"You are my soul," she whispered.

Cheremi sat down, setting packages of sour yogurt and eggs on the floor. Eleanora put the yogurt in their best bowl and heated corn bread from last night, along with water for fresh coffee and hot towels. She set up the table. Cheremi rarely joined her for a midday meal, and she would make him her honored guest.

Cheremi rummaged through his sack and put a book on the table. Neither of them looked at it, instead staring into each other's eyes.

"I love you," Eleanora replied, leaning over and kissing him again. She was almost afraid to ask. "Why did you leave me so early this morning?"

"There was a foreigner who wished to leave town," he said, "to go into the mountains. Near your old village. He did not have government permission, so he had to leave before sunrise. I took him to the Koplik village, set him up with another guide. At first the guide did not want to pay me, but we reached an agreement."

Eleanora served him coffee and put the corn bread on the table with the yogurt. He drank his coffee in one gulp, passing the cup back to Eleanora, which she filled for herself. Then she fetched the steaming towels and wiped each of his fingers before they ate.

She said this now because they could laugh at it. "I was afraid you might have left me. For good."

"Never, my soul," he said, without looking up from the bowl of yogurt.

She did not mind. She liked that he spoke so casually to her about this; his leaving her was an impossibility not worth addressing.

He wiped his hands with another fresh hot towel she fetched for him, and rose.

"Must you go again?" she asked, grabbing his red sash and stroking it.

He sighed. "You know what I must do."

"What if this man you look for is gone?" she asked, looking at his sash still in her hands. "Or if you find him and it turns out it was some sort of accident?"

"You have asked me before, and I tell you again—there are no accidents of this sort." He stepped toward the door, his sash falling out of her hands. "It is possible he has left, but I feel somehow sure he will return here, and when he does I am ready for him."

He came back to her, his hands on her shoulders as he kissed the top of her head. "Do not worry, my soul. Fate will take care of us."

She wanted to cry, but at least everything was softened by the fact that he had returned to her; he always would.

She spent the afternoon completing her chores, scrubbing dishes, dusting the house, fetching water, washing clothes. For some reason she avoided the book. Perhaps just knowing he had brought it to her was enough.

Later that night, after serving Cheremi raki and more sour yogurt, after putting the dishes away and making their bed for the night, she nestled near him.

"Do you like your book?" he murmured, half asleep already.

"I like anything you bring me," she whispered, and she

played the game where she matched her inhales to his, her exhales to his, though his deep-chest breaths stretched longer than hers. She had to count to make her breath match his: *one, two, three* . . .

THE NEXT MORNING she stirred the fire, made the coffee, and Cheremi went without an explanation or a kiss. She sat down to the book. She flipped through a few pages—it was something to do with God. How large, how interesting. Her father had not kept theological books in his study.

As she turned back to the first page, she widened her eyes. The purpose of her life was written in black and white: to obey a man was the highest function of woman, marriage the highest institution she might serve. So many other books said so, asserted the author. So it must be true. And it must be true a woman should not be judged by her beauty—for that might mislead—but by her work and the sons she should bear. Eleanora's body rocked with soundless laughter. She had no sons, but she herself was a man. Or had been. Did that count? She wished she could share this with her father.

When Cheremi came home, she kissed his cheeks, pressed a cup of coffee into his hands, then set up the table for dinner. She sat with him on the floor, and, smiling as she picked up a small chunk of corn bread from a new hammered copper bowl, told him the book he had brought her was the most ridiculous she had ever read.

His brow clouded.

"I am sure it is by a very respected man," she continued, "but it says the silliest things about women—"

"I asked the librarian for a book suitable for a woman," Cheremi interrupted. "And he gave me that one."

"I am sure the author has considered what it means to be a woman more than I have," Eleanora said, rolling her eyes.

"Likely," Cheremi said. "How could you question a man who is as respected as that?"

He took the rest of the bread and sopped up the last of the yogurt.

He often fed her the last bite of dinner. Eleanora felt her eyes sting with tears, but she dug her fingernails into her palms and breathed deeply. She could not talk freely with anyone. She must hold back. She moved closer to Cheremi so their thighs touched.

"Perhaps," she said, "if I finish the book I will understand his whole point of view."

"I did you a nice thing to bring you a book to look at," he said.

He rose from the table.

She had hurt him; she had not meant to hurt him. She had been boorish to forget there was no way he might have known the book was ridiculous, since he likely did not even know the language the book was written in. She got up and hugged him hard, trying to smother the pain between them, and he pulled her to the floor so they lay together.

Their hurt disappeared into the darkness; the blanket they lay underneath together smothered their differences. To be in his arms was to experience the world as she always imagined she should, but never thought she would—an exaggerated reality so beautiful she lost herself feeling each moment, each second stretching into its own eternity. Their hearts beat in sync with each other and some otherworldly silent music. When she touched him he responded in equal measure, so sometimes she was not sure if the pleasure she felt was due to his touch on her skin or hers on his. And when she opened her eyes his face mirrored the pleasure she felt, and hers his, so they created a little infinity.

"Do you know how much I love you?" he whispered, his hot breath making her ear burn.

"Yes, yes," she breathed. "At least as much as I love you."

What was the escape she had sought in books, the idealized world she had sought to create with her paintings, compared to this? She was living what she had imagined. Life was actually beautiful.

And unlike when she returned to the everyday from her fantasies, disappointed with its dullness, the light Cheremi gave her lit up the rest of the world, erasing shadows seeping in after her father had been taken from her. Cheremi's love shone from his eyes onto her and everyone else, and suddenly she found the world worthwhile, people pleasant, the grass greener than she could have captured in paint.

Maybe she did not need to go to Italy with Cheremi. Perhaps Cheremi was her Italy.

Her days felt full, and if they sometimes felt small, she told herself it was because they were filled with so much feeling. Even the muted hours of monotonous chores were bright, because they served as contrast to the highs when she was in Cheremi's arms. They made love every moment they were together, even if it was just the way his eyes met hers over dinner, reminding her of his head looming over hers as he gasped. Most every morning before he left he touched her belly and asked if a son grew there. Eleanora would blush and kiss him goodbye. She had never thought of children before, of creating anything outside her art, but she saw the beauty of a new life sparking from those moments of wordless pleasure she felt when he filled her.

When she considered her old thoughts of escaping to Italy, it seemed a childish dream, like when she would read a book and want to climb into the novel. How could life hold more happiness than this? She would like to see more of the world. But she had time, and she wanted to see everything with Cheremi.

"Where would you like to go that you have not been before?" she had asked him again.

And his eyes had locked with hers. "Why should I want to be anywhere but here, now, with you? Do you know how beautiful you are?"

And she, who had always thought of her looks as some separate possession that meaningless people might comment on, began to guard her beauty. She splashed milk on her face in the evening when she thought Cheremi was not looking, and she was careful not to pull her skin with the rag she washed her face with in the morning. She tried to keep the charcoal of her drawings from getting under her nails, and took care to make sure her clothes were as clean and neat as possible again, though she never went out now except to fetch water and for occasional trips to the market. For if she wanted a book now, she told Cheremi and he brought her back something with a story. Most of the time.

Thus every day Italy faded further away. When she did ponder her dream of going there, all she felt was a slight twinge of sadness that she no longer regretted not going. She now could draw between her chores, which she hardly thought of as chores—it was work that brought her closer to Cheremi. She was making a home for him.

This home that was also now hers was so different from the one she had grown up in, not just because the windows were fewer and smaller and it was so close to neighbors she rarely nodded hello to, but because she tended it, made it her own, and she felt the responsibility of keeping it comfortable. Once, when Cheremi brought over an old friend, she even washed his feet as a woman should, and hovered in the background of their conversation like a ghost, silent except for the crack of a lit match she offered so they might smoke, or the soft splash of freshly poured raki. It was a role she smiled about as she played it. After their guest left she would command Cheremi, with her mouth, with her hands.

She hardly ever thought of the first time she had come to this house, before she had known Cheremi. When she looked out the window, she only meditated on the shifting sunlight of spring, and how close to home Cheremi might be; sometimes she tried counting the white blossoms on the lone tree. Through daily use and her taking it for granted, the house had become a new home to her—and she a new woman.

Her days and nights were filled to the brim, and it was rare that she thought of Italy or her old home in the mountains, where she told herself Meria was well, if lonely. It was even rarer still that she thought of how she had been the man who had killed Cheremi's brother, though Cheremi still searched for him every day.

The man who had killed Cheremi's brother had made a grave mistake, and this mistake was made so long ago, and so much had happened since then, that the few times Eleanora allowed herself to remember this man, she could barely believe she had been him. She understood him, though, and she felt Cheremi would understand him, too—Cheremi had the same goal this man had had, really. If only she could tell him what that man she had been knew—revenge led to nothing.

And yet it had led to Cheremi.

She felt a pitiful ache for him, and for her old self. She had been afraid and so lonely.

Chapter 25

Wednesday was market day, when towns and tribes flooded the bazaar, and for the last two weeks Cheremi had encouraged Eleanora to go and shop for food, while he sought work at Hotel Europa.

"So many other women go," he had said, "so why not you as well, my soul? Some bold women even sell things! But you do not need to do any such thing while I am here for you, and I am grateful you would not want to display yourself in such a way." His voice teased her. "I would be so jealous to think of other men looking at you, looking at my . . ."

"At your what, my soul?" she asked, her hand on his cheek.

He grinned, looking like a shy boy. He gulped down his coffee, pressed coins into her hand, and left for the day.

Eleanora peered out the small window at the flowering tree and smiled. What might she wear today to the market? She looked through the clothes from the chest, sifting through the carefully folded, freshly laundered garments. She would not have ordered such clothing for herself, but the costumes were beautifully made. She held up the sheer white blouse with wide bell sleeves. It was as light as a cloud, and the white ankle-length skirt she pulled on was full and heavy enough to keep her warm in the spring morning. Over this went a cream vest, nearly as long as her skirt and stiff with swirls of gold embroidery, then a heavy silver-studded belt of a married woman. She tugged on her shining leather sandals, freshly conditioned with butter. She patted her pockets to make sure she had the coins, locked the door, and left.

She tipped her head back and smiled into the sunshine as she walked through the olive groves and dewy, flowering fields dividing the houses from the commercial part of town. Through the fields there was a line of flattened grass, as if someone had been chased and trampled a wild trail into it. His face would have been whipped by the grass; it was so tall now. It looked so different from that late-fall day she had run through these fields to get back to the mountains, but then those had been different fields, had they not? Eleanora frowned as she kicked a rock in the path.

Why think of that today?

She was young and the spring air was fresh; she was loved and in love. She wanted to cherish these days, so she could remember them when she was far away with Cheremi. Surely she could convince him to leave soon; he must sense the impossibility of finding the man he hunted.

She wondered if Italy had olive groves. Who knew, and how would she ever know? She was stuck here until Cheremi found his brother's killer. She dashed ahead with a burst of nervous, high energy, escaping her thoughts in the joy of her healthy body, and two women carrying kindling strapped to their backs stared at her. Eleanora slowed only when she reached the slippery cobblestones of the wide street lined with the town's tall buildings. Merchants yelled greetings at the crowds, which began to thicken.

She thought wistfully of the library. She would not go that far today. It was fine to be here, at the market, where there were plenty of women to get lost amongst. Two elegant ghosts in head-to-toe cream lace strolled by, and a woman in a black-and-red bell-shaped skirt ambled on, spinning wool with a howling baby strapped to her back. Clumps of men strolled together, laughing loudly. No one paid any attention to Eleanora in this busy street, but she would not risk the attention she would bring to herself going to the library or to one of the cafés filled with men discussing politics and business. How much she would love to taste that orange cake again. She missed Baba, she even missed Meria. She would have been in school by now, and the three of them might have enjoyed such a bustling scene across the sea, in Venice. Her eyes welled up, and she dug her fingernails into her palms.

"Do not be such a fool," she muttered. "You do not deserve what happiness you have."

She talked to herself at home sometimes during the many hours she spent alone. She must stop.

The bustling market seemed grimy and sad suddenly. These were merely people who had been her neighbors in the mountains, and people who were her neighbors now, jostling for overripe food and cheap goods and stale gossip. She walked more quickly, weaving between the shoppers, while careful not to step in the murky gutter, focused on finding the fruit stall she had been to last week.

But why must she go to the same one again? She wanted something new, and when she saw the polished wood of an elaborate cart, nearly out in the middle of the street, with people snaking around its rainbow of fruits and vegetables, she smiled. She walked up to the cart, drawn to a new fruit the color of a ruby. She picked it up.

"What a beautiful fruit!" she exclaimed, grateful for the distraction from her confused thoughts. "What is it?"

"It is a very special fruit," the young seller said.

He wore white pants, a white turban, and a white shirt, like all other men, except instead of a short jacket he wore a vest that flared out like a woman's skirt around his knees, and his shoes forked at the tip like a serpent's tongue.

"This fruit, you cannot bite into for its flesh. You must cut it open and eat its juicy seeds."

A large man edged up to the stall, close to her. She ignored him, her mind wandering ahead to tonight. She would feed these seeds to Cheremi, spoon by—

The man bumped into her. She looked at him and he met her eyes, and in a voice so low she thought maybe she had imagined it, he muttered, "A woman without shame." He clucked his tongue at her.

Eleanora stared at him in disbelief. His eyes' whites were strangely bright, giving him a boyish look despite the wiry white hairs peppering his thick black brows and mustache. He stepped to the side so he was no longer touching her, brushing off the black braiding on his white trousers as if she had soiled them. She had seen that braiding before. Her heart began to pound. No, it was not the one Edi's family wore. She looked more carefully, but her concentration was broken by the man's voice hissing in her ear again. "You dishonor your family."

"Who are you to judge me?" she asked, her voice shaking.

"Excuse me, madam? Madam?"

The vendor called back her attention. Was it possible he had not heard the strange man's growls?

"Do you want the fruit or not?"

The market noises flooded her ears again as Eleanora looked at the vendor. Relieved, indignant, she turned back to ask the strange large man what he was talking about. But he had disappeared into the crowd.

Eleanora paid for the fruit and ran most of the way home.

After she closed the door behind her, trying to catch her breath, she reached to take off her headscarf. She patted her bare head. Perhaps her scarf had fallen off in her dash through the fields, or maybe she had forgotten it altogether. Was that why that man had called her a woman without shame? Eleanora felt the warmth of anger at this petty man's insults. Oh, if she told Cheremi about it, that man would not live to see the moon rise.

But she knew she would not tell Cheremi. She told herself it was because she did not want to waste any more time on that stupid man. She would rather imagine biting into one of the juicy seeds and kissing Cheremi so he could taste it.

She looked toward the tiny window. How many more hours till she would feel his lips on her forehead, her nose, her mouth? As she walked over to the window she tripped, barely catching her balance. She cursed her throbbing toe, which felt warm and wet.

"What is that?" she murmured to herself. Looking down, she saw a rough stone with a ragged piece of paper tied around it. She carefully unwrapped the paper, more curious than afraid, even when she saw the childish scrawl. *We know who you are, and you see that we know where you are.*

"So someone in Edi's family could write!" she murmured.

She imagined her father laughing with her about that, and her face crumpled into tears. She took a jagged breath and wiped her eyes.

"What should I do, what can I do?" she said, pacing.

She should show Cheremi, of course. But to have to remind him of what she had done—the troubles she had brought into his life! She shook her head, no, no. She could not be completely blamed. She had defended herself from Edi and his brothers. She had defended Cheremi. But had she not also put him in the position to need defense? She had always suspected that since he was not from the mountains he had not known how serious her vow was. Perhaps she had not known. She would not think of the man she had been. She could not think right now, when all her mind drowned under the image of Edi lying in his own blood on the floor of her father's study—blood gurgling from his mouth like a spring from the ground, like blood soaking the white shirt Kol had worn, soaking the floor of this room, its beaten ground not so different from the dirt road that her own father had lain upon. Those same open eyes, staring.

But they were not the same. They were all so different. So different, but with one major commonality—her.

She unfolded the note, which had crumpled into the size of a pebble under the pressure of her fist.

She would have to show Cheremi.

As soon as he walked through the door, she told him.

"Look what I came home to," she said in a toneless voice, pressing the paper into his hands.

He looked at it, and her cheeks burned when she remembered he could not read it. She read it aloud to him.

He shook his head.

"I knew you should not have shown your face around town," he said.

"You had known, had you?" When he had urged her to go to the market! She threw the fruit she was peeling to the ground, watching its bleeding pulp stain the floor.

He pulled her toward him, pushing her head into his shoulder.

"But how could you have known, my soul?" he whispered. "It is hard for you to understand these things."

"You are the one who told me to go! I did this for you, for you." She sniffled into his shirt, her hands at her side as he held her.

She felt frustrated she could not stop the tears blurring her vision.

"For you," she sobbed. "You are the one who told me, and for you . . ."

"Shush, shush, shush," like the sound of rushing water.

His strong hands rubbed her back, and she clutched at his shirt. Her father's shirt, his bloody shirt. She let out a low wail, clinging to Cheremi. She had been unable to say goodbye to Baba. And what about Cheremi? What if she found him lying in the street, too? Just as Baba had left her. He had left her, but she was buried as well: under Kol's death, Edi's death, her own near death. She did not want to die yet, and to be the cause of Cheremi's death, too. She meant to go on living, really living.

She must. It was what her father would have wanted. Not her trapped here, in a stupid little town, just like her village, even if the houses were larger, even if the fences were made of smooth stone instead of rough spears. They were still fences, shielding the people from realizing how small their lives were. How small her life was. And yet she could not leave Cheremi. She must save him, at least she could save him. He kissed her face, and then she tasted the salt of her tears on his tongue. He pressed against her. She was grateful they were to be one again, and tried to ignore the sneering voice in her head: he believed he was right to have yelled, and if he forgave her for anything it was for being a woman.

When she climbed on top of him and he looked her in the eyes and apologized for fighting with her, she knew she underestimated him. Not only was she saved from being alone, but she remembered how beautiful it was to be alone with him. She stared into his eyes and he closed them, moaning. Did she hold the same power over him he held over her? She must suck him over the sea, to be with her and free from this stupid danger . . .

She blinked into the dark room. Waking or dreaming? How had she gotten into bed? She shut her eyes again, nuzzling her chin into Cheremi, her chest sticking to his ribs, her arm tangled and numb beneath him. She loosened her arm, twisted onto her back, and felt herself falling backward into a darkness that was part of a picture in one of her books. She tried to grab Cheremi and pull him with her. She tried to yell his name, but she could make no sound and she began to panic. She felt sure if she was left alone in this blackness she would die and yet—

Her heart was pounding as she blinked awake. The window was a gray glowing rectangle. Cheremi was sitting near the hearth, waiting for her to serve him coffee. She got up, cajoled the smoldering flames into a real fire, made the coffee, and kissed Cheremi goodbye.

She thought of running after him, to use her presence as a woman to shield him from being shot. But she was the one who had broken her vow. She would be shot, too.

She waved a small piece of firewood through the flames. What would it be like to be shot?

"How much could you feel a thing if you did not know it was coming?" she murmured to herself.

But Cheremi. What if he was shot first? And she saw him, lying there, dying, as she had seen her father. What if he was shot and not killed instantly? What if he did not lie still in the dirt with his eyes still and open to the sky, but writhed, choking on blood spurting between his lips as he begged for death?

The pain. Just end it now. Please.

She squeezed her eyes shut—tight, tight, tight until everything was black.

It was her fault he went out every day endlessly searching, her fault he might be killed.

She thought of Meria, desiccated and alone near a dying fire. That would be her fate as well if Cheremi were killed in the street. No one would know to come to tell her. She would waste away waiting in the house, hoping Cheremi might return, frightened to even fetch water in case Edi's family waited for her at the door.

Knock knock knock.

She jumped up. She chuckled at herself. This was the life she had made for herself: a shot of terror at the knock of a neighbor. She shook her head as she walked the short distance to the door, but before she could open it and greet whoever stood there, the door rattled as someone banged on it again. Her heart began to pound despite the bright sun and the fact that customs decreed any man or woman was safe from harm inside their own home.

After all, that had not saved Cheremi's brother.

She fought her fear and tiptoed toward the small window. Perhaps she could stick her head out and see how many people were outside. Then she froze—

What if someone looked back at her? Might that be the confirmation they needed to break through the door? One was supposed to be safe in their home. Women were supposed to be safe. She laughed to herself. Customs acted as shields—so long as they were not dropped midway through the game everyone had agreed upon, and one of the basic rules being everyone must carry the shield while facing other players. She had always thought the shield an unnecessary weight. And perhaps she was right, when plenty of people who embraced traditions were killed, people with large families and ties to other tribes, people of consequence. She had none.

The banging on the door started again, harder, punctuating her thoughts. The knocker knew all about her. The bolt jangled, like her earrings as she shook her head now. She had changed from wearing skirts and headscarves to pants and a hat, back to another woman's dresses and headscarves again, but her eyes were certainly the same.

But if the knocker could not see her eyes, if her eyes never met his, he simply could not barge into her home, could he?

She stepped backward, stifling a gasp as she tripped over a floor cushion and fell onto the hard floor. She sat there, staring at the dusty floor, hypnotized by a small spot a shard of sunlight highlighted: despite her daily scrubbings she saw in the harsh sunlight a stain. She looked at the door and imagined a stranger walking into her home, towering over her with a gun.

But Kol had fought her, and she would fight, too. She grabbed her rifle, rubbing its smooth metal with her thumb. The door began to shake, buckling slightly every time it was hit, and she saw bright blue sky for a moment when it bent. Her first fear was that the person on the other side might see her in that second. The door's pounding stopped. She was as still as possible, a part of her panicked and wanting to avoid detection, and the other part watching and waiting to see what would happen.

"We know who you are," called a deep voice from the other side. "And we know you are here."

She wondered how many sets of fists and how many butts of rifles were battering her door. It did not matter. One was one hundred; they were the same man. If she rid herself of one, another would come, and another. How closely might they resemble Edi?

She sighed.

Until this moment she had never allowed herself to realize how much Cheremi looked like that man that had lain on this floor the first time she had been in this house.

"You see you can never leave," called the voice.

The door was pelted afresh with hammering.

She thought of shooting through the door, but that might give them license to shoot back. It was better to pretend as if she was not home. As if she was not the person they were looking for—as if she was not the person Cheremi was looking for. And so, she crumpled into the corner of the room, her back against the wall, facing the door, locking her finger on the trigger, hearing the door shake in time with her pounding heart.

Suddenly silence.

She began to rise when the banging on the door began again. As it went on and on, she was able to feel as if she had always existed with this noise, and she even grew slightly bored, wishing she had paper nearby so she might sketch to pass the time.

She almost did not realize when the banging stopped. But when it did, she simply got up and put her gun back in the chest, rearranged the floor pillow she had stumbled on and sat on it. She opened a book she had nearby and stared at it, and when her stomach grumbled, she found a chunk of stale bread to nibble on.

The book was still open in her lap when Cheremi came home. The rest of the day had passed so slowly that when she thought of the morning she felt she had dreamed it, until Cheremi returned at dusk and asked why the front door was splintered.

"The door?" Eleanora asked, dropping dried branches into the fire. "Oh, yes, that. Someone came here and banged on it. They said . . ." She trailed off, too ashamed to tell him what they had said to her.

"How long did it go on?" Cheremi asked.

"I do not know," she stammered. "It felt like hours, but I do not know."

"How many men were there?"

"I could not see, I was too afraid . . ." How could she explain it to him? "It could have been one, it could have been one thousand."

"One or one thousand, minutes or hours." Cheremi's laugh

was forced and dry. "You do not know. What do you know, then?"

"That we must leave," Eleanora said, latching on to his arm. "That we must go to Italy, we must get away to anywhere but here." She began to cry, not even trying to be strong and stop. She would do anything to persuade him to go along with her, even if simply out of indulgence. He merely hushed her and petted her hair.

Cheremi looked down into her face, and she felt his wide rough thumbs wipe away the tears on her cheeks.

"I would swim with you across the sea," he said, "anything to stop you from crying like this."

Eleanora closed her eyes, nodding, letting herself become limp in his arms.

He tilted her head up to his, and he searched her eyes with his.

"Only, my soul, I must find whoever murdered my brother first. Even as a woman, you must understand. It is bad enough for him to have been killed, but in his own home . . ."

Eleanora began sobbing again, without any thought of her tears persuading him, and every time he told her to shush and called her his soul again, she cried harder.

The next morning Eleanora refused to rise, even while Cheremi was snapping branches he tossed into the hearth, clanking the spoon against the pot as he made his own coffee, nudging her despite her closed eyes, asking her if she wanted coffee. Cheremi left for the day, and as Eleanora lay she felt a deadweight like that of a body on top of her chest, making her breathing shallow. To let Cheremi walk out the door, when she knew they were out there, so close. When she might tell him the truth and save him the pain of his fruitless hunt. What would he think of her if he came across someone who remembered a sworn virgin from the mountains searching for his brother the day he was killed? How could he ever forgive her for not telling him?

Would he kill her?

No, he could not. She knew by the way his eyes met hers. And she had shut her eyes and let him go today when they were nearby, with society's blessing to kill him.

She rolled onto her back and looked up at the dark ceiling.

She must tell him the truth.

Chapter 26

That night Eleanora lay next to Cheremi, her eyes wide open in the dark, and she felt, without turning sideways to see, that his eyes also stared at the black ceiling, which seemed to be lowering itself upon her.

She squeezed her eyes shut as if that would stop it. And those eyes that haunted her drawings flashed in her mind again.

Baba's? Kol's? Edi's?

Cheremi's?

All of them.

Cheremi's eyes had been wide and white when he returned home that afternoon, earlier than usual. His hand trembled slightly as he took the coffee she offered.

"I heard a man asking for my name in the street," he said, his voice toneless. "There were three of them. And they did not look like Englishmen wishing to explore the mountains."

His trying to bravely joke for her sake hurt her more than if he had panicked.

Warm wetness trickled down her cheek, tickled her nose. She was afraid to move; Cheremi might realize she was crying. She sucked her breath in, choked on a sob. Cheremi held her against his rib cage, petting her hair.

"My soul, we are safe. You are safe here with me," he murmured.

She squeezed her eyes tight, hot tears absorbed by his shirt and pressed back into her eyelids, and he held her so tightly she could barely breathe, asking her again what was wrong and then telling her to hush. She clung to him, to the memory of her father holding her like this as a little girl, asking her what was wrong, so ready to understand, already forgiving her for breaking one of his cherished things, and she cried harder, reminding herself he was dead. He was dead. He was dead. He was dead.

"I killed him . . ." she whimpered.

Chapter 27

I killed him," Eleanora whispered again.

"Yes, my soul," Cheremi said, the flat of his palm heavy on her head as he petted her hair. "I know, do not think I do not know."

He squeezed her more tightly to his chest.

He knew?

"I know, I know, my soul."

She felt lightheaded as she stared at the ceiling. It had stopped moving, and she felt as if she might float up to it. He knew. He had only waited for her honesty. Now they could leave and begin their new life together, they—

"Shush," he said softly. "Do not cry so, my soul. You did what you had to. You had to kill Edi and his brothers. You had to defend us. You saved your life. My life. Do not think I forget that. And he deserved it, coming into our home to kill us—"

"No, no, no," Eleanora cried, shaking her head, the movement muffled by Cheremi's arms. That was why he was grateful to her? Because she had defended them from Edi's insulting break from tradition?

"No," she said, her gulping breaths slowing. "I killed Kol. I killed your brother. I cannot lie to you any longer and let you risk your life. But I can explain!"

She felt a sudden space between their bodies.

"What do you mean?" Cheremi laughed, his voice angry. "How could you ever, ever begin to explain such a thing? If you think you can say this to me and think things will be the same . . . I know you are scared and want to leave, flee to your stupid Italy where neither of us have friends or family or can make a living, but where you can draw pictures and look at books . . . If you think you can say something like this to me, even if you are a woman—"

"Yes, I am a foolish little woman. You cannot believe a stupid little woman could have the revenge you could not. Whatever stupid vow I made or broke, at least I have my honor." She shrank into herself in disbelief of what she had said, clamping her hand over her mouth. He sat up and she remained lying, though she turned her back to his, her arms wrapped tightly around herself.

"So explain." The voice of a stranger. "Tell me how you did it."

"I shot him," she cried. "But I did not mean to, I—"

"You did not mean to, the way you did not mean to shoot Edi and his brothers so expertly."

She sobbed.

"Do not be so ashamed. I admired your shooting."

"It was not like that, at all. You do not understand."

"So help me to understand."

"I came here, to the city, last fall, looking for the man who killed my father. I merely wanted answers, that was all! I swear to you."

She tried to steady her voice, but she choked on her breath.

"I ended up here. And he admitted it. He told me he would do it again if he could. And then he attacked me! Your precious brother. He pulled me into this room, he tried to—"

"He was not perfect, my brother, but he would do no such thing. Perhaps he was drunk and joking."

"Drunk and joking! Perhaps he was drunk and joking when he shot my father in the street in the daylight and announced his deed, according to the code of honor."

"He killed your father for honor?" Cheremi asked in disbelief. "I heard, when I went around your village, he had been killed, but I assumed it was long ago. Your father? Your father was Fran?"

He laughed, and kept laughing.

"Fran of Gucis. Was that his name? You never spoke of him to me, until now."

That was not her father's last name. Eleanora shook her head, though Cheremi probably would not see or feel it. He was so far from her.

"His name was Fran, yes, but that was not where he was from," she said. "You see this has all been a mistake, one terrible mistake after the other!"

Yet Cheremi said, "Yes, his name was Fran of Gucis. Answer me honestly. Did—"

"I have been honest with you! If you dare think—"

"Quiet, quiet. Now tell me, did he have a scar down his cheek?"

"Yes," she whispered. "How did you know?"

Cheremi laughed, a rolling laugh repeating as an empty echo of itself, not the rising chuckle that she knew. Eleanora hated it.

"And your mother?" Cheremi insisted. "Your mother is not Meria, of course. I would have known that even if she had not told me. Who was your mother?"

"I do not know," she said bitterly. How was it after Cheremi became a stranger to her he knew so many painful secrets? "I never knew my mother."

"You never knew your mother, and yet you are just like her. Beautiful like she was. So cool on the surface, like a frozen lake that somehow has fire below if you can crack the ice. She was wild, too."

"How dare you speak of my mother."

Cheremi laughed and lay back down again, still far away but the space between them was suddenly relaxed.

"Ah, Elise. And you are far from me—now anyway—just as she was. She—"

"How did you know my mother?" Eleanora demanded. Who was he to talk about her mother like this? Baba would have shot him.

"I knew your mother, Elise, when she was a girl," Cheremi said. "About your age, perhaps a little younger. You see, I knew your mother when she came to live with my family as my wife."

Eleanora's heart stopped. She did not realize she was holding her breath until she felt her heart pounding fast again. She gulped for air.

"Oh, and I knew your father, Fran, too," Cheremi continued, "though only by reputation. And now that I think about it, I cannot believe how I missed the similarities you share. I barely knew him, I only saw him once, but I quite admired his spirit, even if I hated him."

"Do not dare talk about him," Eleanora said, before she could catch herself.

"Oh, I think I ought to," Cheremi said. "In fact, I feel it is only fair, given what you have just told me about my brother. Your mother and I were betrothed before she was born. My father had saved her father's life, and on the spot her father swore to give my father his daughter. And so when she was born, gifts were exchanged, promises repeated, and that was that. She was of course to live with her family until they were ready to marry us, which kept being delayed, and finally my mother needed extra hands in the house sooner, and so Elise came to live with us. That was her name, but you must know at least that?"

No one had told her until now. Her father had not even named her in his journal to her. *My soul, my soul*, he had called her. He had sworn Eleanora was so important to them both, and yet he had never even told her her mother's name. Eleanora squeezed her eyes shut, but tears slid down her cheeks.

"She lived with the women and shared their work," Cheremi continued, "and I barely saw her, except across the room, or when she lit our cigarettes. Once her hand brushed mine . . . Her fingertips were like silk, her beauty was unbelievable. When I saw your face the first time when I was sick, it was the same, and I thought I was delirious. So beautiful, but so wild. She would stick her tongue out behind my mother's back. She made me laugh. I fell in love with her. When she should have stood silent in the corner, she spoke to my sister, who only called her new bride, and said, 'My name is Elise.' My sister slapped Elise, and Elise laughed and sat on the floor, saying she was tired otherwise she would slap my sister back. And she would have!

"I was so shocked. She looked like an angel and acted like the devil. Before she had come to live with us, there was talk she was in love with another man, that was partly why our marriage was delayed. There was so much talk her father offered to take her back before the marriage, and give my father another daughter, rather than have my family feel dishonored by this. But my father said it was fine, he did not want to insult his friend, and besides, he had already grown proud of Elise's beauty . . .

"Anyway, I caught Elise one day, when she went to get water from the well, talking to a man. I was wildly jealous. They spoke standing close to each other, sharing this secret sort of smile. You smile the same way. Your father was very handsome, despite the scar down his face. He met my eyes and watched as I walked over, bold as anything! But by the time I had reached the well, he had started walking away, down an alley, so casual, and Elise stood there, brave like you . . .

"I did not say anything. I was young and in love with her. I suppose that was the problem. I did not say anything to her, and I said nothing to my family, who would have had her beaten or worse. Most men would have said something, but I could not bear the idea of that face of hers bruised. We walked back to the house together, in silence, Elise finally apologizing. The man was a cousin of hers, she swore, and she begged me not to tell anyone. How could I deny her? That voice, that face, those eyes . . . You know how it is. You are the same."

Eleanora felt dizzy though her body was rigid against the bedding.

"We went home, and after dinner I watched her make her bed to lie on across the room, and in the darkness she smiled at me, and I felt so happy I had a secret with her. That night I dreamed of the special marriage we would have, what a gracious husband I would be to her. The next morning she was gone. Run away. I was a complete fool. Her family was ashamed. They said they would put a bullet in the man she ran away with themselves when they found her, that her father would beat her himself and return her to us. I searched as best I could to find her before anyone else . . .

"I never told anyone but Kol that I had seen her with Fran, though soon enough we all knew who Fran was. When I heard they were in the mountains, I took up work as a guide, hoping I might find them, though I mostly traveled to escape the shame of my family. We lost so much. My father could not show his face at the market without being mocked for his weakness, for his eldest son's weakness. I felt so guilty. Only Kol was friendly to me after that, and he was the only one who knew the whole truth. If I only had said something. A few bruises and it would have been over, instead of everything we went through."

The bedding rustled against Cheremi's shaking head. Eleanora heard a metallic click in her ear.

"Now leave," he ordered.

Eleanora squeezed her eyes shut, biting her lip until she

tasted blood. "You want me to leave? But it is finally all over! After all we have been through, all you can tell me is to leave? Shoot me then. I have no one. No one loves me, and I do not care to live without you."

She sobbed, crying harder as she realized she did not mean it. The pain only went so deep, and somehow that made her sadder. And yet she loved him so much. Who else had she?

"Yes, you can. You never needed me, do not think I did not feel that. You liked being petted and loved, but you never needed me."

His voice cracked, and she felt the cold pistol tickling her ear, so different from his soft mustache, his breath, his lips.

Tears slid down her cheeks, but she did not move.

"How can you say such things to me?" she begged. "You saved me as well as I saved you. Let us leave together. Everything that happened were crazy mistakes, and the only goodness being that we came together."

"The only mistake made was that I let you go the first time. My whole family was ruined because of that. And here you are again, wanting to leave me. Why else would you tell me what you had done?"

"But I am not she! I only wanted to save you, and for you to come with me."

"You do not need me. You only want to leave as she did. Leave now, before it can hurt me any more."

The cold gun pressed hard against her temple until it hurt.

Eleanora slowly rose to her knees, lifted one heavy leg at a time, until she stood.

"You make me into someone I am not," she sobbed.

Her palms pulled at her cheeks as they wiped them.

"May I at least take the few things that are my own?" she asked stiffly.

She had never spoken so formally to him, even when he was a stranger lying unconscious in her house. But he was gone from her now, a cool ghost, like the other ghosts he had revealed to her.

Cheremi did not answer. He no longer cared.

She crept to the chest, picked out an ivory headscarf, and found two gold coins she had kept hidden on the bottom. Why had she kept them? Perhaps she had always known he would leave her. Or was she leaving him?

She stumbled to the door, dragging her feet, hoping at any moment Cheremi's light touch on her arm would stop her. Perhaps he would shoot her. Anything but him doing nothing.

He did not move. The firelight flickered over his sitting form. The gun in his hand gleamed.

She bought time pulling garments out of the chest—anything. She supposed these were her mother's. Elise's. Strange. Had her father admired her mother in one of these dresses?

She looked up again, hoping Cheremi was near. He stared at her, and she saw his cheeks were wet with tears. She began to stumble toward him, but he shook his head.

"Do not make me," Cheremi said, his voice a choked whisper. "I cannot forgive you for what you have done. For leaving me."

"But I am not she," Eleanora cried. "I am not she."

"You are too young to understand that you may as well be. You must go."

The gun trembled but remained pointed at her.

Eleanora crawled to the door, her hand leaden on the wooden bolt. She slowly turned her head back one last time, and the gun kissed her lips.

She staggered out the door. Why was she shivering and so cold? Was she barefoot? What did it matter?

She was halfway to the well, which was halfway to the field dividing the homes from the town, when she heard steps behind her. She began to run, but a heavy hand clamped on her shoulder. She tried to twist away, but he held her arms pinned down, smothering her lips with his.

"I cannot let you go again, my soul."

She was in Cheremi's arms, and they were holding each other as they walked, taking limping steps back to their home, limping steps like when she had found him on the trail and she had taken him back to her house in the mountains.

They tumbled through the door, Cheremi bolting it shut, shoving Eleanora onto the ground, his mouth slamming against her, their teeth clicking as he kissed her and pulled her skirts up. They were panting and moaning, and she had never felt so close to him as when their heaving, climbing breath became one shared gasp. Cheremi clutched her to him.

"I will always keep you safe," he whispered. "Always. Wherever we go, I will keep you safe. Even when we are here."

"Here, my soul?" Eleanora murmured. "Where?" What did it matter when her ribs stuck against his chest, as if she were a piece of him?

"Yes, I promise you I will keep us safe here," he said.

He breathed into her neck.

"You need not worry. And now that I know . . . well, that is all over, as you said. I will take care of Edi's family, and figure out how to tell people my brother's—I will figure it out, so that it will be behind us completely."

"But I do not care what anyone else thinks," she whispered, nestling deeper into his arms. "All that matters is you."

"Yes, of course," he said, a smile in his voice. He spread his hand on her belly. "All that matters is you, and that we will have a son one day. And that means we must consider others, for the sake of his future."

"Yes! The future. That is exactly why we must leave."

He chuckled indulgently, kissing her hair. "Is Italy all you think of? There are many good artists here. I believe I even heard of one who studied in Italy. I only wish I had thought of it sooner. I will find you a teacher."

His hand on her head became heavier, his breath deepened.

"It is not only Italy I think of, my soul," Eleanora said, stiffening in his arms. She struggled to name another place they might go. "It need not be Italy, but . . ." Her voice broke as she thought of a child growing in her while she lived in this small dark house, where she would always live, especially if they made peace with Edi's family. The child's only bits of beauty would be the patch of sky or the olive tree out the tiny window, or exposure to her own drawings, never actually great but offering glimpses of her potential for greatness. Lessons for her! More important was that she make enough money to send the child away for school . . . But Cheremi could never let go of a son or spoil a daughter like that, and where would such a plan leave her anyway? She might as well not have a child, while she lived most hours alone in this box, her aspirations for art reduced to the indulgence of a soft husband she would come to resent, no matter how many concessions he made to his eccentric wife. They had to leave. She could only keep loving him by leaving.

"We must leave here," she whispered, near tears again. "It need not be to Italy."

"Italy?" he murmured, as if she had woken him up. "Always Italy. I will take you there one day."

She realized she was holding her breath, and she forced herself to exhale. He would take her there. But they would not go there together. Cheremi's words replayed in her head as she lay there, even as his arms relaxed and fell to the ground.

Eleanora carefully crawled out from his hold. She pulled the blanket from their bed and tucked it around his body. Should she get him a pillow, too?

No, it might wake him. She wiped her eyes before she kissed his lips; she did not want her tears to fall and disturb him. She looked at him in the low firelight. Was he still breathing?

Ah, yes, his chest rose, slowly. He did not stir.

She took her wrinkled headscarf from the ground and put it around her head, patted her pockets, and found the thick coins were still there. They would be enough. She slipped on her shoes and took her father's rifle, which was leaning against the door where Cheremi had placed it when he had come home today. She would call extra attention to herself if she carried it, for what woman carried a gun, especially one so unique? She rubbed the sterling silver etchings, recalling the sworn virgin admiring her father's gun so long ago. Let them look—she knew its power now. She had defended herself before, and she would do it again.

She was silent as she unbolted the door and stepped out into the darkness, tears blurring her sight, making the path she had trodden so many times for so many days feel foreign. She glanced back at the little house.

She survived it before. She would survive it again.

Acknowledgments

I have the deepest gratitude for my husband, Matt, who often reminded me that "done is better than perfect" and encouraged me to complete this novel, which I might otherwise still be working on. For my mother and father, who supported my dream of becoming a writer while teaching me that storytelling is a craft requiring hard work. For my teachers Irene Park and Patricia Estrin, who encouraged me to keep writing. For Bedi Singh, Cathryn Michon, and her husband, W. Bruce Cameron, whose belief in this story buoyed my spirit for more hours than they will ever know. For Ralf Jackson Walters, whose editing sharpened this tale, and for Tessa Woodward, who graciously guided me in the mysterious magic of making Eleanora come to life.

I am greatly indebted as well to Dr. Robert Elsie, who was indispensable as my consultant on everything from artists active in Shkodër in the 1910s, to the particular fabric of women's costumes of northern Albania. That said, I take responsibility for any creative license that is interpreted as historically inaccurate.

All of Dr. Elsie's deep knowledge of the customs of Albania could not be included in this novel.

I want to thank readers in advance for understanding that *The Sworn Virgin* is the story of Eleanora, a fictional young woman who is of unique character, living under exceptional circumstances. I have tried to make her as true and realistic to the world of her time as possible. Nonetheless, this book's span or depth is not enough to contain all of the wonders of Albania, and the beautiful bravery of the Albanian people.

About the author

About the book

Insights,
Interviews
& More . . .

Meet Kristopher Dukes

Matt Jacobson

KRISTOPHER DUKES was born and raised in Los Angeles, California. She has been a nationally published writer since she was in high school. Her work has been featured in the bestselling book series Written in the Dirt and fashion bible *WWD.* She has been profiled in Vogue.fr, NYTimes.com, *Fast Company*, Forbes .com, and *WWD. The Sworn Virgin* is her debut novel. She lives in Manhattan Beach, California, with her husband, Matt, and Doberman, Xena. ❧

Behind the Book

Q: How did you discover the tradition of the sworn virgin?

A: I first read about the tradition nine years ago, in a *New York Times* article about the last living sworn virgins in Albania. I was fascinated by these women who had exchanged their sexuality for the social and legal powers of a man.

Immediately, I wondered what would happen if a sworn virgin fell in love. Would she be putting her life at risk? Would she regret giving up her social standing, her economic equality as a man? The idea became more intriguing as I read more: not so long ago, in parts of Albania, a woman's life was worth little more than an ox's—while a sworn virgin's life was worth the same as any man's. To gain the rights of a man in this part of the world was to gain more than I even imagined. On top of that, if a sworn virgin went back on her vow, she could be killed by her own family, and, if applicable, the family of her past betrothed.

As a novelist, you must be a masochist to write regularly, and a sadist to write compellingly. Every morning you ask yourself: How many ways can I convincingly put off staring at a blank ▶

3

page today? Every afternoon you finally ask yourself: What is the worst conflict my imaginary people can find themselves in?

And what is worse than forcing someone to choose between their life and their love?

True love is a rare gift, and I could not imagine my story people, especially in as hard a world as the mountains of northern Albania were, passing it up and enduring life alone. Sexuality is such a primal part of who we all are, but would an otherwise unimaginable independence make romantic love worth giving up? For many sworn virgins, it was considered a fair trade. How many of us have wondered what it would be like to be in the same situation, only to be heard as a man instead of seen as a woman? For sworn virgins in Albania, this was the chance they were given, with their vows acting like magic.

Equally intriguing, then, was wondering if a sworn virgin took the leap into love, might she come to resent no longer being the equal of the man she loves? Might she come to grieve her loss of independence?

I was fascinated and saw within what first seems like an otherworldly tradition a layered metaphor for the emotional journey of any woman, living yesterday or today, in a village or city.

Q: Do sworn virgins still exist?

A: Yes, sworn virgins still exist, though last I read only forty are estimated to be living, and most of them likely made their vows half a century ago. The custom, along with others, gave way when the communist government fell and Albania opened up to the rest of the world and Westernization.

Q: How did you research the world of the sworn virgin?

A: I spent over five years researching the intricacies of northern Albanian customs and culture, through travel journals, letters, and correspondence with the incredibly gracious and knowledgeable Dr. Robert Elsie, who answered my questions about whether Eleanora would have known what a fork was, used pastels or pencils to draw, and if she and Meria would have dyed their clothing while mourning for Fran.

I studied postcards from early twentieth-century Shkodër (spelled Shkodra in the novel, as I believed that is how Eleanora would have mostly referred to the city) to understand how the roads were paved and how the buildings looked. Countless times I read amateur anthropologist Edith Durham's *High Albania*, a fascinating ▶

Behind the Book *(continued)*

account of her travels deep into the Albanian mountains, and Rose Wilder Lane's entertaining *Peaks of Shala*, detailing her travels from Shkodër and into the mountains. I read Lord Byron's letters describing his time as the guest of Ali Pasha of Tepelena. I found a travel article, written during Eleanora's time, describing Shkodër's bazaar, its merchants, and its geographical location within the city.

The mountains of Albania had a culture as rich and variegated as the slanting limestone and crumbling shale that stacked up to make their indescribably steep peaks; and like any other region, parts of its rhythms and rules were seeming contradictions.

The tradition of a sworn virgin feels especially oxymoronic. The custom existed because men and women, by both genders' shared belief, were not equal, and a woman was unable to take the place of a man in a household. But the fact that any woman could become a man, and become revered as the manliest of men by the same people who knew this sworn virgin when she was a woman, proved any woman was equal to any man.

The old laws of the Albanian mountains are no exception to people's universal ability to hold contradictory beliefs.

How much are we capable of when

others—and more important, we ourselves—have already decided what we are capable of?

Q: How did you come up with the story?

A: This story took nine years to develop—which any writer will find reassuring, appalling, or both.

After I first read about the tradition, I immediately began writing, with my only idea that a sworn virgin would fall in love, and this, naturally, would create vital conflict.

After a few starts and stops, I quickly realized I needed to better understand the world that would shape my characters. It's one art to create a reality out of thin air and develop its laws, and another to strive to re-create a world that existed and was—however faintly— documented, often by foreigners enchanted by the mountaineers' intricate costumes, dedication to honor, and everyday bravery.

As I began to understand the laws, which are, in any time and place, only idealized guides for behavior, I also began to understand where there could be exceptions and how Eleanora, without becoming a feminist anachronism, could be bold and passionate—one of the rare people of any era and country who sees beyond what exists to what is possible and ▶

Behind the Book *(continued)*

yearns and strives toward the illusory world of her imagination. One of the largest Albanian communities, during her lifetime, was in Venice, Italy, and often men from Shkodër traveled to Italy to study art there.

Funny enough, if I had to pick the least historically accurate character, it might be Cheremi. It was considered quite unrespectable for a man to fall in love with a woman, even his wife, but love stories and songs popular during his and Eleanora's time make the case that it was not completely uncommon, and the passion and living ghosts that brought the two together fated them for love.

Q: What is your connection to Albania?

A: My connection to Albania is a deep fascination with the country and its culture after dedicating years to learning about a very particular time and place within it. Albania, like any country, contains a multitude of cultures, and that of the northern mountains enchanted me. To travel into it was, at least until the early twentieth-century, to travel into a land before recorded time. Early twentieth century visitors felt to climb into the mountains was to climb back one thousand years in human history, to communal tribes that valued familial honor above all, for better or worse. I believe early adventurers were attracted to this part of Albania for the same reasons I was drawn to writing about it: as much as it was this obscure otherworld, there was a feeling they were witness to a shared ancestral history playing itself out. Written technology was so far away that drawing was considered a sort of magic. Men swore they knew men who had married *ora*, those spirits of the woods that are believed to be the basis of the Greeks' myths. Women could become men. ∾

Reading Group Guide Questions

1. One theme *The Sworn Virgin* explores is the gap between what society expects from men and women. How would Eleanora's life have been different if she had been born a man? Do you think she still would have wanted to leave Albania and become an artist?

2. If Meria had been raised with the same privileges and education as Eleanora, do you think she would have supported Eleanora's dream to be an artist, or would she still have thought it idealistic?

3. When Eleanora and her father, Fran, witness a bride being dragged away to her new family, Fran tells her he tried to interrupt a scene once when he was much younger and the bride slapped him for the shame he had caused. What do you think Fran's point was?

4. When Meria first tries to arrange the marriage between Eleanora and Edi, do you think she is sincerely trying to help her stepdaughter or does she have ulterior motives?

5. Meria and Eleanora represent traditional and nontraditional women. How do they deal with the death of Fran differently? What are

the contrasting ways they approach survival?

6. Do you think Meria would have sold Eleanora into marriage if Eleanora had been her biological daughter? Why or why not?

7. After Meria's betrayal, do you think Eleanora could have acted differently? How would you have acted?

8. How does Eleanora and Meria's relationship change after Eleanora becomes a sworn virgin and the head of the household?

9. What other ways does society treat Eleanora differently when she is a sworn virgin?

10. Considering Eleanora's going back on her vow might leave Meria to starve, do you think Meria was right to warn her stepdaughter?

11. When Eleanora says to Meria, "You always blamed me for my father's death. . . . But it was you, you and everyone like you who killed him," what do you think she means?

12. When Eleanora meets Cheremi, they are social equals, and Cheremi is grateful to Eleanora for saving his life. As their relationship develops, do you think Cheremi continues to treat Eleanora as an equal? ▶

13. Do you think Cheremi acts defensively because he finds Eleanora's independence threatening, or does she have unrealistic expectations of what their relationship can be?

14. Why do you think Eleanora ultimately leaves Cheremi? Do you believe she did the right thing?

15. The last lines of *The Sworn Virgin* are: "She survived it before. She would survive it again." What did Eleanora survive before? Does "she" possibly refer to another character, and if so, whom?

16. Symbols for infinity (such as the ouroboros bracelet Eleanora wears that originally belonged to her mother) and history repeating itself appear throughout the book. What are the ways that characters repeat their previous actions or their own history? In what ways do characters repeat the history of other characters? ∾

Discover great authors, exclusive offers, and more at hc.com.